Items should be returned on or before the last date
shown below. Items not already requested by other
borrowers may be renewed in person, in writing or by
telephone. To renew, please quote the number on the
barcode label. To renew online a PIN is required
This can be requested at your local library.
Renew online @ **www.dublincitypubliclibraries.ie**
Fines charged for overdue items will include postage
incurred in recovery. Damage to or loss of items will
be charged to the borrower.

Leabharlanna Poiblí Chathair Bhaile Átha Cliath
Dublin City Public Libraries

Baile Munna
Ballymun
Tel: 8421890

Baile Átha Cliath
Dublin City

Date Due	Date Due	Date Due
1 0 APR 2015		
18 MAY 15		
3 0 JAN 2016		
2 9 AUG 2016		

THE RETURN OF FURSEY

The Return of Fursey

by

Mervyn Wall

The Swan River Press
Dublin, Ireland
MMXV

The Return of Fursey
by Mervyn Wall

Published by
The Swan River Press
Dublin, Ireland
in March, MMXV

www.swanriverpress.ie
brian@swanriverpress.ie

Dust jacket and cover design by Meggan Kehrli from
"Their Blood Shall Be Upon Them" (2015)
and "Drink the Cup of the Lord and
the Cup of Demons" (2015)
© Jesse Campbell-Brown, MMXV

Title page drawing from the original dust jacket
for *The Unfortunate Fursey*; designer unknown

Set in Garamond by Ken Mackenzie

ISBN 978-1-78380-006-3

The Return of Fursey
is limited to 300 copies.

Contents

INTRODUCTION

L earned books have been written about "the Irish comic tradition", which ranges from the tales of Finn Mac-Cool and Brian Merriman's ribald *The Midnight Court*, to the classic plays of Shaw, Wilde, Synge, and O'Casey, to Joyce's rumbustious *Ulysses*, Flann O'Brien's head-spinning *At Swim-Two-Birds*, and the desolate comedies of Samuel Beckett. To this distinguished Gaelic company belong Mervyn Wall's two novels about the misadventures of an ex-monk and inadvertent wizard, the ever hopeful and usually hapless Fursey.

Fursey's misadventures began in *The Unfortunate Fursey*, available from Swan River Press as a companion volume to this one. While you should certainly read that earlier book before starting *The Return of Fursey*, a quick précis of the story so far is hardly out of place, if only to reintroduce our hero.

Back in late tenth-century Ireland Satan and his forces mounted a determined siege on the monastery of Clonmacnoise. To thwart this onslaught of demons and succubi the brothers were compelled to exile a rather simple-minded monk named Fursey, in part because the Devil had taken a shine to him. Unhappily out in the world, Fursey rapidly encountered witches, corrupt clergymen, a lecherous king, sexy elementals, a holy anchorite, Joe the poltergeist, and various representative citizens of medieval Ireland. Having admitted to intercourse—social not sexual—with demons, the unfortunate Fursey was righteously sentenced to immolation at the stake. In the end, this apprentice sorcerer escaped his punishment by flying off on a broomstick, hoping to start a new life in Britain.

The Return of Fursey opens three months later. Wall's mock Augustan prose is even more coolly ironic than before:

> It is not generally known that the first Letters of Extradition issued in Western Europe were those addressed to the court of Mercia by Cormac Silkenbeard, King of Cashel; and they related to the notorious sorcerer Fursey, recently fled across the Western Sea to Britain. They set out in elegant Latin his manifold crimes and villainies, and politely requested that he be returned to Ireland for judicial burning.

As it happens, Ethelwulf, the king of Mercia, is a monarch of volatile temper and battle-hardened ways. He hesitates to comply with the extradition request. The Abbot Marcus patiently explains that "Fursey surrendered himself to the authorities of the Kingdom of Cashel, and made a full confession of his affliction, asserting that he had become a sorcerer by accident; but no sooner did we inform him of our charitable intention of securing the safety of his immortal soul by burning him on a pyre, than he began to behave in a manner altogether at variance with his known character for gentleness and humility. He immediately proceeded astride a broom to the roof of the Bishop's Palace and set flame to the thatch with such thoroughness as to gut completely that valuable and desirable residence. Not content with having wrought this great mischief and evil, he swooped on a neighbouring church, interrupted a marriage ceremony, disabled the bridegroom by a sudden kick in the stomach, and carried off the bride to the great distress of her friends and relations."

After some reflection, Ethelwulf agrees that the jilted Magnus—who has accompanied Abbot Marcus on this mission—may retrieve his runaway bride, if she wishes to return to him. But no one is to touch Fursey. The shrewd king of Mercia recognises that a good sorcerer could be of considerable assistance in his upcoming military ventures.

Meanwhile, Fursey has become a quiet and well-fed provincial storekeeper. By using his magic rope, he can readily produce whatever foodstuffs or delicacies his customers desire. Though Fursey's domestic life with Maeve has remained properly chaste, she has nonetheless assumed an increasingly wifely, even shrewish, manner. "He had learnt during the two months he had lived with Maeve that a woman fussed by her household duties is a different sort of creature altogether from the girl one remembered standing beside a lake with the wind blowing through her hair."

That passage already hints at the prevalent tone in this second Fursey novel: disenchantment. In *The Unfortunate Fursey* high spirits and picaresque adventure predominated; here, Wall—without losing his sense of comedy—emphasises the shattering of illusions, the undercutting of romantic dreams by quotidian reality. When we first see Fursey again he is sitting under a tree, Buddha-like, reflecting on the nature of human happiness. As the novel progresses, he will again set out on the open road, but the sunniness of the first book will now be tinged with an autumnal melancholy.

After Maeve is persuaded to return to the soldierly Magnus, the distraught Fursey immediately forgets the domestic spats of the past months. Suddenly, unexpectedly lost to him, Maeve once more becomes his idealised beloved without whom life seems meaningless. To destroy Magnus and win back the woman of his dreams, Fursey—who has never actually done anything sinful in his life—now resolves to serve the dark side, to become "a most depraved character". As he operatically declares, "I'll turn wicked."

So, shivering with fear, he makes a Dantesque journey through a haunted wood to summon up his old chum, the Devil. Yet when a rather broken-down figure appears, Fursey is taken aback. The poor fellow has clearly fallen on evil days:

> On the couple of occasions on which the Enemy of Mankind had previously appeared to him, seeking to purchase his immortal soul, Satan had manifested himself as a suave, debonair personage, dressed in the latest fashion and irradiating good fellowship and *bonhomie*. Fursey recognised the lineaments of the Prince of Darkness, but it was with difficulty; for the dark-complexioned fiend presented the appearance of a very decayed gentleman indeed. His countenance seemed tarnished with malignant vapours and his black cloak was singed and smelt abominably of brimstone. In fact, the Archfiend was a hideous piece of wreckage, very rickety as to his legs, and generally very much in need of repair. Fursey gazed at him in amazement. A melancholy smile played about the Devil's aristocratic features; then he emitted a sigh that seemed laden with all the heartbreak of history.

I'll say no more: Readers should discover on their own why and how Satan has managed to lose his customary suavity and self-assurance.

While *The Return of Fursey*—like the second part of *Don Quixote*—presents a litany of repeated disappointment, Wall nonetheless keeps matters consistently amusing. When Fursey agrees to lead a ship of Viking marauders to Clonmacnoise, he grows friendly with one-eyed Snorro. On the night before the raid, Snorro explains that the crew members usually take the omens, which involves "the examination of entrails for the purposes of divination." But their chief has decided to temporarily put off this ritual.

"I don't understand," said Fursey. "I'm sure it's an interesting ceremony, but I don't mind missing it."

"You won't miss it" said Snorro patiently. "It's your intestines that are to be consulted."

"*My* intestines!" ejaculated Fursey. "But will I survive the ceremony?"

"I never heard of anyone that did," replied Snorro gloomily.

Later, this odd couple look out from a hidden vantage point at the monks they are about to attack: "Are they happy?" Snorro asks. To which Fursey answers, and you can almost hear the sigh, "Ah, who is happy?"

This stoic resignation—very much in the key of Beckett—runs throughout these pages, as our hero learns that all hopes are soon dashed, all dreams only mirages. The satire, too, has grown harsher. *The Unfortunate Fursey* ended with the Devil making a cleverly diabolical arrangement with the clergy of Ireland. Here, a censor visits Clonmacnoise and—before the eyes of its Librarian—incinerates all the monastery's most precious manuscripts, including "four copies of the Old Testament, which he had denounced as being in its general tendency indecent." The censor represents the worst sort of modern bureaucrat:

"What some of you people don't realise," he explained to the mournful Librarian, "is that in this country we don't want men of speculative genius or men of bold and enquiring mind. We must establish the rule of Aristotle's golden mean. We must rear a race of mediocrities, who will be neither a danger to themselves nor to anyone else."

Given such bitter, even Swiftian touches in *The Return of Fursey*, there's little wonder that Wall's later novels, starting with *Leaves for the Burning* (1952), deepen his repudiation of Ireland's narrow-minded orthodoxies.

If being a Viking wasn't dangerous enough, Fursey soon encounters a cinematically spooky vampire. The weary ex-monk is marching along at midnight when "he turned a corner and came to a stretch of vacant road along which the trees were spaced like soldiers. He experienced a sudden fright as he saw a few yards from him a raven perched on a gatepost. It cocked its glossy head and looked at him wickedly. Fursey passed by trembling and entered the avenue of trees. The shadows lay in grey bars across the road. He became conscious of a fluttering movement in the air above him. He stopped and glanced up. Innumerable bats were fluttering up and down between the trees. As Fursey watched, one of them, larger than the others, fluttered down and, alighting on the road ten paces ahead of him, resolved itself into a gentleman wrapped in a black cloak."

Vampires, or at least vampires like George (for that is his name), are not usual in Celtic folklore, which is one reason why some stringent critics faulted Wall for employing European, rather than Irish, supernatural beliefs. Such purism seems out of place, especially given George's charm and Wall's own insouciance. As the author once explained:

I brought vampires into *The Return of Fursey*, if you remember, and, really, why I don't know. They just came into my head, that's all. There was no solid reason behind it. You see, they're not even believed in in these Western countries at all. So it just came into

my head and I shoved it down. I wasn't very responsible in these matters.

George and Fursey enter into an uneasy friendship as they
walk along, discussing the loneliness that besets them both.
Before they part, George sounds once again the minor
chords of romantic melancholy. "Turns in the road are attractive . . . because one can never be quite certain of what
one may encounter round the bend. Of course, in point of
fact, there is never anything round the bend; but when a man
ceases to believe that there may be, it is time for him to die."

Fursey continues on his way, determined to reach a mountain fastness inhabited by witches and diabolists. En route,
he passes some of the "pillarstones" of ancient pagan belief,
gloomily remarking that "wherever there was strong religious
conviction there was blood-letting and oppression." Increasingly, the satire of *The Unfortunate Fursey* has begun to morph
into something approaching misanthropy. At one point Fursey even declares, "If only man were absent . . . how beautiful
the world would be."

While in residence at this witches' hideout (in some ways,
a mirror image of his old monastery), Fursey tries to persuade
the sorcerer Cuthbert—another carryover from his earlier
adventures—to create a poison that will destroy Magnus and
a philtre that will win back Maeve's affections. Yet Fursey's
moonings over his lost love, Wall suggests, are just as ab-
surd as the amorous mooings of an infatuated cow that has
become fixated on the apprentice sorcerer. In the end, after
resisting an impulse to commit suicide, Fursey pulls himself
together and resolutely presents himself at the small farm-
house where Magnus and Maeve live. More surprises await.

Critic Darrell Schweitzer has observed that the Fursey
books, especially this one, "become deeply moving as they
unfold . . . Scenes of merriment give way to tears. Wall's tech-

nique is one of using comedy to approach subject matter so bleak that it would be unbearably depressing if handled any other way. Life is so painful, these books tell us, so terribly futile, that all one can do is laugh at it while one can. It is a difficult balancing act. The two novels seem all the more robust and emotionally wrenching for their slapstick. On the surface, they sparkle, but they are dark at heart."

Yet, let me stress, they do sparkle. Wall once wrote, "it was words I was interested in always—words; just like a painter's interested in the pigment. It's not a matter of what happens, but to use words as they've never been used before is what's important, it seems to me." Given such an aesthetic, Wall was always a slow writer, as meticulous as Flaubert: "I have to weigh every word, sound and everything." Sometimes, working from nine till midnight, he would compose a single paragraph and "the following day I'd come along and I'd correct that paragraph, because I wanted every sentence to be perfect."

Those efforts paid off. Both Fursey novels are, as literary scholar Brian Stableford rightly remarks, "beautifully polished comedy". They also belong to that rare class of books that one can reread periodically with unalloyed pleasure. Brother Fursey's expulsion into the world may have been a sore trial for him, but it was—*O felix culpa!*—a fortunate fall for lucky readers. Fursey forever!

Michael Dirda
Silver Spring, Maryland
February 2015

The Return of Fursey

To
RIA MOONEY
my good friend these many years

CHAPTER I

It is not generally known that the first Letters of Extradition issued in Western Europe were those addressed to the court of Mercia by Cormac Silkenbeard, King of Cashel; and that they related to the notorious sorcerer Fursey, recently fled across the Western Sea to Britain. They set out in elegant Latin his manifold crimes and villainies, and politely requested that he be returned to Ireland for judicial burning. The Civil Service of Mercia was a small, bald-headed man, whose administrative cares increased yearly as his warlike master pushed conquest further and further into the neighbouring territories, but the Civil Service of Mercia was tenacious, and after three weeks' study came to a full understanding of the document and of its implications. He appointed a day for the reception of the Irish delegation and carefully coached the King of Mercia in what was expected of him.

Ethelwulf was a gloomy, big-boned warrior, at home only in the saddle. He had begun to realise the drawbacks of conquest. It was very pleasant to overrun and annex territories during the summer months, but during the autumn and winter you had to settle down and give your time and energies to arranging for their administration; and this work he found in the highest degree tedious. Other things, too, contributed to the steady decay of his temper. He was blessed with a wife shapely of body and gracious of address, but her extravagance was past all belief. To keep her clothed in the latest Byzantine fashion cost more than would maintain an

1

army of the hardiest warriors. And on the day on which he received the Irish delegation, he had even more than usual cause for moroseness and gloom. His only son, on whom were based the hopes of the dynasty, had but a few days previously disgraced himself by eloping with a molecatcher's daughter. The molecatcher had been immediately seized and hanged, but this act of tardy justice had afforded but little solace to the afflicted father. So it was with a brow of more than usual sternness that Ethelwulf entered his Hall of Audience on the day appointed.

On his entry the assembly of nobles and warriors rose to its feet as a mark of respect to their sovereign, and a flock of long-haired harpers in a corner struck up a welcoming tune. Ethelwulf stalked across the hall, mounted the dais and seated himself gingerly on his carbuncle-studded throne. When the company had once more resumed their seats, the Civil Service cleared his throat and began to read the day's manifestos and proclamations prior to passing them up to the monarch so that the royal mark might be made at the bottom of each.

During these preliminaries Ethelwulf rested his black chin on his fist and gazed gloomily along the rows of forked beards that filled the hall. How he hated the silks and effeminate trappings of peace! How ridiculous they looked, those fierce swordsmen of his, dolled up in coloured cloaks and ribbons! His eyes travelled the length of the hall and came at last to rest on a little group of strangers near the door. His face brightened with a momentary gladness as he bent his gaze upon the group of tall, fierce-looking men with lank locks tucked into their belts—the Norse traders. They had come a few days before and from their long dragonship in the harbour had discharged a cargo of salted hogs. The king smiled slightly. They were no traders. He noted the twitching fingers on the pommels of the great swords, the scars, the broken noses and the places where ears had been lopped off.

Those were not accidents that befell simple traders on board ship. Unless he was very much mistaken they were men after his own heart, Viking raiders, some of the few who had so far escaped Christianising. He wondered what they had in mind. The cargo of salted hogs was obviously a blind. It paid their expenses, of course, and brought them thus far into the Western Sea. Doubtlessly they would slip away some night without a return cargo, but with an empty dragonship to cruise along the coasts with irregular and villainous purpose. Despite the Viking raids of the previous centuries there must still be many a fat Irish monastery worthy of their attention. Hardy warriors, he told himself. He could use such men in the coming spring, when he planned to burst like a hurricane into the kingdom of Strathclyde.

The shrill droning of the Civil Service ceased, and Ethelwulf awoke from his day-dreaming. He turned his eyes to where the Civil Service was bowing and smiling blandly so as to secure his attention. When the little man saw that Ethelwulf was listening, he puffed out his chest importantly, unrolled a scroll of parchment, and announced in ringing tones: "Request from Cormac Silkenbeard, King of Cashel, for the extradition of the unspeakable sorcerer, Fursey, recently fled to Mercia in Britain."

"Where's Cashel?" asked the King suddenly.

"I have searched my encyclopaedias," replied the Civil Service, "and discovered that it's a small kingdom in Ireland."

"Where's Ireland?" enquired the King.

"It's an island lying far distant in the Western Sea."

"I've heard of it," said Ethelwulf grimly. "A land of abhorred pirates, who constantly raid these coasts for the purpose of carrying off honest men into slavery."

The Irish delegation stirred uneasily. The Civil Service, well aware that the King was as likely as not to order the immediate removal and hanging of the delegation, proceeded hurriedly:

3

"Cashel is an inland kingdom many miles distant from the seas. The delegation is a most respectable one. Step forward, gentlemen, and state your name and condition."

Two men moved forward to the foot of the throne. The elder was an ecclesiastic, whose dress proclaimed him a man of some rank. Although he was advanced in years, he held himself upright and moved with simple dignity. His face was the face of a student; there were tiny lines about his eyes, the legacy of long hours spent by taperlight poring over illuminated manuscript and obscure scroll. Ethelwulf noted the gentle dignity of the face and the noble carriage of the head. When the King spoke again, his voice was subdued.

"You are welcome," he said. "You may speak without fear."

The ecclesiastic bowed slightly. "My lord king," he began, "there is in the island of Ireland a great river which we call the Shannon. Beside that river, in a lonely countryside of marsh and low green hills, a place remote from men, there is a famous monastery called Clonmacnoise, where for more than four hundred years simple men have sought to serve their God in quiet, far from the strife of mankind. My name is Marcus: I am the abbot of that monastery."

There was a hush throughout the hall. There seemed to flow from the silver-haired abbot a winning grace, which affected every one of the savage warriors present. They, to whom gentleness was weakness and old age a joke, looked across at the stranger, their fierce countenances strangely softened as they watched the changing light and shade in his face.

"My companion," continued the abbot, "is Magnus, an honest soldier. We have come to your court, my lord king, he to request the return of his bride lately carried off by a deplorable sorcerer named Fursey; and I to request the surrender of the sorcerer's person so that he may pay the penalty of the law for his crimes and for his misfortunes."

Ethelwulf glanced from the abbot to the brawny young soldier who accompanied him. Then he sat back in his great chair.

"Relate your story," he commanded.

"What I shall relate," began the abbot, "is a strange and marvellous tale. Scarcely three months ago the terrible Emperor of Night, Satan himself, grown rabid with hatred of our holy settlement, launched a determined and sustained attack upon the monastery. To forward his unhallowed purposes he drew on all the dread forces which surround mankind. The assault began with certain curious and unaccountable happenings. By daylight showers of fish fell from the heavens like hail. At night the bedclothes were suddenly switched away from the beds in which my monks were peacefully slumbering. The monastery echoed to the baying of giant hounds, a sound all the more dismal in that it appeared to proceed from some invisible source. As these happenings are out of the course of Nature, we began before long to suspect that there was devilry afoot. It was not, as you may imagine, that the monastery is situated in a particularly sorcerous neighbourhood. On the contrary, a clear, cool air of unmistakable sanctity pervades the entire territory. We gave ourselves to fasting and prayer, but the Evil One in his struggle for empire redoubled his efforts. In every corner of the monastery pestiferous demons could be heard snorting and snuffling most hideously. There were no bounds to their detestable behaviour. An unspeakable company of female devils of the most luscious character imaginable strove sedulously to tempt my hard-praying brethren to improper thoughts. When this damnable behaviour proved ineffective, we were plagued with demons of hideous aspect in the form of loathsome worms and hydras. Ounces and pards came sloping down the corridors and used my unfortunate brethren most foully. For three long weeks Satan haunted the settlement, contriving all manner of wickedness, until

5

at last by prayer and exorcism we drove him and his evil-working minions forth."

As the abbot paused to wipe from his forehead the small beads of perspiration which had broken out at the recollection of these terrible happenings, his fascinated audience stirred and breathed again. The abbot's voice dropped as he turned once more to face the King.

"I have said that we succeeded in ridding the monastery of these unwelcome visitants. That is not altogether true. In one cell they remained. There was in Clonmacnoise at that time a laybrother named Fursey, a man of sparse intelligence, though nimble and courteous in the performance of his duties. It's my belief that he was a good man, but definitely thin-minded. This unfortunate fellow had an impediment in his speech; and being so circumstanced, was unable through sheer fright to pronounce the necessary words of exorcism, so that in Fursey's cell the demons knew themselves to be safe. There was only one practical solution: we expelled Fursey from the monastery. He went; and their bridgehead gone, the demons went with him."

Once more the abbot paused, whether to weigh his own responsibility in the matter or to conquer his emotion, his hearers could not say. When he took up the thread of his story again, he spoke so low that only those near at hand could hear him.

"He was an unfortunate man, this Fursey. After he had left the monastery, he permitted himself through stupidity to be married to a witch, an aged, spent and decrepit hag; and, through a deplorable lack of attention to what was happening around him, he inadvertently inhaled her sorcerous spirit as she lay dying, and so became unwillingly a sorcerer himself. That is the story which Fursey tells, and I believe it. Others, including my companion Magnus, deny its truth and assert that Fursey has been a complicated villain from the very beginning."

Magnus the soldier spoke for the first time. His words came out in a low growl.

"I don't believe that tale. Fursey is nothing but a malevolent wizard of the lower sort. Didn't he carry off my bride on the very day of her marriage? The whole countryside saw the two of them ambling and capering through the air on a broomstick as they flew eastwards to this country."

Ethelwulf stirred so as to obtain a less uncomfortable position on his carbuncle-studded throne before addressing himself to the abbot.

"I don't quite understand the character of this man Fursey," he said. "From what you assert he appears to be some sort of doting monk, yet he has enraptured at least two women in as many weeks. Is he then a man of such resistless charm that no woman can look on him and preserve her virtue?"

"On the contrary," answered the abbot gloomily, "he's a man whose brain is naturally moist. I have said already that he's thin-minded. Nor can it be truthfully claimed that he's a model of manly beauty. He's about forty years of age, small and plump. His hair is snow-white, and his visage is one of exceptional foolishness."

"How then," queried the King, "do you account for the fact that in the course of several weeks he won for himself a wife, albeit she was a witch; and succeeded in so enchanting the bride of this well set-up young man that she fled hither with him from your interesting country?"

"His wife," replied the abbot, "was nigh on eighty years when she married him, and was very nearly blind. How he persuaded the maiden Maeve to flee with him, passes my comprehension."

"He beguiled her with his extravagant wizardings," growled Magnus.

"Do you know aught of this remarkable man Fursey?" enquired Ethelwulf, turning to his Civil Service.

"Yes," answered the Civil Service importantly. "I have had diligent enquiry made. He runs a small grocery business at the edge of the wood just beyond the town. I detailed two graduates from our College of Spies to watch him over the fence for the past couple of weeks. He seems to be plentifully supplied with foodstuffs, though where he procures them nobody can say. He does little business, due, I am informed, to the science of economics, which is defined as the relating of supply to demand; but he has every appearance of prosperity. He is always prepared to undercut our own traders by producing, seemingly from nowhere, vast quantities of food and drink, which he readily exchanges for articles of lesser worth. Last week he deprived a passing charcoal burner of a pair of pigskin trousers, giving as payment countless hogsheads of wine."

"These things I can explain," interrupted the Abbot Marcus. "Fursey, although he possesses the powers and capabilities of a sorcerer, has only learnt how to practise two forms of sorcery. He is able to fly on a broom, and he can produce an infinite quantity of food and drink by the simple operation of throwing a rope over the branch of a tree and pulling on it. In all other forms of wizardry he is quite helpless. These things he has confessed to me himself."

"Does he present in his manners or conversation any symptoms of frenzy?" enquired the King.

"No," replied the Civil Service. "I've seen and spoken to him myself. He is friendly, anxious to please, and of a somewhat scattered intelligence."

"Remarkable," said the King.

"Yes, Your Majesty," concurred the Civil Service.

"Have you aught more to add?" asked Ethelwulf, turning once more to the abbot.

"I have, my lord," answered Marcus. "As long as Fursey continues to live, my people in Cashel will shake and sweat with fear. We are civilised men, and we live according to the rule of law. It's a well-known fact that to cure a man of being a wizard is beyond the competence of the most skilful leech or surgeon. Only by the cleansing action of fire can a cure be effected. Fursey surrendered himself to the authorities of the Kingdom of Cashel, and made a full confession of his affliction, asserting that he had become a sorcerer by accident; but no sooner did we inform him of our charitable intention of securing the safety of his immortal soul by burning him on a pyre, than he began to behave in a manner altogether at variance with his known character for gentleness and humility. He immediately proceeded astride a broom to the roof of the Bishop's Palace and set flame to the thatch with such thoroughness as to gut completely that valuable and desirable residence. Not content with having wrought this great mischief and evil, he swooped on a neighbouring church, interrupted a marriage ceremony, disabled the bridegroom by a sudden kick in the stomach, and carried off the bride to the great distress of her friends and relations."

"Maybe," said the King mildly, "he was not unnaturally incensed at your high-handed proceeding in deciding to burn him without consulting his convenience in the matter."

"But, my lord king," remonstrated the abbot. "It is the law. We are a civilised people living according to the rule of law. Surely in your enlightened kingdom you also put sorcerers to death by fire?"

"Not always," said Ethelwulf absently. "Sometimes they have their uses."

"Uses, my lord?"

"In warfare," answered Ethelwulf. "Let us suppose a king were contemplating warfare, a wizard might be useful in raising an enchanted fog on the battlefield. Even the sight of a sorcerer muttering spells powerfully affects the morale of the opposing forces."

"I have no more to say," replied the abbot shortly. "I demand the extradition of the sorcerer Fursey, that he may return with me for condign punishment in his own country."

There was a silence in the great hall. Ethelwulf sat back slowly in his chair and contemplated the abbot.

"No doubt your suggestion is," he said sweetly, "that I should send twelve of my hatchet-men to apprehend him."

"Something of the sort," replied the abbot, "but permit me to add that my studies have taught me that in order that wizards may be bereft of their execrable powers, it is necessary to remove them from contact with the earth. Therefore, when Fursey is arrested, he should be carried away in a basket or on a plank."

The King sat suddenly upright.

"Presumptuous cleric!" he thundered. "Do you realise that you have used the word 'demand' to me, Ethelwulf the Unconquerable? Your request is refused. Fursey remains in my dominions. Show the gentleman out." The abbot seemed about to remonstrate, but four of the royal hatchet-men moved in upon him and conducted him to the door. Ethelwulf watched, and the thundercloud slowly drifted from his brow. When he turned his head again he saw that the soldier Magnus was on his knees before the throne.

"My lord king," pleaded the soldier, "do what you will with the unspeakable Fursey, but give me permission to take my bride back with me to my own country."

Ethelwulf looked at Magnus. He noted with approval the great hands and muscles, the broad shoulders and the bullock-like simplicity of countenance of the born soldier, the sort of man he understood and with whom he felt at home.

"Marriage is a folly," he said sympathetically, "but it's a respectable one. Take the woman if she is willing to go with you, but do the sorcerer no violence."

CZ

Beyond the town, but not quite as far as the fringes of the forest, a small, plump man sat under a tree pondering the problem of human happiness. He was a tubby man with a fresh-complexioned face, round and moonlike, crowned with a wealth of prematurely white hair. Nearby was a snug cottage with walls of cunningly interwoven rods and twigs carefully plastered over with clay. A trickle of smoke drifted meditatively from a hole in the thatched roof. The track from the town passed the door and wound away into the forest, already aglow with the mellow loveliness of autumn. Some hundred paces from where Fursey sat were the cliffs, which fell sheer into the untranquil sea.

For some moments the little man sat listening to the seas fussing among the rocks, then his thoughts came back again to the problem that was exercising him. "I have a neat house," he said to himself, "the best of food and drink, and a pleasant woman on whom I am sore assotted. And yet I am not conscious of being actively happy." He sighed, and his eyes strayed across to the long line of cliffs against which the sea was tossing its white breakers, and thence to the winding track and the chequered countryside, coming to rest finally on the stretch of nearby trees, the outposts of the forest. He noted appreciatively the autumn colouring, green, amber and gold. "Nature is beautiful," he said to himself. "If any man should be happy it is I, who possess all that I can possibly desire—and yet I am not conscious of happiness. I am only conscious of sitting under a tree thinking about these things."

He shook his head gloomily and began to think about his friend the molecatcher. It had been a beautiful friendship. Twice a week he had walked over to the molecatcher's hut to sit at the molecatcher's feet and listen to him talking philosophy. But on the previous Wednesday when he had gone over to put to his friend the problem of human happiness, he had been surprised to find the molecatcher hanging from the crossbeam over his own front door. Fursey, knowing that it was unlucky to meddle in matters which did not concern him, had crept away without a word. But for the past few days a certain depression had weighed upon his spirit. He had begun to worry not only about human happiness, but about the uncertainty of continued existence. His thoughts were interrupted by a clear, pleasant voice from the cottage:

"Fursey! Supper's ready."

Fursey rose obediently and ambled across the grass to the little wickerwork hut. He ducked his head in the low doorway and entered the cottage. Inside there was a woman bending over the fire, her face somewhat flushed from the heat. She straightened herself and glanced around as he entered. She was about thirty-two years of age, fresh and gracious in appearance.

"What's for supper?" enquired Fursey pleasantly.

"I have made you a pie of escallops," she replied, pointing with the ladle to the place where he was to sit at the table. Fursey rubbed his little, plump hands contentedly.

"A beaker of ale is needed to make smooth its passage to the stomach," he remarked, and going to the corner he gave a sharp chuck to a rope which hung from the rafters. Immediately a beaker of ale appeared from nowhere, slid down the rope, was caught deftly by Fursey and conveyed to the table. Maeve threw a glance at him over her shoulder, a slight frown upon her face.

"I hate to see you engaging in sorcery," she said.

"Why?" asked Fursey blithely. "Isn't it the foundation of our fortunes? Anyway, producing food is practically the only sorcery I know. I know nought of conjurations or any kind of complicated wizardings."

"Sorcery of any sort doesn't seem to me to be very respectable," retorted Maeve.

"But we'll starve unless I produce food and drink."

"You could get a job."

"A job!" ejaculated Fursey, his mind becoming immediately engloomed.

"Yes," continued Maeve determinedly. "Now that the molecatcher is dead, I'm sure you could get his job if you asked for it."

"But I don't know anything about catching moles," bleated Fursey.

"You could learn," replied Maeve tartly as she turned once more to the fire. "At least it's much more respectable than being a wizard."

Fursey relapsed into abstraction, his spirits much affected by this sudden suggestion. He ate his pie in silence, for he could think of nothing profitable to say. Besides, he had learnt during the two months he had lived with Maeve that a woman fussed by her household duties is a different sort of creature altogether from the girl one remembered standing beside a lake with the wind blowing through her hair. But the silence in the room became at last so painful that when he had finished his beaker of ale he ventured to speak once more.

"I was talking to the charcoal burner yesterday," he said, "and he told me that the world is going to end in the year 1000. It's the talk of the town, he says."

"It'll probably last out our time," snapped Maeve.

"It's a very serious thing for humanity," said Fursey, shaking his head.

Maeve did not deign to reply, but sweeping the pie dish from the table, began to scour it thoroughly. When she spoke again, she astonished Fursey by her sudden change of subject.

"I wish you wouldn't sit around on the grass," she said. "You'll ruin your new pigskin trousers."

It was Fursey's turn to be silent, and he sat for a long time brooding on the sore change that had so suddenly befallen their relationship. He was aroused from his thoughts by a sudden commotion outside the cottage. All at once the door was kicked open and, as the startled Fursey rose to his feet, he beheld the man whom he had wronged, outlined in the doorway. Magnus appeared to be struggling to break from the restraining grip of the two other men, the Civil Service of Mercia and the Abbot Marcus.

"Is this the abode of the accursed sorcerer?" shouted Magnus. "Let me go. I am resolved to make a skeleton of him."

At these alarming words, Fursey sprang across the kitchen as if to burst through the far wall and so make his escape; but, finding no exit that way, he fled into the corner and hid behind Maeve. Magnus continued to give tongue to the most gross and horrid epithets of abuse and insulting comparison, but made no real attempt to break from the feeble grip of the two elderly men and precipitate himself into the sorcerer's cottage. He seemed to be struggling in the most furious and formidable manner, but in fact he deemed it wise to keep as great a distance as possible between himself and a man of such unwholesome fame as Fursey.

"Go in and restrain Fursey," said the abbot to the Civil Service. "I fear me that if these two come to grips the combat will be terrific beyond all description and will doubtless result in their mutual destruction."

The Civil Service did as he was bid, but when Fursey felt the persuasive hand laid on his arm, his confusion of mind was such that he fell on the floor. When Magnus beheld the sorcerer on his hands and knees he did not doubt but that an operation of a magical character was imminent, and he was with difficulty restrained by the abbot from taking to his heels. In this scene of indescribable confusion, Maeve seemed to be the only one to keep her head. She stepped lightly across to the door.

"You are welcome, gentlemen," she said. "Won't you come in and take a seat?"

Marcus inclined his head politely and, keeping a tight grip on Magnus' arm, entered the kitchen. The soldier was put sitting on the edge of a chair, panting heavily. Fursey was helped to his feet and stood leaning against the far wall, from which he cast agonising glances across at the door. Fursey knew himself to be in evil case. He knew that one cannot carry off a bride from the foot of the altar, live with her for two months, and then on one's next encounter with the outraged bridegroom expect him to behave with courtesy and reason. He knew Magnus to be a man of hard temper, and he was under the most painful apprehension as to the outcome of the affair. It seemed to him that he would be lucky if he escaped with no worse hurt than a couple of broken limbs.

"Yes," said the abbot to the Civil Service of Mercia, "this is Fursey, the unfortunate man to whom the Devil manifested himself in Clonmacnoise, and who afterwards became unwillingly, he asserts, possessed of sorcerous powers. Those powers are fortunately of a very limited nature."

As the Civil Service contemplated him with interest, it was borne in powerfully on Fursey that his one hope of safety lay in convincing his hearers that he was a man more formidable than they imagined. He passed his tongue over his dry lips and addressed himself to the abbot.

"My lord," he quavered, "since we last had the pleasure of meeting I beg you to believe that I have become most learned in occult devices. I regret to say that my disposition has altered for the worse, and I am now a man prompt to violence. I am subject to sudden storms of rabid fury."

The abbot stared at Fursey doubtfully, but the Civil Service moved back his chair hurriedly.

"It may be," he said in an awestricken whisper, "that this man, to all appearances tame and tranquil, is in fact possessed of a wily, treacherous and fierce disposition."

A ghastly smile spread over Fursey's visage as he strove to assume a look of preposterous depravity. Magnus rose shakily to his feet.

"Let us go," he whispered. "His countenance and complexion are scarcely of human aspect."

Maeve laughed suddenly, and Fursey experienced a stifling feeling as he felt the tension in the room relax.

"What is this nonsense, Fursey?" said the abbot, bending forward. "Sit down, Magnus. Would you forego your bride?"

"I can ill endure his presence," muttered the soldier. "He seems to me to be forming some atrocious design, he sits there so still."

The abbot shook himself impatiently. He arose and taking Maeve gently by the arm, drew her into a chair.

"My dear lady," he said, "why did you run away with this man?"

Maeve glanced up at him with surprise. There was such a winning kindness in the old man's face that she suddenly knew that she could not tell him a lie. She flushed slightly and looked down at the floor.

"It all happened very quickly," she answered in a low voice. "I thought he needed me. He seemed so helpless and without friends."

The abbot nodded understandingly.

"You know," he said gently, "your life with him here is not very respectable."

Maeve flushed again. "I suppose not," she admitted in scarcely audible tones.

"Not respectable at all," repeated the abbot. "If people thought you went with him voluntarily, they'd be inclined to talk."

Again Maeve looked at the old man with surprise.

"Do they not know I went voluntarily?" she asked.

"Oh, no. They believe he bewitched you by an insidious spell and carried you off against your will. Everyone has the greatest sympathy for you. If you return to Cashel, no one will think the worst of you."

Maeve put her head down suddenly on the abbot's shoulder and began to cry. He patted her arm soothingly.

"Respectability is a very precious thing. The good opinion of our neighbours is worth more than gold. This young man, Magnus, is willing to take you back."

Maeve raised her head and looked with streaming eyes at Magnus, who nodded to her awkwardly.

"Do you think that Fursey still needs you?" whispered the abbot.

"No," wept Maeve. "He can get everything he wants with that magic rope of his. And I don't know that he even cares for my company. He spends half his evenings drinking with a disreputable molecatcher."

The abbot made a sign to Magnus, who arose and put his hand around the weeping girl.

"Take her to the boat," said the abbot, "I will follow you." As they walked through the doorway, Maeve threw one glance back. Through a film of tears she caught a glimpse of Fursey sitting dead still in the corner, his face ashen and his forehead damp with sweat. Then the door closed behind them.

"Our journey to this land has not been altogether in vain," said the abbot. "One wrong at least has been righted. Fursey, I have little to say to you. I demanded of the stiff-backed ruler of this territory that you should be surrendered and go back with me to Cashel, there to stand trial; but my reasonable request has been refused. The King seems to think that he can make use in warfare of such knowledge of the darker arts as you possess, though I did my best to persuade him that you possessed none worth talking about. I must now take my departure; but before I go I urge you once more to repent of your manifold crimes. Goodbye, Fursey."

When the door closed behind the abbot, Fursey gave vent to a moan that accorded with his forlorn situation. The Civil Service of Mercia coughed importantly and addressed himself to the little figure huddled in the chair.

"With reference to what has just taken place," he began, "I am instructed to inform you that the application for your extradition to the Kingdom of Cashel has been refused. I am to inform you further that you are forbidden to quit this territory under pain of His Majesty's displeasure. You will hold yourself in readiness at all times to give service and to perform such duties as may be assigned to you."

"I'm afraid I don't understand you," replied Fursey. "My spirits are in too great disorder."

The Civil Service regarded him disapprovingly. Then he relaxed and seated himself on a chair.

"If you will oblige me by removing that wild and vacant look from your face I shall endeavour to explain your position to you. His Majesty has saved you from the fate of most sorcerers, death on a funeral pyre, an end which is without comfort or honour. You will be grievously lacking in courtesy and gratitude if you fail to place at his service the experience which you have gained in the practice of the darker arts."

"But I'm no good as a sorcerer," wailed Fursey. "All I can do is produce food by pulling on a rope."

"Is that all?" asked the Civil Service suspiciously. "I find it hard to believe you."

"I can fly on a broomstick if it's ready prepared and anointed for me. But I've no magical oils or ointments, and I don't know how to make them."

The Civil Service breathed severely through his nostrils as he rose to his feet.

"You would do well to make rapid progress in your studies," he said coldly. "The King has little patience with charlatans. Last summer he employed a most well-spoken wizard with a satchelful of testimonials, but the wretched man failed lamentably to live up to our expectations. In the first battle in which he was employed, although he succeeded after much labour in inducing a shower of thunder-stones, they fell, not on the enemy, but on our own commissariat two miles in the rear. His ability to produce an enchanted fog when required cannot be called into question, but the poltroon was unable to control it, and it kept floating up and down the line of battle, impeding the vision of our slingsmen."

"I suppose His Majesty was annoyed," ventured Fursey.

"Annoyed! The fellow was nothing but a quack, and he got his deserts—a fate worse than death."

Fursey swallowed. "I see," he said.

The Civil Service paused at the door. "I'd brush up my magic if I were you. You know not the day nor the hour when the King may call upon you."

Alone in the cottage, Fursey rested his arms on the table and buried his face in his arms. He sat for a long time thus; then he stirred and placed his right hand on his heart as if to support its intolerable weight. It felt like a heavy stone in his chest.

"For a week," he said dully, "I was so idle that I had nothing better to do than try to explain to myself the nature of happiness. Now I know. Happiness is no more than the absence of unhappiness, and it is a sufficiently blessed state."

As he sat alone hour after hour the realisation of his grievous loss waxed until it possessed his whole body. He squirmed as he thought of the woman he loved so dearly, and he beat his fist impotently on the table—hard, hopeless blows. Then he was still, and bitterness crept into his mind as a thin sliver of light creeps across the surface of a lake. He remembered what she had said, that she had only gone with him because he seemed helpless and without friends. It was pity that had stirred her, not love. For a moment he felt that he hated her, but something suddenly broke down inside him. The tears coursed down his cheeks and he knew that he could never hate her. But feeling the necessity to hate someone, his thoughts stretched out and encompassed Magnus—a strong, self-confident bully, he told himself. And he began to hate himself for his weakness. "I'm a born coward," he reflected bitterly, "without the strength or the courage to put out my hand and take what the world has to offer, without even the resolution to hold what I already have." But self-hatred is a whip from which we turn and twist until we escape, and Fursey began painfully to justify himself in his own eyes. After all, he had never in his life willingly done any wrong. He had been expelled from his Monastery, released from his vows and flung into the unfriendly world because a horde of unwelcome demons had attached themselves to him. Through no fault of his own he had swallowed the sorcerous spirit and powers of a witch, and when he had made known his misfortune, the authorities, instead of striving to cure him by spiritual or surgical means, had coolly set preparations in train to burn him. And at last, when he had seemed to find happiness in another land with a dear, good woman, they had coaxed her away from him with talk of respectability and virtue.

"Damn respectability and virtue!" exclaimed Fursey, and suddenly took his resolution. "Henceforth I will serve Evil. I'll become a most depraved character. I'll turn really wicked."

He sat for a moment, his troubles forgotten as he turned over in his mind a new idea. After all, his entire life had been spent in the pursuit of goodness, and where had it got him? Into a proper fix, with the probability of having to face any moment "a fate worse than death". He rose to his feet and swaggered around the room. He looked around the kitchen as if challenging opposition. Then he seized a pie dish and smashed it to pieces on the floor. He was rather startled at the crash it made and skipped hastily out of the way of flying pieces. But he recovered himself quickly and kicked the broken shreds across the floor. Then he seized the ladle and flung it into the fire.

"I'll show them," he said. "I'm tired of being the football of destiny. I'll earn myself a terrible reputation as an evil-working fellow. I'll behave in a preposterous manner so that people will say that my like for depravity has never been seen in the world before."

He took up the chair and, opening the door with one hand, flung the chair out on the grass outside. Then he came back and seated himself at the table so to think out a plan of campaign.

"There are three things I must do," he said. "I must recover Maeve. I must do Magnus an injury, and I must remove myself and Maeve to some place where she shall be secure. No, there's a fourth thing, most pressing of all—I must remove myself with the utmost dispatch from the dominions of this monarch before he starts asking me to do magical sleight-of-hand for him. The results of any such attempts on my part would certainly be deplorable."

Fursey shuddered as he remembered the beady eye of the Civil Service as the words "a fate worse than death" were enunciated. He spurred on his thoughts to think out a course of action, but despite the simmering inside his head, of which he was conscious, no plan presented itself. Then he remembered that he was a sorcerer and as such never entirely alone. He bent forward and whispered a name.

"Albert!"

For a moment nothing happened. Then there was a thickening of the air beside the fireplace, and ever so slowly there appeared a creature like a large dog, covered all over with rusty black hair. It was tailless and had the paws of a bear. The creature was of an unnatural leanness and seemed in very poor condition. It fixed on Fursey a pair of smoky red eyes of unutterable melancholy.

"Is that you, Albert?"

The stranger opened his snout, and his voice came out in a hoarse croak.

"Who the hell do you think it is? Haven't you just summoned me?"

"Don't be impertinent," said Fursey.

"You called my name," the creature insisted obstinately. "What did you expect to appear? A buck rabbit with a ribbon round its neck?"

"See here," said Fursey severely. "You'll have to learn to be more respectful. You're my familiar, and a sorcerer's familiar should treat his master with respect. It's not sufficient that you should always be at hand to carry out my orders. I expect you to be courteous as well as nimble in my service."

Albert's smoky red eyes regarded Fursey mournfully, but he volunteered no reply.

"What have you been doing with yourself during the two months since I last saw you?" enquired Fursey. "You've allowed yourself to become very emaciated."

The light of indignation flickered for a moment in Albert's red eyes and then was suddenly drowned in a look of watery despair. Two large tears welled up and ran down each side of his snout.

"Oh, Albert," said Fursey, bending sympathetically towards his familiar.

Albert took an uncertain step forward and laid his chin on Fursey's knee. Great husky sobs came up from the depths of his shrunken chest and he slobbered all over Fursey's new pigskin trousers.

"Accursed be the black day on which I first became attached to you as your familiar. I'm slowly starving to death."

"But I thought," said Fursey diffidently, "that spirits feed on quintessences and other matters of an ethereal nature."

The look which Albert threw at him was so full of pathos that Fursey's heart turned over within him.

"You know perfectly well," said Albert heartbrokenly, "that a sorcerer must feed his familiar with his own blood. I explained it all to you when you first became a wizard. It's your criminal neglect that has reduced me to my present lamentable state."

For a little while Fursey sat brooding sadly while Albert slowly mastered his emotion. At last the familiar raised one of his bear's paws and dried his eyes.

"Things are going to be different from now on," said Fursey gently. "When you first introduced yourself to me and informed me that I had inherited you as well as a magician's powers, I was so revolted at the thought of being a wizard that I could not bear the sight of you. Nor did I entertain sympathetically your repeated demands for my blood. But things are going to be different from now on. I am resolved to live a life of unexampled depravity."

"If you wanted to do me a good turn," suggested Albert, "you could either sell me or make a present of me to some full-blooded enthusiast who is embarking on a career of sorcery. That's my only chance of survival."

"No," said Fursey determinedly. "I won't part with you. You're the only friend I have."

Albert emitted a despairing moan.

"To others," said Fursey, "you may be a terrifying citizen of the spiritual world, but to me you are my familiar, personal to myself, and my very dear friend."

"That's all very fine," said Albert lugubriously, "but as things are going at present, I don't think I'm long for this world."

"But I need you," insisted Fursey. "Never have I stood so much in need of advice and assistance. My affairs have taken a very sinister turn and are at present in a state of grave detriment."

"It's no use expecting nimble service from me," replied Albert. "At present I haven't the energy of a ninepenny rabbit."

"Will my blood restore you?" asked Fursey.

Albert raised his head expectantly. And then in the half-light of the cottage Fursey deliberately did evil for the first time in his life. He took a knife and, making an incision in his thumb, fed some drops of his blood to his familiar. When the ghastly ceremony was over, Albert sat back on his hunkers, far from satiated, but filled with optimistic expectation of brighter days to come.

"Now," said Fursey, "to business. I am much in need of advice."

Albert had no tail, but he wagged his hindquarters courteously.

"I have an enemy," began Fursey. "He has just carried off an amiable young woman on whom I am sore assotted. How will I get even with him?"

Albert thought for a moment.

"You don't happen to have a hairless cat?" he enquired.

"No," replied Fursey. "I'm sorry."

"If your enemy was here," said Albert, "you could imprison him in a leather bottle, or alternatively you could spread the venom from a toad, or other baleful juices, on his linen. But, of course, he's not here."

"No," said Fursey. "I don't know where he is."

"If we had some eggs," said Albert, "we could labour them in a pail of boiling water and see what happens. But, of course, you'd need to know how to do it. Unless a wizard is very expert in the weaving of a spell he cannot always be certain of immunity from danger to himself."

Albert paused and gazed for a moment thoughtfully into the fire.

"I have it," he said suddenly, slapping one clenched bear's paw into the palm of the other. "You should hide under his bolster a rope composed of the hairs torn from the head of a raging hyena. That will cause his fingers and toes to rot and fall off."

"I wish you'd be practical," replied Fursey shortly. "I haven't got the head of a raging hyena."

"Well, have you got the marrows of an unbaptised babe? They're very useful in inducing delusions and insanity."

"I haven't," said Fursey peevishly. "I haven't got any of those things."

"Well, why not simply afflict him with a lingering and painful disease?"

"Because I don't know how."

"Do you not even know enough," enquired Albert hopefully, "to afflict him with a lameness?"

"No," replied the exasperated Fursey. "You know perfectly well that the only magic I'm competent to perform is the production of food and drink by pulling on a rope."

"And I heard you this evening," said Albert, shaking his head reprovingly, "telling Abbot Marcus that you had become most learned in occult devices. I'm afraid you're an extreme liar."

"That was a defensive stratagem," answered Fursey.

"Do you even understand the powers of seven and nine?"

"No."

Albert shook his head despondently. "I'm afraid you're a sad sorcerer."

They sat for a while in silence, Fursey watching his familiar's face anxiously, while Albert gazed broodingly into the fire, occasionally shrugging his shoulders and muttering to himself as he dismissed some plan that had suggested itself to his mind. Finally he raised a hairy paw and scratched his head.

"I can't think of anything," he said. "After all, if you don't know any sorcery, there's nothing to be done in that line. You'll have to proceed by ordinary natural means."

"You're not much help to me," said Fursey.

"What's the use of trying to help a shiftless fellow like you?" snapped Albert. "You've been a sorcerer for three months and you've learnt nothing. I don't know what you've been doing with your time."

Albert rose and shook himself like a dog. Then he shambled over to the door and back again.

"Of course, there's one thing you might do," he said.

"What's that?" enquired Fursey eagerly.

Albert threw a quick look at his master. "There's an old acquaintance of yours in the neighbourhood," he said slowly.

"Who?"

"Satan."

Fursey sat back slowly in his chair and his eyes met those of his familiar. Albert was squatting on his hunkers and gazing steadily at his master.

"I'm not acquainted with Satan myself," he said diffidently. "We belong to different mythologies. But I understand that he is an affable gentleman, always willing to oblige a friend."

Fursey said nothing.

"I don't want to seem inquisitive," continued Albert, "but it would clarify matters considerably if you would tell me the exact relationship in which you stand to the dread Emperor of Night."

Fursey had become suddenly wan. He passed his tongue over his dry lips before he spoke.

"When I was a laybrother in the monastery, Satan appeared to me and sought to persuade me to sell him my soul. I refused. He appeared to me several times afterwards before I fled to this country, and each time he repeated his offer. He always treated me with courtesy, asserting that he had taken a liking to me, but how do I know whether or not to believe a being whom mankind calls 'The Father of Lies'? He insisted on doing me several services, in order, I suppose, to ingratiate himself with me. It is sufficient that I have always rejected his offers."

"Would you reject them, now that you have determined to live a life of iniquity?"

Fursey said nothing for a long time, but sat brooding on his forlorn situation. His mind hardened as he remembered how the good and the pious were seeking his destruction.

"How do you know he's in the neighbourhood?" he asked at length.

"You forget that I'm an elemental spirit," replied Albert. "In my capacity as an ethereal essence I get to know a lot of things."

Still Fursey hesitated. Then be suddenly envisaged the exasperation of the King of Mercia on discovering that the wizard whose life he had saved was unable to perform the simplest magical operation. He did not doubt but that a wealthy monarch like Ethelwulf had in his dungeons a repertoire of the most exquisite tortures. He shuddered.

"Yes," he said huskily. "I'll seek out Satan and ask his help. Where is he to be found?"

"There are things happening in the forest to-night," replied Albert darkly. "He is there—with his friends."

"The forest is vast," quavered Fursey, "and it is an uncouth place in which to wander alone and after nightfall. How will I find my way to him through the profound darkness that will obtain?"

"The moon is full to-night. You will find your way by moonlight. You know the broad track that enters the forest?"

"Yes."

"Four hundred paces along that track a bridlepath branches off to the left. You must follow the windings of that bridlepath until you penetrate deep into the wood."

"Wait a minute," interrupted Fursey. "The week before last a merchant who had lost his way took the track of which you speak. The unfortunate man had to run a distance of five miles, pursued by a numerous banditti."

"It is true," admitted Albert, "that the forest abounds in dishonourable fellows of the robber class, but you will be lucky if it is only human beings that you encounter."

"What do you mean by that statement?" demanded Fursey. "Is the woodland frequented by wolves and wild boars?"

"They are present in force," conceded Albert; "but it was not such creatures that I had in mind."

"Please be explicit," said Fursey. "I may as well know the worst."

"I said that there were things happening in the forest tonight," replied Albert. "You may find your road incommoded by the presence of ghouls."

Fursey looked at him. "Maybe it would be as well to call the thing off."

"Nonsense," rejoined Albert, "you're not the sort of man to be alarmed by a vague wraith or two."

"Amn't I?" interjected Fursey. "I'm glad you think so."

"The truth is that certain tenants of the tomb are abroad. As you proceed along the woodland path you will probably be conscious of unseen intelligences about you. If they materialise, you would do well to have no conversation or dealings with them, as all spirits are of a variable disposition and inclined to deceit."

"You needn't fear," retorted Fursey, "that I'll force conversation on them. I'm not proceeding into the forest at all. I'd prefer to surrender myself to the King and let him torture me into a knot."

"Don't be silly," rejoined Albert. "All you need is a stout heart."

"But that's a thing I haven't got."

"I wish you wouldn't always be making such capital of your poverty," said Albert crossly. "It may be effective in argument, but it gets you nowhere in life. I'm only trying to help you."

"You're a great help," snapped Fursey. He sat for a while gazing into the fire in much dejection of spirit.

"Suppose," he said at last, "suppose I do commit myself to the dangers of the forest, and succeed in escaping destruction by bandits, wild boars, wolves and the ghastly inhabitants of the tomb, what happens after that?"

"Deep in the forest," replied Albert, "you will come to a rude bridge of hurdles flung across a chasm."

"And I suppose," said Fursey gloomily, "there'll be a couple of poltergeists waiting there to throw me over."

"I don't think the matter is a suitable one for joking," said Albert huffily.

"I assure you that I don't feel a bit like joking," replied Fursey. "All that you tell me is most dismal to my ear. What will I encounter at the bridge?"

· "You may not encounter anything," said Albert stiffly, "but in its neighbourhood you will very likely espy a dark, low-sized fellow with the face of an ape."

Fursey breathed heavily through his nostrils. "You seem to be acquainted with all the riff-raff of the World of Shadows," he said severely. "What is he? Some class of unclean spirit, I suppose?"

"He's the demon Elemauzer," said Albert with dignity. "You will have no difficulty in recognising him. He has a pair of boar's tusks, which are in the highest degree formidable."

When Fursey spoke again it was in a strange hollow voice: "The whole affair seems to me to wear a dismal aspect."

"You mustn't let ideal terrors influence you," urged Albert.

"In the long run," replied Fursey, "the adventure might well prove a bootless undertaking."

"You must act in the matter as suits your convenience and pleasure," answered Albert coldly. "Take thought."

"I'm taking thought," said Fursey, "and the whole business seems to me to be in the highest degree unwholesome."

"I admit that once you are in the forest it will be necessary for you to behave with uncommon caution."

"You're very glib," said Fursey, "but it seems to me that I'll be very lucky if I succeed in advancing one hundred paces into the forest without being torn into small pieces by someone either spectral or mundane. As for you, there's no need to maintain that black and sulky aspect; it's I, not you, who must face these manifold dangers."

"So you're going to go?"

"I don't see what else I can do," responded Fursey. "I'm in imminent danger of destruction at the hands of the Christian monarch who rules this territory, and it seems that Satan is the only one who can advise me. I feel moved to much cursing and swearing, but unfortunately I don't know how."

"When you encounter the demon Elemauzer, you should address him courteously and ask him to direct you to the Prince of Darkness. He will not hesitate to do so."

"I will," said Fursey glumly, "if I get that far. I'll enter the forest well charged with ale. It may serve to allay my trepidation."

"Before you order me to disappear," said Albert, "I would remind you that I will be due for another feed of your blood at latest the day after to-morrow."

"Kindly vanish," ordered Fursey, "and don't bother me further. I've enough worries of my own."

Albert disappeared slowly with a wriggle of indignation, and Fursey was once more by himself.

CHAPTER II

It is unlikely that Fursey would have ventured into the forest at all that night but for the courage artificially induced in him by the consumption of large quantities of ale. Although it was not yet dark when he left the cottage, he held a lighted lantern high above his head. He had a length of rope slung over his shoulder and his gait was somewhat uncertain. It was a couple of miles to the edge of the woodland, and by the time he arrived among the occasional trees that were the outposts of the forest, he had sobered considerably. The shades of evening had deepened between the trees and, as Fursey stood peering into the green gloom, an indefinable fear gripped him. Even the trees seemed to him to wear a look of conscious mystery. The path which he must take was murky and in the highest degree uninviting. He stood in an agony of indecision. He was sorely tempted to retrace his steps, and it was only by keeping constantly before his mind the elaborately equipped torture parlours of the King of Mercia, that he hardened his courage sufficiently to enter the forest. He told himself that he would be wise to hasten so as to complete as much of his journey as possible before the light faded altogether from the sky. This thought seized on his mind so powerfully that he began to run. It seemed an age before he reached the spot where the fatal bridlepath wound off to the left. Here he paused, the prey of the most painful imaginings. With a shaky hand he flung his rope over one of the lower branches of a tree.

"A large beaker of ale," he whispered. The beaker slid down the rope, and Fursey took a long pull, half emptying the vessel. Then he secured himself a second beaker, made an attempt to damp down his terror, and started to tiptoe down the bridlepath, filled with dismal foreboding. It seemed to him a profound forest and very dusky, but he did not dare let his mind dwell on its secrets. Instead he sought to conjure up an image of himself being introduced to a company of the King's most expert torturers. Once, as the pale glimmer of his lantern lit up a space between the trees, he thought that he saw something very frail moving in the black depths of the wood; but in the dubious twilight he could not be certain. He stopped to take a swig from his beaker before hurrying on. He had gone a long distance along the crazy track when he was brought to a standstill by the sudden appearance of a dingy phantom leaning against a tree. It turned on the quaking Fursey an eager, frenzied eye, and contemplated him for a moment before suddenly springing eight feet up the bole. The wonder was that Fursey retained his wits. As it was, he staggered uncertainly and with difficulty kept his feet. The phantom was of peculiar aspect. He seemed a sullen, rancorous fellow and had piercing eyes like those of a water-rat. It was quite apparent to Fursey that he was a demon of the lower sort, but in spite of his uninviting aspect he seemed to be a knacky and ingenious fellow, for before the eyes of the startled Fursey he began to climb the tree with his teeth. This unusual behaviour was little calculated to allay Fursey's disquiet. He became suddenly galvanised into action and began to run with such violence that he dashed himself against a tree. In a flash he was on his feet again and scuttled down the track as fast as his legs would carry him. He was conscious of mad laughter accompanying him as he ran. It seemed to come not only from behind the trees and from the undergrowth, but to be all around him. Fursey ran faster than he had ever run in his life before, and as he ran he raised the beaker to his lips and strove to drink at the same time, spilling most of the liquor in his efforts. He had turned a corner and run right through a meagre gentleman in a shroud before he noticed him. When Fursey realised what had happened, he did not pause to make any explanations, but ran all the harder. When he stopped at last through sheer exhaustion, the blood was pounding in his temples and his heart felt as if it might at any moment burst through his chest. He leaned against a tree to recover his breath.

"By God," said Fursey, "this is a sombre business."

The wood was quiet. Between the treetops came the random light of the moon, shedding over all a dismal sepulchral illumination. But the wood was quiet, and Fursey allowed himself to hope that he had passed successfully through that area of it which was haunted. But before long his hopes were dashed, for he had no sooner recovered his breath than he observed something approaching him, flitting from tree to tree. Whatever it was, it seemed of flighty and unsettled character, and very bristly. Fursey did not wait to scrutinise it further, but hastily finished his beaker of ale and took to his heels once more.

It was fortunate for Fursey that he was drunk during the latter part of his progress through the wood. It was true that he was inclined to see the subsequent phantoms and demons as pairs of twins instead of singly; but the alcohol seemed to give him an unexpected second wind at the moments when he most needed it. Moreover, it served to dull his senses. Had he to run such a gauntlet when sober, it is unlikely that he would have succeeded in doing so without becoming deranged in his intellects.

All at once he found himself in a small clearing. Now that he was clear of the trees it was less dark, and Fursey stopped to peer left and right around the open space ringed irregularly by the black forest. The atmosphere of the place, the air tremulous in the twilight, filled him with peculiar foreboding. As he stood hesitating, he was suddenly conscious of a furtive breeze that seemed to come slipping around a mass of lichen-crusted rock which lay athwart his path. A chill breath of air struck him in the face, and a moment later he became aware of a small wind of an uncommonly pestilential character. Above the whispering of the forest he could hear the sound of water close at hand. As he stood with a beating heart listening, his senses strained to the utmost, there came suddenly skipping around the pile of rock a strangely disreputable-looking demon. It was covered with matted hair and seemed to Fursey an apparition of a particularly unlucky looking character. It paused on the path about ten paces from where he stood and, fixing its eyes upon Fursey, displayed a double set of teeth. Then it bent down and started whetting its fangs on a stone. Fursey was much affected by this baleful sight, and it was borne in powerfully upon him that the creature was bent on doing him a personal mischief. He felt that it was no empty phantom, and the conviction grew in him that this was something he had better not have seen. The creature suddenly wagged its head in Fursey's direction.

"What would you have?" it asked.

Fursey grew pale about the lips and was too overcome to vouchsafe an answer. The demon, its fangs having now been sharpened to its satisfaction, stood once more upright and began to skip and gambol to and fro among the rocks, around and around Fursey, in ever diminishing circles. Suddenly as the phantom wagged its head, the soft moonlight fell full upon its face, and Fursey noticed that from its countenance sprouted a formidable pair of boar's tusks. A flood of relief swept over him.

"Stop," he said in a thin voice. "Aren't you the demon Elemauzer?"

The hideous apparition ceased its capering and stood stock still.

"Yes," it answered, surprised. "Who are you and what are you doing in the forest on a night such as this?"

Fursey, as he answered, made a mighty effort to interlace authority with his words.

"I do not tell my business to underlings. Kindly take me to your master Satan, who is present in this forest to-night."

The demon seemed startled. It stood looking at Fursey for a moment rather crestfallen.

"Follow me," it said at last, and, turning, made off across the clearing. Fursey followed, quaking.

They came to a narrow rustic bridge, beneath which a torrent sighed and roared. Fursey hurried across in the wake of his guide, not daring to glance down at the white water foaming in the hollows between the thirsty crags. They continued across another stretch of open ground until they came to a long, low grassy mound. Fursey recognised it as a barrow, the burying place of some old pagan king, who, before the beginnings of history, had been here laid to rest with fabulous ceremony. The demon stopped and turned its unattractive visage to Fursey.

"Satan will manifest himself here, sir," it said. "You have only to call upon him."

"All right," replied Fursey, eyeing the apparition with considerable trepidation. "You may go now about your business. I shall not require you further."

Elemauzer still hesitated.

"I hope it's nothing in the nature of a complaint to the Boss," he said ingratiatingly. "I had no idea you were a friend of his. Anyway, I wasn't really going to harm you. I was only joking."

"That's all right," gasped Fursey. "Please go away."

"Goodbye, sir," said Elemauzer humbly, and he touched his forelock. "I wish you a successful outcome to your business."

He spun himself suddenly on one toe and was gone. Fursey peered left and right to convince himself of the fiend's departure before venturing to lean against a rock and wipe the sweat from his forehead with the tail-end of the hempen rope which he still carried.

"If there's much more of this," he said, "I'll fall into a lunacy."

He let his eyes travel about him so as to ascertain the exact nature of his surroundings. He seemed to be still in the clearing, which was apparently larger than he had at first imagined. It was an area of tumbled rocks and bracken, enclosed by the wide circle of the forest, black, rustling and muttering, never still. In the light of the moon the clearing was filled with a misty splendour. Here and there were grey pools of shadow, but in general the night was blue and luminous. Fursey looked at the low green barrow a few yards away and thought of the pagan king only a few feet down, the black earth packed tightly against his fleshless face. He shuddered; it was surely a place of ill-omen. He remembered his errand and his heart shrank within him. He had endured so much to-night already that he began seriously to doubt his ability to support a prolonged interview with as formidable a personage as the Archfiend Lucifer himself. He was sorely tempted to leave the Devil undisturbed and stay where he was until morning. He could then retrace his steps through the forest by daylight when its dread visitors would presumably have gone. This course of action appealed to him very powerfully, but he forgot completely that the demon Elemauzer had no doubt hastened away to acquaint the Lord of Hell with the fact that a gentleman had called to see him. He was therefore considerably startled when there was a sudden flash of blue light, accompanied by a smell of a very sulphurous character, and a voice addressed him affably.

"Good evening, Fursey. I trust that you find yourself in the best of health."

When Fursey turned his head a yellow vapour was dispersing and creeping away along the ground; and there, lounging against the barrow, was no less person than the Prince of Darkness himself.

"Thank you," ejaculated Fursey nervously. "The truth is that I find myself in the utmost solicitude and agitation, but I trust that you're keeping well yourself."

The Devil inclined his head politely, but said nothing. As he and Fursey gazed at one another Fursey got a sudden shock. On the couple of occasions on which the Enemy of Mankind had previously appeared to him, seeking to purchase his immortal soul, Satan had manifested himself as a suave, debonair personage, dressed in the latest fashion and irradiating good fellowship and *bonhomie*. Fursey recognised the lineaments of the Prince of Darkness, but it was with difficulty; for the dark-complexioned fiend presented the appearance of a very decayed gentleman indeed. His countenance seemed tarnished with malignant vapours and his black cloak was singed and smelt abominably of brimstone. In fact, the Archfiend was a hideous piece of wreckage, very rickety as to his legs, and generally very much in need of repair. Fursey gazed at him in amazement. A melancholy smile played about the Devil's aristocratic features; then he emitted a sigh that seemed laden with all the heartbreak of history.

"Nay," he said gently, "do not enquire solicitously about my health or as to whether things are not going right in Hell. It's true that things are rather disturbed below. We have had our first Irish ecclesiastical contingent, and they are making things hot for the whole of us; but that is only a small part of my troubles."

He gazed into the distance, a look of unutterable sadness shadowing his fine, dark eyes.

"I fear," he continued, "that I grow wilted and old. Soon people won't believe in me any more."

"Oh, you must cheer up," said Fursey. "Things aren't as bad as all that. There will always be some to believe in you."

"I suppose so," replied the Devil, but without much apparent conviction.

There was silence between them for a while. The Devil gazed at the turf between his feet. He looked like a man in whom hope had died. He didn't seem to have a jig left in him. Fursey was suddenly struck by the strangeness of the situation. He watched the Devil round-eyed, and all at once stirred nervously. His companion looked up.

"I may as well tell you," the Devil said heavily. "It's a relief to talk to someone. Sit down on the sward."

"On the what?" queried Fursey.

"On the sward," repeated the Devil.

Fursey sat down on the sward.

"Since I last saw you," began the Archfiend, "I've just missed having *finis* put to my career. And it would have been a pity, for it's been an interesting and adventurous career. It was one of your countrymen that nearly did for me. He was very adroit, far too adroit for me. He comes from your part of the country; maybe you know him. He's called The Gentle Anchorite."

"I've met him," said Fursey hoarsely, "and broken bread with him."

"With a mallet, I expect," replied the Devil gloomily. "He lives on a crust a day, and he's always about two months in arrears with his meals. He's a man of the most formidable sanctity."

"Was he unkind to you?" asked Fursey inadequately.

The Devil's visage assumed a very peculiar character.

"You probably know," he began, "that people of every class and condition come to Hell, but the most numerous are those who have sinned as I have sinned, through pride. And the greatest sinners in this category are those who pride themselves on their virtue. The righteous and the presumptuous are packed into every tenement in Hell in such myriads that the housing problem is becoming very acute. But I always find room for more, and it has ever been a point of honour with me to provide a warm corner for those who have passed their lives presumptuously convinced of their own virtue. Such a one is the man who likes to be called The Gentle Anchorite. Forty years ago he took up residence in an unhygienic cave on a waste and windy hilltop some miles south of Cashel, and there he has since lived on a sparse diet, every day increasing in sanctity. He is a most hardened anchorite, and for many years has subsisted entirely on an occasional crust or a handful of nettles, washed down by a mouthful of water every Saturday night. Some of my liveliest demons tried their hand at tempting him, but all to no avail. Succulent meats were passed to and fro beneath his nostrils, attempts were made to dazzle him with showers of gold and the promise of kingdom, whole platoons of the most engaging females were perambulated up and down before his eyes, a series of poetry readings were initiated in an attempt to beguile him; but for all the success we met with we might as well have been trying to interest a bullock in the intricacies of classical music. He didn't pay the slightest attention. He just sat in front of his cave meditatively prosecuting his researches for fleas, of which he harboured untold myriads. The most alluring visions had no meaning for him. What matter if he had continued to sit there until his death, in this state of pious stupefaction; but he is an ambitious man, and many years ago he decided to take the offensive himself and carry warfare down the avenues of the world of shadows. In short, it became his practice to fling aside his passivity when one least expected it, and hit back at any demon foolhardy enough to approach him. In the course of many years he has become a man very expert at dominating devils. Experienced fiends give him a wide berth, but the fascination of what is difficult has proved an irresistible bait to many of my younger and more adventurous subjects. The net result has been that Hell has suffered grievous casualties at his hands—some fifty of my nimblest and most daring imps have been tied down by him in sundry bog pools in the unattractive moorland on which he dwells."

"I've heard of these things," said Fursey softly. "Prudent demons eschew the neighbourhood."

"The young are always reckless," said the Devil, "and even the most needle-witted imps have fallen a victim to him. Would that I had learnt from their example!"

"Did you venture yourself," queried Fursey, "to knit the issue with him?"

"Unfortunately," sighed the Devil, "I knitted it. I have no one to blame but myself. I knew The Gentle Anchorite to be a sapient man and a performer of many remarkable miracles, but my accursed self-confidence betrayed me. You know," said the Devil, turning a piercing eye on Fursey, "that I am of Jewish origin?"

Fursey thought for a moment. "Of course," he replied.

"Well," continued the Archfiend, "I have all the faults and virtues of my race. I possess in a high degree the ability to take punishment and come up smiling. You may try to subdue me by insult, you may think you've rid the land of me and my companions, but you might as well try to put a cork permanently under water. The moment your heavy hand is removed, I bob up again. This quality I account a virtue. I am one who recovers heart quickly, therefore can truly boast that my spirit is indestructible. But there is another side to it. I am artistic and wayward, qualities the possession of which I account a vice. As far as The Gentle Anchorite was concerned, I should have left well alone; but the danger attracted me. What artistry, I thought, to bring about this man's ruin by giving him cause for such pride as never Christian heart had felt before. He has overcome some fifty minor demons,

I said, and his pride in his achievement is great. Let him imagine that he has wrestled with and overthrown the dread Emperor of Hell himself, and his very heart and brain will burst with overweening vanity. So confident was I of success that before I set out upon my mission I ordered a special pit to be dug in Hell and paved with glowing anthracite for the reception of the man who had wrought such havoc among the battalions of the lost. Then I winged my way to Ireland, and for a whole week I hovered in the air above the hermit's cave. I watched him as he squatted on his lean hunkers in the cavern mouth, a long rusty beard enveloping the lower part of his face, and the rest clothed with dirt of various kinds and colours. I watched the tawny wolves who came from the holes in the hillside and sat at his feet without fear. I saw him take his daily exercise, an amble around a nearby crag and back. I endured with fortitude for seven days the chill winds of the upper air, while, with all the will power which I have at my command, I insinuated into his mind the insidious temptation. 'You have tied down nearly fifty filthy demons,' I urged. 'Why not tie down the Prince of Darkness himself, and so gain the glory of having rid mankind of him forever?' At length my efforts were rewarded. I saw him dismiss his friends the wolves, bidding them go as he wished to meditate. I saw him walk up and down thoughtfully with tempered gait. I saw him dig a mighty cavity in the ground to hold me. I watched his preparations, and at the proper moment I manifested myself. I came as Lucifer, striding across the mountains in all my panoply of terror, while the miserable hermit in his rags took his stand on the bare hillside to receive me, quite unafraid. I had a clever plan. I meant to allow him almost to overcome me, and it was my intention at the last moment to substitute an airy phantom in my place."

"The combat must have been of a nature terrific beyond all description," remarked Fursey, round-eyed.

"It wasn't," said the Devil lamely. "I rolled the thunder around the sky a bit in keeping with my dignity, but I was afraid to make too much noise for fear of frightening him. Also I reduced myself to my natural size and took my stand ten paces distant from him."

"What happened then?" asked Fursey with bated breath.

"To tell you the truth, I don't exactly know," replied the Devil gloomily. "I only know that I got the worst of it from the very beginning. He had some religious sleight-of- hand up his ragged sleeve, and he shouted something at me in Latin, which had the effect of rendering me earthbound. I found myself suddenly bereft of my power either to rise into the air or to disappear, nor was I able to transform myself into a hare or other animal noted for its speed, which would have enabled me to make my escape. He then ran at me and smote me about the head so shrewdly with a club, with which he had armed himself, that to the present day I have a singing in my ears. For his age he was remarkably agile, and no matter how I doubled and ran, every time I turned my head, there he was cantering close behind. He seemed full of advantageous devices; that is, they were advantageous to himself. Finally he caught up with me, and with his club struck me a buffet that left me all bemused. While my brain was still beclouded, he tripped me and set about rolling me in a bed of furze. I need not tell you that by this time I was in a state of sore vexation but I was in no mood to grapple with him: my sole concern was to make my departure with the utmost despatch. I succeeded at last in this, and fled down the hillside with The Gentle Anchorite in close pursuit. I had to endure the indignity of precipitate flight along many miles of country road. All the children of the countryside were waiting for me, and they pelted me mercilessly with stones. At last the hermit's wind gave out, and he fell exhausted at the fourth milestone. One little brat of about seven years of age kept following me for a mile further, but fortunately his aim was poor. He only registered one hit, when he took the tip off my ear with a piece of slate."

Fursey sought to assume a sympathetic cast of countenance and shook his head disapprovingly.

"One thing is certain," concluded the Archfiend as he looked down at his torn and shabby garments. "Never again will I put a foot in the holy land of Ireland." He bent a steady gaze upon Fursey. "I don't like your countrymen," he said. "They're too rough."

There was a silence between them for a few moments. The Devil shifted himself on the barrow so as to attain a more comfortable position, and crossed his knees nonchalantly. He glanced at Fursey and then began to study his finger nails, which emitted pale sulphurous flames. Fursey, sitting on the sward with his parted legs stretched out before him, gazed at his toes and said nothing.

"I assume," said the Devil at last with a show of indifference, "that you didn't come here through courtesy merely to enquire about my well-being. Am I correct in assuming that it was business brought you?"

"Well, yes," conceded Fursey awkwardly. "In a way."

"I suppose you want something of me," said the Devil, with a trace of hardness in his voice. "No one ever seeks me through a desire for my company. I suppose you want me to do something for you."

"I have put the pursuit of good behind me," burst out Fursey. "I have come over to your side. I am determined to become a man of violent and atrocious character."

The Devil glanced at Fursey's innocent, moon-round face, and a slight smile flickered across his own countenance and disappeared beneath one of his pointed ears.

"Why?" he asked solemnly.

"The virtuous have done me great injury," replied Fursey. "They're still intent on tying me to a bundle of faggots and burning me with colourful ceremony. Any moment the King of Mercia may decide to demand impossibilities of me; and when I disappoint him, as I undoubtedly will, he will mete out to me a fate worse than death. I understand that he is very practised in meting out such fates."

"He is," grinned the Devil. "Ethelwulf is a playful lad, and very ingenious."

This remark seemed to Fursey to be in bad taste, having regard to his unenviable situation; but he ignored it and continued:

"Lastly, they have taken from me and carried away to Ireland the woman without whose company life seems to me dull and unprofitable."

"Wait now," said the Devil. "Are you certain you want her back?"

"Of course I want her back," retorted Fursey.

"Do nothing rash," advised the Archfiend. "You have lived with her for two months, and it's not as if your heart was still palpitating with the first tumults of love."

"I want her back," replied Fursey determinedly.

The Devil shook his head disapprovingly. "I advise you not to be too hasty," he urged. "You may be in love with her now, but cast your eyes twenty years ahead. Just imagine the old muzzle of her staring across the table at you three times a day. It gives one furiously to think."

"I don't care what you say," asserted Fursey. "I am determined to recover her."

The Devil shrugged his shoulders.

"May I ask a question?"

"Certainly," replied Fursey.

"Was your union consummated?"

"Certainly not," said Fursey indignantly. "We both had a good Irish Catholic upbringing, and we don't know how."

The Devil seemed impressed and lapsed into silence.

"Her laughter was part of the loveliness of the world," said Fursey, striving manfully to overcome his emotion. "The taking of her from me was a maimed business. But I mean to become apt in the practice of sorcery, so that I may transfix and utterly destroy Magnus, who has carried her off to Ireland to make her his bride."

"Sorcery," said the Archfiend meditatively. "You mean learning how to sweep the dust of the street towards his door so as to inflict him with the palsy or something equally unpleasant. You may succeed in annihilating him by sorcery if he's a man accessible only to coarse influences. I don't set much store by magic myself. It's old-fashioned stuff and belongs properly to a period prior to my era, though it survives here and there."

"I possess the spirit of a sorcerer," replied Fursey. "My trouble is that I'm lamentably inept in the practice. In fact, I may as well admit that I'm acquainted with no occult devices whatever. I'm no good at wizarding at all."

"I suppose that there's a certain amount to be said for sorcery," said the Devil. "One may learn the most arcane secrets and wander at will through the abysses of the unseen world. But time passes. What do you want of me, Fursey?"

"I want to know how to get to Ireland, how to recover Maeve, how to consume subtly and altogether destroy the baneful Magnus (or at least how, by the operation of magic, to afflict him with monstrous boils and warts), and lastly how to escape and live happily ever after."

"You're asking a great deal," replied the Devil testily. "I can neither recover Maeve for you nor instruct you in conjurations and charms. I might also add that the recipe for happiness is unknown to me. All I can offer you is two pieces of advice. I can advise you how to get to Ireland and I can advise you as to the present whereabouts of the master sorcerer Cuthbert, to whom you would do well to apprentice yourself. The rest is up to you."

"I suppose I must be satisfied with what I can get from you," replied Fursey hesitantly. "The state in which I find myself at present is so benighted that any help is welcome."

"You realise, of course," continued the Devil, looking at him hard, "that I am first and foremost a business man. You must pay my price. I shall require your soul in exchange for my advice."

"That's barefaced robbery," ejaculated Fursey indignantly. "My soul is worth more than two pieces of advice. Not so long ago you offered me in exchange for my soul, kingdoms, troops of females of the most lively and amiable character, and even a reputation as a man of letters."

"My poor Fursey," replied the Archfiend sympathetically, "you have little wit. Is your brain so moist that you do not realise that circumstances have changed? On those previous occasions when you refused my offers for your soul, it was I who was the petitioner. Now it is you who stand in need, and are the bidder. You need my advice. I fix the price. Take my offer or leave it."

"It's a black market operation," muttered Fursey.

"I don't know why you hesitate," said the Devil irritably. "Just now you told me that you were determined to become a man of violent and atrocious character. What better beginning can you make to a life of iniquity than the sale of your soul to me?"

"That's true," said Fursey despondently.

"Well?"

"All right," said Fursey glumly. "I suppose I have no choice. What do I do?"

"Well, we should really begin the ceremony by devouring the boiled bones of a black cat," replied the Fiend; "but as I don't suppose you have a black cat about you, we can dispense with that preliminary."

He raised his hand and made a mysterious pass in the air. Immediately a thick, dun vapour came rolling from behind a rock and came to rest at his feet. The Devil pulled up his sleeve and plunged his arm into the vapour. When he withdrew his hand, Fursey saw that he was holding what seemed to be a small chunk of sulphurous mist. This he parted delicately and drew out two pieces of goat's skin parchment, an iron pen and a small knife.

"It's necessary," he explained, "that the agreement be written in your blood. Are you not feeling well?"

"I don't know why," replied Fursey, "but I begin to feel peculiarly indisposed."

"The night airs and the damps of the forest affect some people adversely," said the Devil smoothly. "Oblige me by rolling up your sleeve."

The quaking Fursey did as he was bid. He emitted a short, sharp yelp of pain as the Devil, wielding his knife dexterously, made a small incision in his arm.

"Can you read or write?" enquired the Archfiend.

"No," replied Fursey mournfully.

"Then I better indite the agreement. All that will be necessary will be for you to affix your mark."

The Devil wrote assiduously for a few minutes.

"I wish you wouldn't keep jabbing the pen into my arm," complained Fursey. "If you do it again I'll call the whole thing off."

"I've got to dip the pen in the ink," retorted the Devil. "Will you kindly stay still. I never knew such a complaining fellow."

At last the documents were completed, and the trembling Fursey affixed his mark to each.

"Why do there have to be two copies?" he enquired.

"It has to be in duplicate," explained the Devil. "One copy is filed in my closet in Hell and the other must be swallowed by you."

"Swallowed?" repeated Fursey faintly, fixing his eyes on the thick goat's skin parchment.

"Yes," said the Devil briskly, "and swallowed entire. No chewing or biting bits off. I once let a robber captain from the County Cork consume his agreement in bites; and when I wasn't looking he bit his signature off and spat it out. "Oh, he was a tricky fellow all right."

Fursey gave a wan smile and continued to contemplate the bulky parchment.

"It will have a most adverse effect on my digestion."

"Nonsense," rejoined the Devil, "you'll have it down in no time. Go on, try."

A moment later Fursey was lying across the barrow choking while the Devil thumped him on the back.

"Is it up or down?" queried the Fiend, turning Fursey over.

"Up," gasped Fursey.

"This is very vexatious," said the Devil. "Try it again. Grip it firmly with your gullet and give a sudden swallow."

Fursey tried again, while the Devil pushed hard at the rolled end of the parchment which protruded from Fursey's mouth. A corncrake-like rattling came out of Fursey's throat, and he evinced every sign of imminent suffocation. The Devil removed the parchment and peered down Fursey's throat.

"The passage seems somewhat narrow," he said in disappointed tones. "I'm afraid I'll have to let you tear it into pieces and swallow a little at a time."

Fursey seated himself on the barrow and addressed himself to this unappetising meal.

"I don't see why all the chewing is necessary," declared the Devil, who was watching him closely. "You'll have all the ink washed off."

Fursey turned on him eyes full of pathos and slowly swallowed the last fragment.

"How do you feel?" asked the Fiend when the operation was complete.

Fursey did not answer for some time, but sat staring in front of him with his eyes glassy.

"I admit to a certain depression of spirit," he said at last.

"That's nothing," answered the Devil, giving him a hearty slap on the back. "Now for my part of the bargain. You may succeed in recovering this woman to whom you are so honourably attached, by learning the ingredients and use of love philtres from the sorcerer Cuthbert, who as a wizard is at the very summit of his profession. Similary, you can learn from Cuthbert how to overcome and demolish your rival Magnus. But you must be assiduous in your magical studies, otherwise you will never succeed in quenching Magnus."

"I'll apply myself with the utmost zeal," declared Fursey earnestly. "I'm determined to quench him, preferably with the greatest pain and inconvenience to himself."

"You are already acquainted with Cuthbert," continued the Devil. "For many years people believed him to be a highly respectable sexton, most sedulous in the performance of the duties of his state in life; but recently strange happenings of a magical nature in the neighbourhood of Cashel, enchanted cats and the like, gave rise to suspicion. Accusations had been levelled against Cuthbert, and the authorities, deeming it wiser to be sure than sorry, decided to burn him forthwith. He succeeded, however, in making his escape into the mountains twenty miles south of Cashel. He has now set up residence in a damp, unhealthy cave in the hillside over a place called 'The Gap'."

"I know 'The Gap'," replied Fursey.

"Well, seek him out and ask him to take you on as an apprentice sorcerer. You may mention my name if you think it will help."

"Very well," answered Fursey. "But how do I get back to Ireland? I came here flying on a broom, but brooms require to be anointed with a magical ointment. The little I had is exhausted and I don't know how to manufacture a further supply. Moreover, I doubt if flying conditions are now favourable in view of the approaching equinox."

"Have you not heard," enquired the Devil, "that there are at present some alleged Norse traders in port?"

"I have," responded Fursey. "In fact, I've seen some of them."

"How did they seem to you?"

"To tell the truth, they looked to me men of gloomy and ferocious disposition."

"So they are," the Devil replied happily. "They are Viking raiders, intent on a sudden onslaught on the Irish coast."

"I hope you're not going to suggest," put in Fursey nervously, "that I should have dealings with them?"

"I am," replied the Devil dreamily. "They would welcome a man like you, who knows the country, to guide them to some sleek Irish monastery."

"But," said Fursey shakily, "will I not be in certain danger from them? They are men of proud temper, who look as if they might be unkind."

"Sigurd the Skull Splitter is their captain," continued the Fiend, ignoring Fursey's feeble objections. "It will be a most promising start for you in your life of depravity. Tell them that your one ambition since you were a boy has been to become a Viking, and offer to pilot them to the rich monastery of Clonmacnoise. A little exaggeration will be advisable. Tell them that the monastery is piled high to the roof with gold plate and similar valuables. You can confide in them and tell them that you're a wizard and that through your control of the winds you can secure them a smooth sea passage."

"But," protested Fursey faintly, "I don't control the winds."

"You're a terrible man for raising difficulties," said the Devil shortly. "What matter whether you do or not as long as you succeed in convincing them? Bring a few stones with you wrapped in a piece of cloth and tie it to the mast with due ceremony. You can inform them that you have favourable winds tied in the cloth."

"But if they should discover the deception," objected Fursey. "Is it not the case that these Northmen are rather hasty of temper?"

"A little snappish sometimes," conceded the Devil. "But I don't know any other way you can get to Ireland. I'm afraid you've no choice."

He regarded Fursey for a moment, and then added sympathetically:

"Would you like a few minutes to let your thoughts dwell on the King of Mercia's College of Torturers before you make up your mind?"

"No," responded Fursey hurriedly. "I've made up my mind. I'll do it."

"Good," said the Devil briefly. "Goodbye now, Fursey. I have other work to do. I advise you to get back through the wood to your cottage and make your preparations."

"Just a minute," said Fursey.

The Devil, who had begun to disappear rapidly from the feet up, manifested himself once more in his entirety.

"What is it now?" he asked impatiently.

"As I came here," said Fursey nervously, "the wood was populous with shadows of most uninviting aspect. I would be greatly obliged to you if you would convey me rapidly to my own door and thus free me from the painful necessity of proceeding once more through the forest on foot."

"Certainly," replied the Fiend, and seizing Fursey by the hair, he sprang two hundred feet into the air. Fursey emitted a scream of mingled pain and fright.

"I declare to goodness," muttered the Devil between his teeth, "I never knew such a complaining fellow. Some people are never satisfied."

He glanced to left and right, and then shot across the ceiling of the forest, still holding Fursey by the hair. Fursey thought his last moment had come, and he kicked wildly as his dangling feet trailed across the treetops. It was a painful and terrifying journey, but it had at least the merit of celerity. He found himself suddenly deposited on his own doorstep, his legs too weak to support him. The Devil did not stay to bid him goodbye a second time, but returned the way he had come, in a delicate streak of lightning.

"By god," said Fursey, as he arose shakily to his feet, "I appear to have embarked on a business of strange and fearful import."

CHAPTER III

It was the turn of the tide, an hour before dawn, and the Vikings were preparing to launch their long dragonship on to the waters. Fursey cast an apprehensive glance at the never-tranquil seas and, summoning all his courage, approached the group of Norsemen that stood on the shore. By the fluttering torchlight he could see that they were hardy fellows, in aspect wild, brutal and terrific beyond description. They wore coarse woven cloth beneath their armour. Their helmets were distinguished by horns and wings, and their corselets of thick leather were covered with chain mail and iron scales. Those in authority wore necklaces and arm-rings of gold, while the ratings had to be satisfied with heavy beads of amber and glass. Shields, swords, spears and battleaxes were piled suggestively on the beach. But it was not their barbaric appearance which dismayed Fursey; rather it was their intent visages, which seemed to him devoid of candour and kindness. But he knew there was nothing for it, and he approached with a quaking heart.

"I beg your pardon," he lisped. "I want to speak to Captain Sigurd the Skull Splitter."

Dark eyes were turned on him, dull and heavy. A man pushed his way forward and confronted Fursey. His limbs were large and uncouth, and there hung from either side of his mouth a pair of moustaches so long that he had their ends tucked into his belt. When Fursey looked up at the visage furrowed with cunning, he felt his blood turn-

53

ing to water. He dropped his eyes, unable to bear the Skull Splitter's scrutiny.

"Well," demanded that personage, "what do you want of me?"

Fursey moistened his dry lips.

"I want to become a Viking," he quavered.

There was a moment's silence, then Fursey heard a series of short, gruff barks, which he took to be laughter; but when he glanced around the circle of fierce faces they were all regarding him impassively.

"Have you run away from school?" asked Sigurd at last.

There was another series of brief barks, and Fursey saw that they were all looking at him, waiting for an answer.

"I'm afraid I'm not making myself clear," he said. "I'm forty years of age and a very formidable wizard. I can be useful to you."

"A wizard?" queried Sigurd.

"Yes," answered Fursey. "Just watch me."

He walked a few paces up the beach to a withered thorn tree which stood beyond the line of shingle. The Norsemen followed him and stood in a circle watching. Fursey uncoiled the rope from his shoulder and flung the end of it over one of the gaunt branches. With a wave of his hand he directed their attention to the boughs naked of leaves.

"You will observe," he said, "that I have nothing up my sleeves. What would you like me to produce for you in the way of food or drink?"

For a moment no one spoke, then a hoarse voice growled from the back:

"A vat of the best Spanish wine."

"Certainly," said Fursey. "A vat of the best Spanish wine."

He gave the rope a sharp chuck and immediately an immense tun fell out of the tree and rolled down the beach into the water. Fursey skipped out of the way just in time to prevent his legs being broken, and the Norsemen scattered in all directions. Sigurd did not run, but Fursey noticed that he bent down and picked up a battleaxe.

"Don't do anything hastily for which you might afterwards be sorry," pleaded Fursey. "Maybe you'd like some mead?"

He pulled the rope, deftly caught the beaker and presented it to Sigurd, who sipped it gingerly.

"It's mead all right," he admitted.

"Maybe we ought to be getting on board ship," said one of the sea rovers nervously.

"I have here," continued Fursey, "a bag in which I have tied up half-a-dozen favourable winds. Fixed to your mast they may come in very useful."

"What is your proposition?" demanded Sigurd.

"I want passage to Ireland in your ship," explained Fursey. "In return my magical knowledge is at your disposal. Furthermore, if you should think of calling at a place called Clonmacnoise, I will be your pilot and guide. I know that country and the monastery intimately, having been a lay-brother there until three months ago, when they expelled me and relieved me of my vows."

The Vikings gathered around again, their faces quickened with interest.

"Why were you expelled?" asked Sigurd carefully.

"A flock of mischievous demons attached themselves to my person. It wasn't really my fault. I couldn't get rid of them."

"So the monks got rid of you?"

"Yes," replied Fursey dolefully. "I was most unjustly treated."

In the silence that followed, Fursey heard a battle-scarred veteran muttering: "He looks like a monk all right. I should know. I've killed scores of them."

Noticing their hesitation, Fursey proceeded hurriedly:

"It would be an exaggeration to say that you can't move around Clonmacnoise without tripping over piles of gold and other valuables; but gold is there, nevertheless, in great quantities. The monastery is situated in the interior on the River Shannon, and the religious settlements on the coast have for many years past sent their treasures inland to Clonmacnoise for safety."

"Describe the exact location of the monastery," commanded Sigurd.

"It's situated many miles inland from the sea and above the Danish city of Limerick," replied Fursey, "but it lies on the Shannon, a great river, readily navigable by ships of shallow draught such as yours."

Sigurd motioned a warrior to step forward. He was a tall, spare man of most uninviting aspect, with only one eye, which was a large, melancholy one. Fursey noticed that he had only two teeth, big, yellow fangs, which dwelt apart.

"Snorro," Sigurd addressed him, "you've heard what the stranger says. Is it true?"

"Yes," replied Snorro. "It is even as he says. I've been in the Danish settlement called Limerick, and I've heard the monastery Clonmacnoise spoken of. It lies in the vicinity."

"Why do you want to lead us to Clonmacnoise?" said the Skull Splitter, turning suddenly to Fursey.

"I want to get my own back on the monks who expelled me."

Sigurd nodded to Fursey and withdrew his men to some distance, where they conversed in guttural whispers. Fursey noticed with foreboding that some of the warriors drew their fingers across their throats before contributing their opinion, while others spoke first at length and then drew their fingers across their throats. He decided that this meant that there were two schools of thought among the Vikings, the first lot was persuaded that it was proper to slit his throat without further delay, while the second school deemed it more sensible to defer the slitting until he had led them to Clonmacnoise. He made up his mind that if the first school prevailed, he would try to make a run for it; but that if they

were outvoted by the second school, he would make a run
for it the moment the ship touched Irish soil. At length the
group broke up, and Sigurd came back to Fursey.

"You can come with us," he said, "but we carry no pas-
sengers. You must become a Viking."

Fursey hastily assured him that to become a Viking had
been his dearest wish ever since he was a small boy.

"All right," said the Skull Splitter. "You're under the care of
Snorro. He's responsible for you."

Sigurd went off to see his men aboard, and Fursey, by
direction of Snorro, went down on his knees and swore allegiance to Thor and undying hatred of the Christian faith.
Then Snorro helped him into a corselet of mail and a pair of
greaves. It was rather difficult to fit Fursey, who was small and
tubby; but Snorro managed it at last, except for the helmet.
Even the smallest helmet fell down over Fursey's eyes when
he nodded his head, but he found that by throwing his head
well back and keeping his eyebrows raised he could keep it
in position. Then Snorro girt on him a long, dangerous looking sword, which incommoded Fursey greatly in his walking.
He found that it took all the strength of his two arms to lift
the weighty battleaxe, but after several efforts he managed to
raise it and rest it in a soldierly manner on his right shoulder.
Thus accoutred he marched down in Snorro's wake to the
dragonship. Willing hands helped him, stumbling and falling, to a place in the narrow waist of the ship, and Snorro
clambered in after him. At Sigurd's request he tied his bag
of favourable winds to the mast, hoping earnestly as he did
so that they would not be required during the voyage. Back
in his place beside Snorro, he raised his helmet from over
his eyes and looked around him. The first grey of the dawn
had lightened the sky in the east. Fursey took off his helmet
altogether and contemplated the two ox horns with which
it was ornamented. Then he wiped the sweat from his brow.

"It should be a pleasant trip," he said to Snorro, who only grunted by way of reply.

"Will there be much murderings?" enquired Fursey anxiously.

"Don't worry," replied his gloomy companion. "You'll get your share of fun. These monks don't fight, but they squeal a lot when you cleave them. Of course we may run into fighting men. That's another matter altogether."

"I expect so," said Fursey. "In that eventuality how would you advise me to comport myself? I have never wielded lethal weapons before."

"Irish fighting men don't fight with any discipline or artfulness," replied Snorro. "They're strangers to wile. They just run straight at you and hit you with whatever they've got. I've known them with one blow to drive a warrior's helmet so far down into his breastbone as to render it impossible of extrication."

"And where was his head?" asked Fursey anxiously. Snorro turned on Fursey his one melancholy eye.

"I don't know", he said. "We could never find out. It must have been in his stomach."

Fursey turned away his face and looked longingly at the receding shore.

"The best thing to do when you encounter an Irish fighting man," said Snorro, "is to receive his first blow on your shield. Then you must hew off his feet at the ankles. This upsets his balance and, as he falls, you can, if you're any good, sweep off his head with a back stroke of your sword. There's nothing difficult about it."

For the first day and a half, during which the dragonship rode up and down across the swelling seas, Fursey lay in the bilge water on the floor of the boat hopelessly seasick. It was only on the afternoon of the second day that he dragged himself up on to his seat in the slim waist of the ship and cast a jaundiced eye over the waters.

"You better have something to eat," said Snorro, passing him a hog's foot and a pannikin of metheglin. Fursey averted his gaze.

"No, thank you," he replied. "I fear that my stomach is in a state of consolidation."

"I never heard such retching," asserted Snorro, looking at him curiously. "And the queer things you brought up. What did you last have to eat anyway? It wasn't a goat's skin overcoat by any chance?"

Fursey shook his head despondently. He pondered Snorro's words for some time, and at last realised that he had probably rid himself of the goat's skin parchment on which was inscribed his agreement to sell his soul. Its loss cheered him considerably, until he remembered that there was a duplicate copy filed in the archives of Hell.

An hour passed, and it became late afternoon—a lazy September afternoon, soaked through and through with sunlight. He had been dreamily watching the thin line of foam in the wake of the ship, spreading left and right; and, as it divided, veining the waters like marble. Now he awoke to the fact that for some time apparently there had been a slackening of speed. The waves no longer ran out to left and right from beneath the keel. He heard a sudden shout from the prow.

"Sorcerer!"

Fursey's heart gave a jump; and, glancing around, he saw Sigurd the Skull Splitter smiling affably as he directed Fursey's attention to the great raven-embroidered sail. It lay against the mast quite loose and relaxed.

"The wind has fallen," said Sigurd. "It's time for you to unloose one of your favourable winds. It's a good thing you brought them with you."

Fursey could see no way out of his predicament. He arose shakily and made his way to the mast. When he pulled the cords and four stones fell from their covering cloth on to the deck, the Vikings looked rather surprised. They said nothing, however, but sat back waiting to feel the brave breeze on their faces once more and to see the raven sail flap and swell. When five minutes had elapsed without anything happening, they began to whisper among themselves and cast dark glances in the sorcerer's direction. Fursey closed his eyes and began to regret that during her lifetime he hadn't been kinder to his mother. The discussion which followed was tumultuous and protracted. It centred mostly around the manner in which Fursey should be ravaged and maimed before he was flung overboard. The Vikings had come speedily to appreciate that in the absence of a favourable wind it would be incumbent on them to resort to the back-breaking business of rowing until a wind should once more spring up. It was obvious to Fursey that he was a grievous disappointment to them, and he listened with dismay to their talk of hamstringing and houghing. The steersman, who seemed a man of particularly irritable temper, impatiently drew a nine-inch knife from his belt and, placing it between his teeth, began to scramble over the benches towards Fursey.

"Drowning is too comfortable an end," he mumbled. "Let us proceed at once to demolish him utterly, but by small stages."

Sigurd took no part in the discussion, but stood by the mast listening to the various expressions of opinion. It was Snorro, who seemed to have taken a liking to Fursey, who restrained the ardour of his shipmates.

"Even the best of wizards," he urged, "can make a mistake. I've been watching Fursey, and I'm convinced that he's the briskest of men, but is at present suffering from a consolidated stomach. Under such conditions no sorcerer can do himself justice. You have all seen him producing wine and mead from the bare branches of a thorn tree. Take care lest by laying violent hands upon him you offend so powerful a sorcerer and he retaliate by starting to beat the sea and thereby raise a storm. Remember, too, his value to us as a guide to the opulent monastery of Clonmacnoise."

The Norsemen hesitated and stood in groups muttering fiery Viking oaths. Snorro stepped up to Sigurd and began to urge him to use his influence on Fursey's behalf. The wretched Fursey sat alone on his bench shivering in every limb. At last Sigurd spoke.

"Fursey," he said, "in this matter I fear that you have fallen appreciably short of success. How has that come about?"

"To tell you the truth," squeaked Fursey, "I'm not much of a sorcerer. I lack practice. I really don't know how to capture and imprison favourable winds."

Sigurd studied him thoughtfully. "Maybe it's just as well," he said at last, "that you know nought of the subject. A little knowledge might have been dangerous and productive of lamentable, and even fatal, consequences. You might have only succeeded in dealing out a hurricane. Go back to your places, men, and take to the oars."

"Maybe the men would like a drink," suggested Fursey weakly, "to make up for their disappointment."

This suggestion had a soothing effect on the crew, and for ten minutes Fursey busied himself producing satisfying beakers of the choicest ale, which he distributed to all. When everyone was carousing merrily, he pulled his rope from the mast and, coiling it over his shoulder, returned to his seat beside Snorro.

"Thank you," he said. "I owe it to you that I have escaped their desperate purposes."

There was a friendly light in Snorro's one eye. "That's all right," he whispered. "I have fortunately some influence with the Captain. My mother is promised to him in marriage. You can do something for me when we land," he added. "I would deem it a friendly act if you would so work magically on my coat of mail that through it no steel may bite."

"Certainly," agreed Fursey. "The moment we land I'll work on it with the mightiest charm I know."

So potent was the ale which Fursey had produced and distributed, that there was soon a gladsome change in the attitude of the crew towards him. His name was shouted from all corners of the ship, and when Fursey's eye was caught he was toasted in the foaming beakers. Before long willing hands grasped him and conveyed him once more over the well of the ship to the mast, where he was required to produce a second round of drinks. Fursey, who had a weak man's liking for being liked, worked with a will, producing further beakers, this time as big as buckets. Scents of uproarious joviality followed. Fierce warriors rolled around in the scuppers, engaged in friendly throttling matches; while the ship's skald, who had been brought along so as to compose a poem on the adventure, began to recite at the top of his voice, with tears streaming down his face, an epic of his own composition on the life and deeds of the fabulous Ragnar Ironbreeks. At length Sigurd the Skull Splitter intervened and restored order with a blunted axe half overlaid with iron, which he kept for such occasions. Back in their places, the oarsmen flung their moustaches back over their shoulders so that they would not interfere with the rowing and set to work with a will. For some time the dragonship kept going around in circles to the immense amusement of its crew; but at last matters righted themselves, and the long, slim ship, impelled by its fifty oars, cut its way forward straight into the sunset. The skald, who had fallen asleep with his head in a beaker, was prodded awake with a spear and instructed to recite a heartening lay. To obviate the possibility of his falling overboard, he was placed seated with his back to the mast, to which he was lashed with a length of rope. His timpans, flageolets and whistles were placed in a basket beside him so that his recital might lose nothing in artistic effect. After some moments of gloomy meditation he set his fingers coursing up and down the few strings of the timpan and began the epic account so well known to Viking raiders, of the tyrant Charlemagne, who had decreed death for every Saxon who refused baptism. Some parts of the history he related, some he sang. Hour after hour the tale continued. It told of the banishment of an entire race from their native land to Denmark and the shores of the Baltic, because of their fidelity to the faith of their fathers. It told of Christian fire and sword, of martyrdom and massacre; and it asserted that the faith in the old gods was living still. The faces of the Vikings grew pale and grim, and they tugged harder at their oars, as they listened to the relation of the wrongs of centuries. Fursey, happy in his new popularity, sat in his place amidships listening to the fierce, sad tones of the skald as they filled the ship and then faded away across the evening seas. The recital was in a language which he did not understand, but he thrilled at the emotion with which the passages were charged, and he was charmed by the occasional instrumental accompaniment. He sat, his eyes wandering from the rune-carved weapons and the grotesquely decorated ornaments of his companions to the great carved dragons rising high in the stern and prow. He gazed for a long time into the blood-red glamour of the sunset and watched the incredible play of pearl and copper green and every other imaginable colour on the surface of the water. The sun had disappeared into the shimmering carpet of the sea by the time the skald had concluded his recital; and, as he was now quite sober, he was unlashed from the mast and crept back to his place in the prow, where he sat motionless, gazing with a face of unutterable sadness at the fast shrinking colours in the west. Fursey watched his thin, delicate features covertly, wondering, as every layman wonders, what strange thoughts were gripping his poet's brain. The skald could not have answered the question. His mind was a tumult of faint echoes of all the race's memories of sunsets, of partings and of broken armies. The delicate forehead and intelligent eyes, brooding on the waste of darkening waters, concealed no real activity. The brain beneath was merely attuned to all that in human history had been dignified and beautiful; and because all beauty is permeated with sadness, his mind and face were sad. Fursey's gaze wandered to Sigurd erect in the prow, and thence to the fifty oarsmen, moving rhythmically forward and backward as one man. It was one of those blessed hours when everyone is at peace with his companions, feeling himself to be in perfect union with those near him and with his surroundings. Fursey was indescribably happy. His troubles seemed to be very far away and unimportant. He felt that he loved these men and all mankind. The Vikings spoke little, and that little in undertones. Some time later, when the stars began to come out, Snorro raised to the heavens his one melancholy eye to identify for Fursey the constellations which he recognised, and Fursey in his turn named the few that were known to him. It was an abbreviated conversation though it lasted for hours, a conversation without strain, a dialogue such as is usual between old friends, mostly brief statement and affirmative grunt. When the moon came into the sky, changing the entire ocean to a sheet of silver, Sigurd arranged the relays of oarsmen, and a great part of the crew stretched themselves on the floor of the ship to sleep. Fursey bade Snorro good-night and, creeping beneath his bench, was soon asleep too.

When Fursey awoke he climbed on to his seat again and sat blinking at the misty splendour of the morning. As far as his eye could see was a line of broken beaches and green headlands, backed by forest.

"Where are we?" he asked.

"South coast of Ireland," answered Snorro, "approaching the Saltee Islands." Of course. The little breeze that blew was laden with pleasant odours and heavenly fragrance. It could not be otherwise—it came to their nostrils across the holy land of Ireland. They were rowing close inshore to obtain such protection as they could from the breeze, which was unfavourable. Fursey could see at the edges of the woods droves of pigs feeding on nuts and roots, while the herdsmen, clad in goat's skins, sat blowing patiently through rustic pipes very much out of tune. Here and there, where a woodland track leading from settlement to settlement came for a little space into the open, a traveller on horse or foot paused to stare out to sea at the long oaken ship with its two great dragons rearing themselves from the water fore and aft. By Sigurd's orders all weapons had been concealed, and the banner that was flown indicated trade; but, as the morning wore on, Fursey noticed that excitement was manifested in every settlement which they passed. Horsemen would set out galloping along the roads and little bands of five or six men would run out to the end of a spit of land and even up to their waists into the sea, waving swords and defying the Norsemen to land and fight. The Vikings paid no attention, but continued to bow over their oars. Fursey's heart gave a mighty bound, however, when he witnessed the first of these challenges and watched half-a-dozen starveling natives capering madly in the surf as they brandished notched and rusty swords and howled opprobrious epithets at the disciplined Viking force of ten times their numbers. As the dragonship sped swiftly by there were tears in Fursey's eyes. It came to him that whatever else one could say about his countrymen, no one had ever been able to accuse them of cowardice.

The breeze had been leaning over for some time, and now it was found to have veered sufficiently to justify raising the great raven sail. While this was being done, breakfast was handed around, a hunk of badger flesh, garnished with garlic and kale. Fursey knew that Norsemen were vain of their appearance, but he was surprised to see that now that they were rid of the necessity for rowing they produced bronze razors and small mirrors made of polished steel. Hooking their moustaches carefully back behind their ears, they began to shave the rest of their faces. The older and more wrinkled sea rovers were even provided with large wooden spoons, which they placed in each side of their mouths in turn so as to stretch their corrugated cheeks and so have a smooth surface for the passage of the razor. Then they plaited their moustaches and set to polishing their bronze and amber armlets and necklaces. Only when these offices had been completed did they begin to manifest an interest in the strange shore along which they were travelling. Snorro knew the coast intimately and was able to name every headland and islet. The seaboard was strange to Fursey, though he remembered having heard the names of the larger landmarks and territories. He was able, however, to explain certain phenomena unfamiliar to the Norsemen, as, for instance, the meagre, half-naked creatures, more like some nondescript species of the animal order than human beings, who came to the mouths of their caves or suddenly popped up their heads from behind rocks to stare at the strange ship.

"They're undoubtedly maritime hermits, who live largely on shell fish," explained Fursey to the intrigued Vikings.

"But do they not live in community?" he was asked.

"No," replied Fursey. "Their love of monastic seclusion is such that they cannot stand the sight of one another," and he made a feeble attempt to explain the nature of sanctity. But the Vikings only shook their heads and made the centuries-old joke common to every Germanic tongue, in which Ireland is called "Irre-land"—the Land of the Mad.

On the following morning they rounded the toe of Kerry and started to make their way up the west coast. As they passed under the Skellig and Blasket Islands, places efflorescent with sanctity, the Norsemen gazed with amazement at the headlands on which motionless figures knelt with arms outstretched in prayer. Fursey explained that these were saints, who had taken up this devout position many years before and were in a state of abstraction from the things of sense ever since. One reverend figure, his bald pate covered with a fine green moss, particularly took the sea rovers' fancy; and they became turbulent until Sigurd, to quiet them, steered close inshore so that they could have a good look at him. He knelt on a small grassy plateau at the cliff's edge and was at least a hundred-and-twenty years old. His clothes had been worn off him and swept away many years before by the action of wind and rain, but Heaven had not suffered him to be ashamed, and accordingly a thick, white beard covered every part of his person. In his outstretched right hand a pair of squirrels were laboriously raising a family.

"Are you certain he's alive?" asked Snorro suspiciously.

"Of course he's alive," retorted Fursey indignantly. "Even in my time in Clonmacnoise there was a Father Juniper, a man of such gentleness that ducks came without fear and roosted on every part of his person."

"Was he canonised?"

"No, he was expelled," replied Fursey. "His benign influence was such that he charmed the wolves, and he invariably came back from a walk accompanied by two or three of them. The abbot had to keep armed men permanently posted at the gate. It was an expense, and it was felt to be bad for discipline."

As they sailed northwards towards the broad mouth of the River Shannon, Fursey sat silent in his place amidships, the prey of painful thoughts and imaginings. His conscience was nibbling him. He glanced furtively at the unattractive countenances of the evilly-disposed men with whom he was associated. It was all very well launching oneself into a life of iniquity, but surely there should be some pleasure or gain to be got from it. One had only to contemplate the fierce aspect of his companions to realise that they were men exposed to all the hurricanes of unbridled passions, and their very proximity was alarming to Fursey. Yet these were the men whom he was helping to lead against his own countrymen and, worse still, against his own kind. His conscience told him that he was on the wrong side. "Ill will come of it," he muttered to himself.

"We're passing Ballybunion," said Snorro suddenly. Fursey roused himself to gaze with morbid horror at the little town which had the worst of all names.

"You know the settlement?" asked Snorro.

"No," responded Fursey, "but I've heard of it. I understand that the dissolute inhabitants are entirely given over to pleasure and vice. It's much frequented in the summer months by members of the lower clergy, who spend their time gaming and in the consumption of strong liquors. It's a notorious centre for cockfighting, dicing and other licentious pursuits."

Even though it was still only early afternoon, the night life of Ballybunion was already under way, and one could hear the wicked hum of the settlement, the barking of depraved dogs, the incessant rattling of dice boxes and the indignant howls of drunkards being ejected from taverns because they had no more money. But the dragonship soon left this modern Babylon behind and crept up the estuary of the River Shannon.

It was almost dusk when they arrived at Limerick and, rowing some hundred yards beyond the settlement, anchored in mid-stream. There was much whispering among the crew, and at length a boat was lowered, into which Sigurd and Snorro scrambled.

"Come on," said Snorro to Fursey, "but leave your weapons and helmet behind."

The surprised Fursey climbed into the boat and Snorro quickly rowed ashore. There Sigurd gave his final instructions to Snorro in undertones, and strode away by himself into the town.

Fursey glanced around him and saw that the city consisted of an irregular patch of grass, around which were dotted at intervals some fifty or sixty circular cabins, built of wickerwork and thatched with straw. Beyond the houses he could see in the gathering dusk fields of tillage and pasture stretching away to the outskirts of the forest. The inhabitants, who were mostly Danes, wore multi-coloured cloaks chequered with spots and stripes. An occasional Irishman was to be seen clad in a loose-sleeved mantle of frieze. On the quay beside Fursey a local saint was solemnly shaking hands with his friends before setting out on a perilous journey into the wilds of North Kerry, where he was to make his fourth attempt to convert the robber lord of that territory, known far and wide as The Wolf of Ballybunion. In the centre of the green an idle crowd was listening to a street preacher, clad in a kilt of severe and uncompromising cut, who was urging them to burn something or other of which he didn't approve.

"Come, and I'll show you the city," said Snorro, touching Fursey's arm.

"Why have the others not landed?" asked Fursey as they set out.

"Sigurd is afraid that they'll start drinking in some Mariners' Rest and betray the fact that we're not traders. So he has confined them on board ship until we start upstream before dawn."

"And where has he gone himself?"

"He has gone to the King's House to fix things. That's it over there, the building with the three skeletons hanging from the tree outside the door."

"What do you mean by 'fix things'?"

"Well," explained Snorro, "when we sack Clonmacnoise and pass by here again to-morrow evening the King will expect a percentage in return for keeping his mouth shut and not impeding our passage. After all, he's a Christian, and would normally be expected to oppose a raid on a monastery."

"It's all very bewildering," said Fursey. "I always understood that although this is a Norse settlement it had been converted to Christianity and was notable for its piety."

"It is rather in process of conversion. The King is a Christian, but most of his subjects still cling to the older faith. He does not persecute them on that account, being a liberal and enlightened man. Most of the public institutions are still what you people call pagan. And certainly it is the case that Limerick has always been noted for its many religious institutions. There, for instance," said Snorro, pointing to a cluster of huts within a palisade, "is The Sick and Indigent Sea Rovers' Institution."

Fursey peered over the palisade and saw half-a-dozen ancients doddering around the enclosure.

"All hardy Vikings once," declared Snorro. "Now all they're any good for is eating porridge and yapping about their battles with their toes to the fire. Over there is The Broken-Down Norsemen's Institute. It's necessary to have lost a minimum of two limbs to secure admittance."

"Let's have a drink," suggested Fursey suddenly.

"Certainly," agreed Snorro. "Have you any money?"

"No," replied Fursey, "but I have a rope. All I want now is a tree."

Snorro searched the gathering darkness anxiously with his one eye. At last they detected a tree in a quiet place behind one of the cabins. Soon they were seated on the turf and provided with a flagon of ale apiece.

"Why did you bring your battleaxe with you," enquired Fursey, "if Sigurd doesn't want it to be known that we are an armed force?"

"An odd battleaxe doesn't count," replied Snorro. "A Norseman would look naked without his battleaxe. Besides, in a strange town you have to have something to keep away the dogs."

They sat for some time in silence. If Fursey had hoped to make Snorro drunk and so effect his own escape, his plan was doomed to failure. Snorro continued to drink, but very temperately. At last Fursey spoke again.

"Why have you and I landed?"

"We're to spend the night in the town to pick up any gossip that may be relevant. Before we go upstream tomorrow we must be certain that nothing untoward is happening in the neighbourhood of Clonmacnoise. If there's a war in progress, or any movement of armies, we'll hear it talked of in the place in which we're going to spend the night."

"I see," said Fursey. After a few moments he ventured another question. "I'm not much use to you as a spy. Why did you bring me with you?"

Snorro emptied the beaker before he answered.

"Well," he said, "before an undertaking such as to-morrow's raid it's usual to take the omens. The crew are anxious that this should be done so that they may have some indication of what to expect to-morrow."

"It seems reasonable," remarked Fursey, "but what has that to do with me?"

"Well," replied Snorro, "taking the omens involves the examination of entrails for the purposes of divination, and Sigurd was afraid that the crew might perform the ceremony while he and I were absent on shore. That's why he told me to take you along with me."

"I don't understand," said Fursey. "I'm sure it's an interesting ceremony, but I don't mind missing it."

"You won't miss it," said Snorro patiently. "It's your intestines that are to be consulted."

"My intestines!" ejaculated Fursey. "But will I survive the ceremony?"

"I never heard of anyone that did," replied Snorro gloomily. "But you needn't worry. Sigurd had got it adjourned for twenty-four hours. You see, we plan to anchor the ship tomorrow around the bend below Clonmacnoise, and you and I will land and creep to within sight of the monastery. You will point out to me the dispositions of the settlement; and then we are to creep back and report to Sigurd, who will draw up his plan so as to take the place by surprise."

"I see," said Fursey impatiently, "but what's that you said about an adjournment for twenty-four hours?"

"Sigurd explained to the men that your usefulness will not be exhausted until the attack has been launched. He pacified them by promising to divine from your entrails after the raid whether or not we shall have a smooth passage home. The men are inclined to grumble; they say it's not quite the same thing. They'd rather learn about the probabilities of success beforehand."

"Naturally," was Fursey's feeble rejoinder. "Nevertheless, I trust that Sigurd prevailed."

"He did. Anyway," said Snorro soothingly, "I would not wish you to be put to death until you have worked magically on my coat of mail, as you promised, so that through it no steel may bite."

"That will take some time," responded Fursey hastily. "It will be necessary for me to collect certain powerful herbs and unguents."

"There's no hurry," Snorro assured him as they arose, "you have really until to-morrow afternoon. I wouldn't wish you on any account to botch the job on the coat of mail."

Fursey was very pensive as they walked back through the town. Although it was now quite dark, most of the inhabitants seemed to be out of doors, leaning against the walls of the houses gazing into nothingness.

"What do you think of Limerick?" asked Snorro.

"It seems to be a city of bewhiskered old women," replied Fursey.

"It is," replied Snorro, "both male and female."

They had come to a low, rambling building in the centre of the town.

"This is where we stay for the night," said Snorro, and he read for Fursey the inscription over the doorway. " 'Night Shelter for Unemployed Vikings, under the patronage of Thor the Thunderer'. That's Thor," he added, pointing to where there stood over the doorway an immense statue of a very formidable character waving a hammer. They had to take their place in a queue of Norse down-and-outs in sordid and base attire. It was hard to believe of most of them that they had once ridden the seas in search of adventure, for they were in general low and obscure fellows with squalid beards and dangling hair. They all appeared to be suffering from malnutrition, and those that weren't either lame or halt had broken backs or lacked their full complement of eyes, ears and arms. When the queue moved forward sufficiently to bring Snorro and himself within the doorway, Fursey saw a broad-shouldered warrior seated behind a table in the entrance. He had a battleaxe swinging from his wrist by a leathern thong, and he was entering each man's name in a sheepskin register.

"That's the Superintendent," whispered Snorro.

As Fursey and his companion came alongside, the Superintendent glanced up at them and shot at them a series of questions.

"Newcomers?"

"Yes," replied Snorro.

"Names?"

"Snorro and Fursey."

"Occupation?"

"Able-bodied seamen, at present unemployed."

"Race?"

"Norse."

"Religion?"

"Worshippers of Thor the Thunderer."

"Very well," said the Superintendent. "Battleaxes are to be surrendered at the Office. It will be returned to you in the morning," and he handed a small metal check to Snorro. Then he read aloud to them the regulations, a copy of which hung on the wall.

> "1. The Superintendent has the right to refuse admission to anyone who may reasonably be suspected of being in a rabid state.
>
> "2. Any attempt at stabbing or throat-slitting will render the offender liable to immediate expulsion.
>
> "3. Knives, spears, swords, battleaxes or hatchets smuggled into the Institution under circumstances giving rise to the reasonable suspicion that they have been brought in for an improper purpose are liable to confiscation."

Fursey and Snorro passed into the dormitory. About thirty inmates were huddled over a spark in the fireplace at the far end of the room. The hall was long and narrow, and a long bench ran its entire length. About three feet higher than the bench a rope also ran the length of the room. One slept sitting on the bench with one's hands on the rope. You then rested your chin on your hands like a dog resting its chin on its paws. At sunrise the Superintendent, after a warning shout, cut the rope with his battleaxe and all the late sleepers fell on to the floor. These things were explained to Fursey by a thin, white-faced creature who sat down beside him. Snorro had gone out into the washroom which adjoined the dormitory. The stranger, who addressed Fursey in nervous, intimate whispers, was barefooted and clad in rags. Indeed, the only entire garment he had was a battered Viking helmet. He seemed haunted by some fear, and his eyes kept shifting up and down the room. Fursey realised suddenly that he was in an extreme state of terror and that he had perforce to speak to someone.

"Do you know," he whispered suddenly, "whether they make you say prayers to Thor?"

"I don't know," replied Fursey. "I was never here before. Ask someone."

"I was never here either," responded his companion, "but I've been in similar places."

His eyes roved anxiously up and down and at last lighted on another human wreck who was sitting a few feet away. His elbow was resting on the rope and he looked more like a corpse that had been dried in the sun, than anything else. When questioned he answered in deep, sepulchral tones.

"Oh, yes, this is a very religious institution. Only last week there was an atheist in here, and he hid in the washroom while the rest of us were committing our well-being to Thor. The Superintendent dragged him out and nearly hacked him to pieces before throwing him out. Oh, the Superintendent is a very pious man."

The ragged creature began to tremble so as to set the whole rope vibrating.

"What's wrong?" whispered Fursey.

"I'm a Christian," came out in a terrified whisper. "I got in here under false pretences. But I can't join in public prayers to Thor. I'd be afraid that I'd be stricken dead."

"Well, you better get out quick," advised Fursey.

"But will they let me out?"

"What's to prevent you slipping down towards the door? If you're asked any questions say you're sick and that you want to go outside for a few moments."

"I'll try it," said the little creature. "Thanks."

"Wait a minute," said Fursey, gripping him by the arm. "Look, do you want to do a pious act?"

The miserable creature's teeth began to chatter. "What is it?" he asked at length.

Fursey had taken a desperate resolution. "Listen," he whispered urgently, "did you see the dragonship?"

"Yes, traders."

"No, raiders. They're going to sack Clonmacnoise tomorrow."

The little man uttered a pious ejaculation and looked at Fursey with horror.

"There's not a moment to lose," hissed Fursey. "When you get out of here make straight to Mulligan. He's the chieftain of the territory in which Clonmacnoise is situated, and his is the nearest military aid. Go at once. Don't waste a moment."

"Wouldn't it be better to warn Clonmacnoise?" gasped the stranger.

"No. Time would be lost. The monastery in its turn would have to seek aid from Mulligan. I'll try to warn Clonmacnoise myself. Do you think you can do it? I notice that you've no shoes."

"I'll do it," said the little man. "I'll do it somehow."

"Rouse the countryside anyway," urged Fursey. "But don't tell anyone until you're well clear of this territory. This place is all Norse."

Fursey watched the little man sidling down the hall and then make a sudden rush through the door. Then Fursey bowed his head on the rope with a full heart. He saw in his mind's eye the fluttering rags and the bare feet running through the night, across thorns and sharp rocks. How little the Christians had done for that frail, starving man, and yet he had not for a moment hesitated.

Snorro was standing at Fursey's elbow. "I'm just drifting around to pick up what information I can. I'll be back."

Fursey nodded, and Snorro disappeared once more into the washroom.

"Here's Thorkils," said the corpse who was sitting beside Fursey.

Fursey looked up and saw a huge, red-haired man shouldering his way down the room from the door. He seemed to be sodden with drink, and the other inmates got out of his way hastily. His features were grim and ill-favoured, and his ginger moustaches were uneven and ragged as if they had been bitten off in some struggle to the death. He was of powerful physique and had hands like two hams. He passed Fursey and, going to the fire, threw two aged Vikings into the corner so as to secure a place for himself. He sat for a few moments warming his knees, then he turned his great torso and let his glance travel up the middle of the room. His eyes fell upon Fursey. It was some moments before Fursey realised that he was being stared at. When he saw Thorkils' bloodshot eyes fixed upon him, he averted his own gaze. Thorkils immediately staggered to his feet and came uncertainly across to Fursey.

"Are you laughing at me by any chance?" he enquired roughly.

Fursey assured him that he wasn't.

"Because if I thought you were I'd make the pieces of you fly this way and that."

Fursey again assured him that he was mistaken, and Thorkils returned to the fireplace.

"That's Thorkils," repeated the cadaverous creature seated beside Fursey. "I wouldn't argue with him if I were you. He has the name of being peevish when he's crossed."

"I've no wish to argue with him," responded Fursey nervously. He allowed his eyes to wander all over the room, and it was a long time before he ventured to throw a quick glance across at Thorkils. The big man was watching him from under beetling, ginger brows, and the moment he caught Fursey's eye he heaved himself on to his feet once more and came staggering across.

"Are you quite certain that you're not laughing at me?" he queried. "Because if you are, it's the last thing you'll ever do. By the time I'm finished with you I'll leave you totally bereft of warmth and animation."

"I'm not laughing at you," said Fursey faintly. "I assure you that I'm not laughing at anyone. You can take my word for it."

Thorkils hiccupped. "That's all right then," he said, "but I warn you that I'm not a man to be laughed at. I've formed the opinion that you're of an artful, gloomy and mischievous disposition. I'm well acquainted with your trickeries. So be careful."

Thorkils returned to his seat, and Fursey began to pray desperately for Snorro's return. A few moments later he noticed out of the corner of his eye that Thorkils was once more getting to his feet. All around Fursey the inmates seemed sunk in their own thoughts. Fursey himself arose and with shaky steps walked the length of the room. He took his stand near the door beside the Superintendent. When he looked back he saw that Thorkils was watching him with narrowed eyes. When a few minutes later the Superintendent was called from the room on some business, Fursey began to move idly in the direction of the washroom with the intention of attaching himself to Snorro, but on the way he was intercepted by Thorkils.

"I knew you were laughing at me," said the Viking, and raising his great fist he brought it down with all his strength on Fursey's pate. Fursey uttered a lamentable moan and crumpled on to the floor. It took the Superintendent and Snorro five minutes to remove Thorkils from the premises, and it is doubtful if they would even then have succeeded in doing so, only that the Superintendent lost his temper and rendered Thorkils unserviceable by a sudden blow on the skull with the flat of his battleaxe.

When Thorkils had been thrown out, they began to search among the debris on the floor for the remnants of Fursey. They found him under the bench quite unconscious, but with a languid smile on his face.

"I feared at first," said the Superintendent, "that the vital spark had fled."

They lifted Fursey and put him on the bench with his chin resting on the rope, and trusted that he would be all right in the morning.

CHAPTER IV

On the summit of a small, green hill Fursey and Snorro lay on their stomachs on the grass and gazed down at the monastic settlement of Clonmacnoise. It lay half-a-mile away just above the high flood mark of the river, a cluster of beehive huts and small churches clearly visible in detail in the mild afternoon sunlight. One could even see the tiny, black figures of the monks moving like ants in the passages between the whitewashed cells, and dotted in the surrounding fields. Looking over his shoulder, Fursey could see the dragonship around the bend of the river, drawn in close against the bank. Snorro was grunting to himself as he strove to disentangle one of his moustaches from a bed of thistles. Fursey spoke rapidly in an attempt to hide his emotion.

"It's a most famous monastery," he said. "In the sixth century the blessed Kieran chose this spot for his foundation because it was lonely and remote from men. He knew that his monks could work and pray in this spot, their minds free from worldly imaginings. And so they have during four long centuries, even to the present day. They have lived in close converse with the saints, barricaded in from the world and from worldly follies."

"Are they happy?" grunted Snorro.

"Ah," replied Fursey, "who is happy?"

"We mustn't waste time," said Snorro. "Point out the geography of the place to me."

"The whole settlement is enclosed by a palisade of wooden posts and thorns," said Fursey, pointing. "That is to keep out the wild beasts which lurk in the forest. The gateway, which is of wickerwork, is on the northern side, opening on to the Pilgrims' Way."

"It will be easy to cut our way with battleaxes through the palisade," said Snorro.

"Yes," replied Fursey sorrowfully, "very easy. Do you see the great cross and what looks like a forest of stones?"

Snorro shaded his one eye with his hand. "Yes," he replied at last.

"That is the graveyard where the generations of princes of the neighbouring territories are buried. It's a very high- class graveyard. You have to be an abbot or a chieftain or a very great warrior to get into it."

"I observe that there are two very solid-looking round towers," remarked Snorro.

"Yes," answered Fursey, his eyes coming to rest on the conical caps of the two narrow, tapering buildings of stone which rose high above the surrounding huts like two upright pencils.

"I'm acquainted with round towers," growled Snorro. "That's why surprise is so important. If the monks once get up into those towers with their gold plate we'll never get them out."

"That's the object of round towers," said Fursey softly.

"I think we better attack from the river, having first sent a small landing party to cut off retreat in case some of the fleeter young monks try to escape into the woods with the valuables. What's wrong with you? You're crying."

Fursey passed his fist across his eyes.

"I was thinking of the twenty-four years that I spent in Clonmacnoise as a laybrother. It's the only real home I've ever known. I know every member of the community."

"Don't worry," said Snorro jocularly as he bared his two yellow fangs. "Your friends will all be with the saints to-night."

"I trust so," said Fursey mournfully. "The only one I'd have any doubt about is the cook. He's a man of hard temper. Many the time when I was working in the kitchen he hit me over the head with the ladle; but, then, I suppose I wasn't much good."

"You're against them now?" asked Snorro suspiciously.

"Yes, of course," replied Fursey. "Didn't they expel me without adequate reason, and hasn't the abbot ever since been intent on burning me?"

"We better crawl back and report to Sigurd," said Snorro.

"Wait a minute," said Fursey desperately. "I perceive over there some herbs that I shall require for the spell that is to make your breastplate invulnerable. I won't be a moment collecting them."

"Come back," hissed Snorro. "You'll be seen from the monastery."

But Fursey didn't wait. He scrambled down the incline to the shelter of a hedge about twenty yards away. When he glanced back, Snorro was waving frantically to him to return. Fursey crept along hurriedly until he found a hole in the hedge. He forced his way through, and in a moment was running as fast as his legs would carry him across the fields towards the monastery.

Peace pervaded Clonmacnoise. Father Crustaceous, who on account of his great age was allowed considerable licence and freedom from the rule, was stumping about the settlement with the aid of two sticks, poking his nose everywhere in the firm conviction that unless he kept an eye on everything chaos would inevitably result. He had stood in the doorway of the poultry house sucking hard at his one remaining tooth and finding fault with Father Killian's system of organising the hens. Then he had looked into the bakeries and watched from under his fierce eyebrows the laybrothers at the querns grinding corn. He tested with a large, malformed thumb the loaves of wheaten bread reserved for the use of the fathers, and the bread of poorer quality made from barley, which was for consumption by the laybrothers and for distribution to the poor. In the dairy he dipped his finger into the churns and tasted the butter, and he sniffed suspiciously at the vessels of curds put aside for the manufacture of cheese. He visited the forge and poked at the birch logs with his stick. He looked disapprovingly at the heaps of wood charcoal, which was used by the workers in metal; and asserted that the charcoal had been a different colour when he was a boy. He felt that it was very necessary for some responsible man to keep an eye to things, for the Abbot Marcus had not yet returned from Britain. He should, of course, have been back long ago, but somewhere or other on the way he had been stopped and persuaded to found a monastery, so it was unlikely that he would arrive for another few days. In the meantime it was up to an old watchdog like Father Crustaceous to ensure that nobody was slacking.

In the library six choice scribes were busy illuminating manuscripts. To the leg of each table a goose was tethered, so that each scribe could bend down, without interruption of his work, and secure himself a fresh quill as required. The Librarian himself sat apart sunk in melancholy abstraction. The reason for his ill-humour was not far to seek. In the previous year a Censor had been appointed by the Synod of Cashel to visit every monastery in Ireland and search the libraries for written matter offensive to morals. He was an active and conscientious man, and in each monastery which he had visited he had left behind him a heap of cinders where there had been previously treasured manuscripts of secular or pagan origin. He had been only three weeks in Clonmacnoise, but already he had committed to the flames most of the Greek and Latin manuscripts, as well as four copies of the Old Testament, which he had denounced as being in its general tendency indecent. He was a small, dark man with a sub-human cast of countenance. One of his principal qualifications for the post of Censor was that each of his eyes moved independently of the other, a quality most useful in the detection of double meanings. Sometimes one eye would stop at a word which might reasonably be suspected of being improper, while the other eye would read on through the whole paragraph before stopping and travelling backwards along the way it had come, until the battery of both eyes was brought to bear on the suspect word. Few words, unless their consciences were absolutely clear, could stand up to such scrutiny; and the end of it usually was that the whole volume went into the fire. When he had first arrived at Clonmacnoise he had explained his method to the heartbroken Librarian.

"I've an old mother," he said, "who lives in a cottage on the slopes of the Macgillicuddy Reeks. She is for me the type of the decent, clean-minded people of Ireland. I use her as a touchstone. Whenever I'm in doubt about a word or phrase, I ask myself would such word or phrase be used by her."

There came to the Librarian's mind an image of an incredibly old peasant woman with the wrinkles of her face caked with dirt.

"Can your mother read?" he asked.

"No," replied the Censor indignantly, "she's illiterate. But I don't see what difference that makes."

"And I suppose she never heard of Rome or Greece?" said the Librarian pathetically, as he watched the monastery's only copy of Ovid's *Metamorphoses* curling in the flames.

"No, of course she didn't," replied the Censor. "And isn't she just as well off?"

The Censor had a permanent smile on his face. It didn't denote good humour; he was just born that way.

"What some of you people don't realise," he explained to the mournful Librarian, "is that in this country we don't want men of speculative genius or men of bold and enquiring mind. We must establish the rule of Aristotle's golden mean. We must rear a race of mediocrities, who will be neither a danger to themselves nor to anyone else."

Once a week it became necessary to wash out the filter of the Censor's mind, which otherwise would have become choked with the dirt through which he self-sacrificingly waded for the common good. This office was performed by four sturdy laybrothers, who held him under the pump and pumped water at high pressure through one of his ears.

A stream of filthy, black liquid was forced out through the far ear. The operation was painful, and the Censor screamed throughout; but he didn't mind: he knew that it was all for the glory of God and the honour of his country. When the sieve of his mind had been thoroughly cleansed, it was once more in smooth working order to filter the literature of his people. The Librarian had made several ineffectual attempts to hide under the floor boards manuscripts noted for their antiquity or their beauty, but the Censor, who had a nose which was constantly in motion, sniffing and twitching like that of a ferret, had smelt them out. The Librarian now sat gloomily watching the sub-human face of the Censor as he read his way through one of these tomes, his eyes moving left and right and in all directions, and his nose a-quiver.

As it was not fitting that such a famous monastery should be without its wonders, a daily miracle was to be seen outside one of the cowsheds. There was a brindled cow, and every afternoon at milking time a bird came and perched on one of its horns. The bird sang to the cow during the milking, and the cow, previously reluctant to give milk, gave it freely when thus sung to. The monastery was fortunate also in having an exceptionally nimble-fingered milker, who had followed the profession of pickpocket before his reform and entry into the cloister.

On the little stretch of grass before the great church the Master of Novices walked up and down, giving his pupils the most excellent moral precepts. A final touch of innocence was added to the peaceful scene by three or four rabbits, who sported on the sward at the foot of one of the round towers.

Brother Patrick, the most diminutive laybrother in the settlement, had been sent to collect watercress in a moist ditch some distance from the monastery. He had nearly filled his bucket when the sound of running footsteps made him raise his head. To his great horror and affrightment he beheld a small man in armour and wearing the horned helmet of a Viking, scuttling down the hillside straight towards him. The stranger held a weighty battleaxe with both hands over one shoulder. Even as Brother Patrick stared at him, the long sword which the Viking wore caught between his legs and he pitched headlong. But he was on his feet again in a moment and burst through the hedge to where Brother Patrick was scrambling madly to escape.

"Don't you know me?" gasped the Norseman. "I'm Fursey."

Brother Patrick paused neither for thought nor for discussion, but, seizing his bucket, he brought it down with all his force on the Viking's head, driving the latter's helmet well down below his nose. Then he turned and bolted madly back towards the monastery, raising the echoes from the surrounding hills with cries of "The Danes! The Danes!"

The monks working in the fields heard his cries and looking up beheld an unmistakable Viking on the hillside running around in circles as he sought with both hands to wrench his helmet from over his eyes. With one accord they turned and fled towards the monastery. The Master of Novices at once assumed command. By his direction the gold plate and ornaments and the most precious manuscripts were conveyed into the stronger of the round towers. The monks were fortunate in having time to convey into this refuge nearly everything portable which was of value. The round towers were permanently equipped with the means of defence, so that nought remained to do but quieten the affrighted community and allot each one his task. From the narrow windows the monks watched with horror the long dragonship come creeping around the bend of the river and touch the grassy edge below the monastery. Immediately a horde of fierce warriors swarmed ashore and made uphill towards the settlement. Simultaneously a line of Vikings came into sight on the hillside to the south and ran towards the monastery brandishing battleaxes and emitting shrill and terrible cries. A sudden shout of anguish came from both round towers, "Father Crustaceous!"

He came doddering around the corner of the farm buildings, where he had been inspecting the beehives. He paused and looked about him, evidently astonished at finding the settlement deserted. Then he heard fifty voices shouting his name, and, raising his head, he suddenly saw the Norsemen closing in on the settlement. Then started an amazing race for safety. Father Crustaceous, sucking hard at his naked gums, made what speed he could with his two sticks. He had not hobbled as quickly for twenty years, and the effort nearly killed him. His face was covered with sweat as he reached the nearest round tower, and willing hands dragged him up the ladder to safety. The ladder was withdrawn and the door slammed as the first Vikings hacked their way through the palisade.

Meanwhile the hapless Fursey had succeeded in wrenching his helmet from over his eyes. The first thing he beheld was a horde of savage warriors rushing by him with uplifted weapons and hideous cries. Fursey immediately joined them, as he thought that it was the safest thing to do. When he reached the settlement he ran around several buildings waving his battleaxe in the hope of convincing his companions that he was intent on the destruction of the entire community and would not be satisfied with less. At last he paused out of breath at the door of the poultry house. There was no sign of Snorro, but at that moment Sigurd the Skull Splitter came running around the corner. It was borne in powerfully upon Fursey that it was expedient for him to show himself a man of ferocious and bloodthirsty disposition, so he kicked in the door of the poultry house and started laying about him with his battleaxe in all directions. Sigurd dashed in after him. They were immediately involved in a chaos of flying wings and indignant screeching and cackling.

"Curse of Thor on you!" snarled Sigurd as he strove to remove a desperately struggling cockerel from beneath his corselet. "I thought you were leading me into the treasury."

Fursey was too frightened to reply, but wielded his battleaxe all the more formidably to demonstrate his courage. The entire population of birds made their escape through the open door except for one hen, who hadn't enough intelligence to consult her own safety. The unhappy fowl thought that her last hour had come, and fluttered from one corner to another squawking desperately.

Meanwhile the ill-humour of the Norsemen was growing. They were finding nothing of value in the churches or cells, and they ran with torches hither and thither setting fire to the thatched roofs of the settlement. From one of the round towers Father Sampson hurled opprobrious epithets at them. Sampson was a man of warm temper, who had been a professional wrestler before his entry into the cloister. His muscles knotted and unknotted as he beheld the senseless destruction on all sides of him. At last when he saw a torch being applied to the roof of the monastery brewery, he could contain himself no longer. He emitted a howl of anguish and, tearing open the door of the round tower, sprang down the fourteen feet to the ground. The high cross over the grave of King Flann stood to hand. He wrenched it from its foundations and rushing at the nearest Viking, who happened to be Snorro, he discharged his ill-humour upon him by hitting him with it over the head. Sampson was a powerful man, and the high cross was a formidable weapon. Snorro was immediately telescoped. The upper half of his body disappeared from view altogether, and the remarkable sight was witnessed of a pair of legs running around by themselves for a few moments before they collapsed. Several Vikings closed on Father Sampson, seeking with their battleaxes to hew asunder his backbone, but so politic was he in his defence, and he laid about their shoulders, ribs and other appurtenances to such good effect that the senses and vital spirits of many of them ceased to perform their usual offices. At last Sampson heeded the urgent commands of the Novice Master and returned to the round tower. The ladder was quickly lowered and he was dragged to safety.

Sigurd was more angry than he had ever been in his life; and, rallying his men, he ordered an assault on the round tower. The Norsemen clambered on each other's shoulders so as to reach the door fourteen feet above the ground. No sooner had the two warriors on top begun to attack the wooden door with their battleaxes than thick streams of blazing fat and pitch descended from the narrow windows, followed by a shower of stones. The Vikings fled screaming. Father Crustaceous' head appeared in an upper window, his face wreathed in a beatific, if toothless, smile. Sigurd retreated black-browed and counted his casualties. Half-a-dozen of his hardiest warriors sat around on the grass suffering from scalp wounds and shock, while three others lay wallowing in their death agonies, imploring someone to take a last message home to their mothers. Six other forms lay prone and still. A pair of legs leaning against the wall was all that was left of Snorro. The skald was sitting upon a piece of timber sorrowfully composing a poem about the adventure. Father Sampson, who had an eye for strategy, now began to direct a fusilade of stones at the beehives beyond the farmyard wall. A few moments later an angry swarm descended upon the Norsemen and, before they knew what was happening, myriads were inside their corselets and greaves. But what finally broke their morale was the sudden appearance of a small, swarthy creature in the doorway of the library. The Censor, in the dark depths within, had been quite unaware of what was happening outside. He had been hot on the track of an improper innuendo and had been chasing it from page to page, never for a moment losing the scent, until he had finally trapped it at the end of the chapter disguised as a moral platitude. With a sigh of satisfaction he closed the tome and placed it carefully in the fire. Then he noticed that the library was empty, and that from outside came the acrid smell of smoke and the crackling of flames. He walked to the door and beheld with surprise that the greater part of the settlement was on fire.

The Vikings were already sufficiently shaken by their grim experiences, but when a little, dark creature with a twitching nose and a permanent smile on its face suddenly manifested itself in the midst of the smoke they were gripped by a sudden fear. They knew that monks were powerful magicians in their own way, and when they beheld the sub-human visage and the two eyes rolling at them independently of one another, they did not for a moment doubt but that they were confronted by a hard-featured demon of the trickier sort. Sigurd, realising that his men were on the point of taking to flight, spoke first.

"It's been a dismal catastrophe," he said. "Our fortunes are confounded. Suspend your sorrows, my men, and return to the ship."

They picked up their wounded and their dead, and retired slowly to the river, pursued by catcalls and hoots from the defenders of the round towers. The Censor, being a man of quick understanding, only delayed to cast one glance at the raging fires which threatened the whole settlement; then he returned and set fire to the library. He emerged a few moments later, his permanent smile a little broader than usual as he prepared a speech of sympathy for delivery to the Librarian.

Meanwhile Fursey, peering around the door of the poultry house, watched the Norsemen slowly and sternly making their way towards the river. He told himself that it was high time that he too departed, but in the opposite direction. He knew that he would get short shrift if he fell into the hands of either party; so creeping from his refuge he quickly slipped through a gap in the burning palisade and was soon scampering up the hillside towards the shelter of the trees. At first he was of a mind to shed his incriminating armour and weapons, and proceed on his way in the homely russet which he wore underneath; but remembering that the countryside was greatly annoyed by wild beasts, he deemed it wiser to retain his fighting kit and only rid himself of the long sword, which was more of an encumbrance than anything else. He doubted his ability to wield the heavy battleaxe to any effect, but its possession gave him confidence. His objective, The Gap in the Knockmealdown Mountains, was twenty miles beyond Cashel; and he knew Cashel to be at least three days' journey on foot. He was afraid to take to the road, but as long as daylight lasted he kept it in sight, carefully skirting the scattered clumps of sally trees which grew along the edges of the swamps. As he made his way over the uneven ground, he reflected how difficult it was to live a life of iniquity. His first act on landing on his native soil had been a good one— he had saved Clonmacnoise from spoliation and its inhabitants from slaughter.

His reflections were interrupted by a sight which concerned him far more immediately. He had come upon a heap
of gnawed bones, the souvenirs of some late lamented person.
Fursey turned and made straight for the road. It was the hour
of sunset, and he knew that with the onset of darkness there
would be little danger of meeting individual wayfarers. He
realised, of course, that he was not altogether safe on the road
either. It was not unusual to espy by the roadside a speckled
wolf gnawing the mangled joints of some traveller; still he
felt it was safer to be on the road than in the vicinity of trees,
from the overhanging branches of which a wildcat might at
any moment spring and tear the scalp off him. With the imminent approach of night his fears increased. The countryside through which the thin road wound seemed to him to
be of a very dubious character. It was littered with great rocks
and occasional trees, and on each side there was the incessant
trickling of water. He had no doubt but that the neighbourhood abounded fearfully in wolves, otters, badgers, kites and
eagles. As the last glimmer faded from the sky in the west a
lonely howling in the distance sounded dismally on his ears.
He saw in his mind's eye some accursed spot in which stood a
magician summoning the dead to converse with him, and he
remembered, too, that the distress of dogs or wolves at nightfall indicated the proximity of vampires. He looked anxiously
around for signs of local fog, which he knew to be a sure sign
of their presence. He saw nothing however but the deepen-
ing shadows between the trees. As the distant howling rose
to a most lamentable, mournful note, he tried to persuade
himself that it was no more than the obscene caterwauling of
some lonely cat avid for the company of its kind. When he
came to a place where the trees overhung the road, creating
an inky blackness ahead, he stopped, his heart hammering
with fright. He knew that in such spots one might well encounter anything. He nerved himself to go on. Beneath the

trees the air was greasy. He fixed his eyes on the dark blue patch of sky in the far distance beyond the trees and began to run, fully expecting that before he reached it he would find a tomb in the bowels of some unfriendly beast. But he passed safely from beneath the trees and relaxed into a quick walk, breathing heavily as he stumbled over the loose stones on the uneven track. And so hour followed hour while he forced himself onwards, his way lit only by the indifferent stars.

When the moon came sidling into the sky from behind the far-off hills it shed its light fitfully, obscured from time to time by shredded cloud. With the increased light, Fursey's fear of wild beasts lessened, for he could see further in every direction. He made up his mind that if he saw a pair of yellow eyes looking at him, he would run for the nearest tree. He assured himself that if he could succeed in clambering up in time he would be able with his battleaxe to keep at bay any wildcats which he might encounter in the foliage. Every few minutes he glanced fearfully over his shoulder to assure himself that nothing was stalking him from behind. But if the opaque moonlight, softening the outlines of rock and tree, had lessened his fear of wolves, it served to increase his dread of the possible materialisation of some unsavoury citizen of the spirit world. He heard the bell of a distant church sorrowfully striking the hour of midnight, and he knew that between the hours of twelve and one in the night, in ghostly moonlight on a lonely road, one is apt to encounter presences that are dangerous. He distrusted the empty wind, which made no sound in the trees, but which he could feel from time to time against his face. He turned a corner and came to a stretch of vacant road along which the trees were spaced like soldiers. He experienced a sudden fright as he saw a few yards from him a raven perched on a gatepost. It cocked its glossy head and looked at him wickedly. Fursey passed by trembling and entered the avenue of trees. The shadows lay in grey bars across the road. He became conscious of a fluttering movement in the air above him. He stopped and glanced up. Innumerable bats were fluttering up and down between the trees. As Fursey watched, one of them, larger than the others, fluttered down and, alighting on the road ten paces ahead of him, resolved itself into a gentleman wrapped in a black cloak.

Fursey's heart stopped beating altogether, then it tried to jump out through his throat. He was conscious of a wave of dizziness; but it passed at once, and he found himself clutching his battleaxe with trembling hands as he and the vampire gazed across at one another.

"It's really a beautiful night," said the vampire at last. Fursey opened his mouth and with his tongue, which felt like a piece of wood, tried to moisten his parched lips.

"Is it?" he gasped.

"You have nothing to fear from me," said the vampire persuasively. "Don't you know that my kind are only dangerous to humans in a state of insensibility, either through sleep or fright? You never heard of a vampire so ill-bred as to seek to achieve his purpose by violence?"

Fursey gathered together his quivering wits and told himself, as from a long way off, that this was true. Nevertheless he tightened his grip on the battleaxe. He knew well that, being unaccustomed to the use of the weapon, a sudden cut at the vampire if it approached him would probably only result in his hewing off one of his own legs, with no inconvenience to the phantom whatever. All the same, possession of the weapon seemed to give him courage.

"In any case," continued the stranger, "I am replete as I have just come from visiting a plump archdeacon." The vampire smiled slightly. "An estimable man. He is just beginning to realise that he is suffering from anaemia, but he will last another couple of weeks. I may add," he continued somewhat stiffly, "in case you still doubt me, that I am not one who ravens promiscuously about the countryside. I select good class clients, and I stick to them."

"I'm not doubting your word, sir," said Fursey.

"In that case," replied the vampire, "you will have no objection to my joining you. Our ways seem to lie in the same direction. I reside some miles from here in a churchyard adjacent to the road, and there is nothing I enjoy as much as a walk on a fragrant night such as this with an intelligent companion. Now that my night's work is done I feel that I can allow myself that little relaxation."

Fursey could see no way out of his predicament. The last thing that he wanted to do was to offend the sallow stranger. While he found it hard to believe that a vampire's purposes could be other than malevolent, the gentleman's account of his call on the archdeacon seemed plausible enough; and while Fursey felt that he could not approve of such dissolute conduct, he was glad that the vampire had already paid a visit that night. His only alternative seemed to be to retrace his steps along the road which he had come, and that was out of the question. He threw a quick look at the visage, gaunt, pale and bewrinkled, in the hope of reading there whether or not the vampire had it in his mind to do him a mischief. He observed that the stranger, for all his pale looks, was very iron-visaged, a fact which impressed Fursey very painfully. He felt that if the vampire had set his mind on a walk with an intelligent companion, it would be the height of unwisdom to deny him.

"Very well," said Fursey weakly, "but I should be greatly obliged if you would keep some paces from me and slightly ahead. You will readily understand that, not being accustomed to the company of the undead it will take me a little time to become used to your presence. No discourtesy is intended."

The vampire bowed stiffly and fell into position as Fursey desired, and together they began to walk along the moonlit road. There was silence between them for a long time, and Fursey had begun to reflect that in such an unlucky looking countryside even such a companion was better than none. He kept a nervous eye upon the vampire all the same lest the latter should become sportful or indulge in trickery. At last his companion vented a deep-fetched sigh.

"Human beings are very unkind to us forlorn denizens of the spirit world," he said. "I suppose they don't always mean to be, but they are nevertheless often unkind."

"How so?" asked Fursey.

"Why do you think that spirits manifest themselves to humans at all? Loneliness. A spirit bound to some forlorn spot experiences an intolerable boredom and a homesickness for all that he has left behind him in the world of men."

"Humans are also lonely," said Fursey.

"It's different," replied the vampire shortly. He seemed dissatisfied and changed the subject. He cast an appreciative eye over Fursey's armour.

"I have been admiring your furniture," he said. "I observe that you are a Viking gentleman."

"No," replied Fursey. "I was with them, but I'm not one of them. I'm a Tipperary man, born and bred."

"That Clonmacnoise business has been a sad disappointment. I was speaking to-night to the banshee attached to the Mulligan family and she's very sore about it."

Fursey pricked up his ears. "I'm interested in that. What actually happened?"

"Well, a large scale battle was expected between the Norsemen and the Mulligan clan. A member of the lower orders, a base and abject fellow, who had got a lift in a chariot from Limerick, gave the alarm, notifying the Mulligans of an impending Norse raid on Clonmacnoise. The banshee, who is a lady of great charm and refinement, repaired last night to the residence of the young chieftain in order to give notice in the traditional manner of the impending slaughter. I must say that it was most impressive. I watched her myself from a vantage point in a neighbouring tree. She put up a very good show, if you'll pardon the colloquialism. She walked around the ramparts in her traditional garments of white gauze, wringing her hands and moaning most plaintively. It was interesting to see the tapers being lit in each bedroom of the prince's dwelling and the startled residents sitting up in bed. At every corner of the ramparts she seated herself languidly for a few moments while she combed her white, silken hair, continuing all the while to give tongue to the most lamentable complaint. It was unutterably sad and most touching and did not fail to bring tears to my eyes. But no sooner had she commenced the second movement of the Grand Wail under the prince's window than the craven died of fright. The lady is a very considerable artist, and she is very put out about it. She feels that her professional integrity is besmirched."

"Why?" asked Fursey.

"Well, after all, she had given the traditional notice of impending battle and slaughter, and, as things transpired, there was no battle at all. On the following morning there was no chieftain to lead the doughty Mulligans against the Vikings."

"But at least the young prince died," objected Fursey.

"But he died for the wrong reason," snapped the vampire, "and he died in bed, which is disgraceful to a Mulligan. He was to have died honourably on the following day, his backbone hewn in twain by a giant Norseman." They proceeded for some time in silence while the vampire conquered his momentary ill-humour. When he spoke again it was with affability.

"I judge," he said, "from your alarming furniture that you are walking the high roads seeking adventure."

"Not exactly," answered Fursey.

"When seeking adventure," continued the vampire, "the principal thing is to avoid deep wells, hollow trees and such obscure places. One must always keep in mind that while one's entry therein may be easy, one's coming forth may well be miraculous. When I was of the world of men my mind thirsted after honourable adventures. My name was George, and you can picture me setting out along the crooked roads every springtime in search of adventure, mounted upon a Kerry jennet. The winding roads of this land had an unfailing attraction for me. I loved above all the sight of the road rising and disappearing over a little hill. One never knew what lay beyond the rise. Turns in the road are attractive too, because one can never be quite certain of what one may encounter around the bend. Of course, in point of fact, there is never anything around the bend; but when a man ceases to believe that there may be, it is time for him to die."

Fursey glanced almost with affection at the silent, sad creature who walked a few paces distant from him. He quickened his pace so as to bring himself alongside the vampire and fell into step with his companion.

"Did you never have any adventures?" enquired Fursey.

"One only in a whole lifetime," replied George sadly; "that is to say, only one before my final one."

"Tell me about it," requested Fursey. "I have grown footsore, and it will haply enable me to forget for an hour my manifold pains and aches."

The vampire stared gloomily at the road before him for a while before he began.

"All your life," he said at length, "avoid one thing as you would avoid the very plague itself. Never have dealings with a rowan tree."

"A rowan tree?" queried Fursey.

"Yes, a rowan tree, the tree with small, red berries, which some people call the mountain ash. It's a tree with properties of a magical character, only too often productive of dolour and annoyance. It was in the month of May—the spring had been late and the bushes and trees were as yet only covered with a fine web of green, when one pale, sunny evening I came cantering down a country road on my Kerry jennet, seeking as ever some honourable adventure. In the centre of a patch of grass stood a single rowan tree. The evening air was balmy, and I dismounted so as to rest myself and my steed. It was a pleasant place neighbouring on a small lake, on which, as I lay idly on the grass, I counted twenty sleek ducks and one bedraggled drake who, even as I looked at him, made his way up on to the bank, cocked a knowing eye at me, and staggered away in search of refreshment. In short, it was a pretty, sylvan scene. Suddenly I became aware of a series of strained sighs proceeding from the tree against which my head was resting. Imagine my astonishment a moment later on hearing from the woody depths a voice, which addressed me as follows:

" 'Noble sir, within this tree are bound by wicked enchantment the one-and-twenty daughters with which bounteous Nature graced Mulligan, Prince of this territory. So singular was the beauty with which we were endowed, that it awakened the base desires of a roving magician, as unattractive as he was spiteful. When we each and every one of us had spurned with ignominious words his repeated offers of marriage, he wrought with deadly malice a potent spell, which had the deplorable effect of binding us in this tree in enchanted sleep for a period of five hundred years. The five centuries are now at an end. Do you, good sir, cut down this tree and effect for us our release from our leafy prison.' "

On hearing this eloquent discourse breathed in dulcet tones like to the sound of harps, I was at first deprived of speech. Then I realised my good fortune. It's the dearest wish of every gentleman who wanders the roads in search of adventure, to come upon a distressed lady whom he can free from enchantment or from the foul machinations of a giant or similar depraved character, but to be presented with the opportunity of liberating in the one operation no less than twenty-one distressed virgins exceeded my wildest dreams. This, I told myself, will make me famous throughout the land. I had no axe with which to fell the tree, but I set about the operation with my sword. The bole of the rowan tree is slender, but my sword was correspondingly blunt, and the task was a tedious one. From time to time I paused to rest, but not for long. The other twenty distressed ladies joined in their sister's plaint and, in accents mild but urgent, exhorted me to persevere. I had happy visions of a well-deserved rest when their liberation should be accomplished, my head pillowed in the lap of the stateliest of the virgins, while her twenty beautiful sisters sat couched among the wild flowers, singing melodious songs for my delight. At last, when I had all but cut through the bole, I exercised the strength of my arms and, breaking off the trunk, overthrew the tree. The one-and-twenty virgins issued forth."

"That must have been a memorable moment," interjected Fursey enthusiastically.

"It was indeed," said the vampire sadly. "I had forgotten that the distressed virgins were over five hundred years old. There issued from the stump of the tree the most incredible procession of aged crones, the ugliest creatures that ever Nature formed."

"Bewhiskered, I suppose?" said Fursey.

"Bewhiskered to the knees," said the vampire dramatically. "You never saw their like for decrepitude. Each held one hand at the back of her hip to prevent her framework caving in, as they doddered around me, overwhelming me with their thanks. I all but took to my heels, not leaving behind me as much as a kind look."

"Remarkable," said Fursey.

The vampire shook his head dolefully. "Their visages were so time-shattered that one marvelled that one could look on them and live. They were veritable night hags, yet so strong was their feminine spirit that they immediately hobbled over to a nearby elder tree and began to pluck the sprigs and berries for colouring matter to make rouge for their cheeks. My gallant Kerry jennet shied when she saw them and, breaking her halter, made off in a frantic canter, her hooves beating sparks out of the road. The last I saw of her was crossing the skyline still in full gallop."

"It was very awkward for you," said Fursey.

"Awkward!" exclaimed the vampire. "I can tell you that it was more than awkward when they began to remind me of the respect and honour owed to poor, distressed gentle-women by their saviour. They adjured me to choose one of their number for spouse, insisting that it was customary. They admitted a slight discrepancy in age, but reminded me that their hearts were young."

"It was a choice that I should not care to have to make," remarked Fursey.

"I didn't make it," replied the vampire, "though to all my protestations of my unworthiness of such an honour the reply of the eldest sister was ever the same. 'Nay, proud George,' she said, 'you are our saviour, and you must have the reward hallowed by tradition and immemorial custom. Make your choice. There is not one of us but will rejoice to be your bride.'"

"A ticklish situation for a man of honour," commented Fursey.

"Very ticklish," agreed the vampire, "yet so ardent was their spirit that they followed me around for three weeks to the great scandal of the countryside. The clergy took a poor view of it and spoke very ill of me. Eventually there was nothing for it but to make my escape under cover of darkness."

"Adventure is not all that the writers of romance would have us believe," remarked Fursey sagely.

"It's not," said George, "but my thirst for adventure was not quenched. I sought it afterwards for many years, but only found it once again."

"What were the circumstances?" enquired Fursey.

"I prefer not to speak of it," replied George solemnly. "Suffice to say that I undertook to lay a master vampire. He won."

"So that's how—," said Fursey gently.

"Yes," was the reply. "I am now the father and grandfather of many vampires, both male and female. It's not a bad life if only human beings would leave us alone. But they're always messing around with pointed stakes, fresh garlic and wild dog roses, so that you're never quite certain when it'll all end."

They had come to the low wall of a churchyard. The vampire stopped.

"Here our ways part," he said. "I reside over there in the building inscribed 'Family Vault'. Would you care to come in for a few moments to meet the girls?"

"No, thank you," said Fursey hastily. "I have to be on my way."

"Goodbye then," said the vampire with a wave of his pale hand. "And don't think so badly in future of us who belong properly to your world, but have lost our places in it."

CHAPTER V

The day was ebbing. The entire arc of the sky was curtained with cloud. A grey, monotonous light occupied the countryside. The wind had pressed against Fursey all the morning and afternoon while he toiled along the crazy track which wound up the hillside, and he was conscious now of a wintry chill in the air; so that when he came to a grassy bank crowned with a tangle of thorn, he crept gratefully into its shelter. He seated himself with a sigh of thankfulness and, resting his elbows on his knees, stared down at the Tipperary plain, which lay beneath him like a vast carpet, patterned in varying shades of green and crisscrossed by lines of hedges and boundary ditches running in all directions. He could just discern in the green distance a fluffy ball of smoke, which hung in the air, marking as with a dot the site of the city of Cashel. It was three days since Fursey had parted from the vampire beside the broken wall of the churchyard, and ever since then he had been travelling in a wide circuit so as to avoid the road which crept across the plain, and to avoid above all the settlement of Cashel, which was the seat of the ecclesiastical and civil government. It was scarcely three months since the authorities at Cashel had sought to cure Fursey of his sorcery by the simple expedient of tying him to a strong stake of faggots and burning him, and he knew that in the neighbourhood of the settlement he would be readily recognised. Although he was tired he was reasonably content: he had circumambulated the danger zone successfully and was near his objective. Two days previously he had rid himself of his armour and his battleaxe, realising that by now news of the Norse raid on Clonmacnoise must have spread far and wide, and consequently that as long as he wore the incriminating Viking dress he was in far greater danger from his countrymen than from a wild beast which might come strolling out of the forest. He knew that if he were seen by one of those lank shepherds clad in sacking, who were to be met with mooching around in the most unexpected places, the hue and cry would be raised; so he had shed his martial furnishings and had proceeded on his way clad in his homely cloak and pigskin trousers.

Fursey was tired and very lonely. Indeed, as he rested his chin on his cupped hands, it was his extreme loneliness that occupied his thoughts. All his adult life he had lived in community, and he now found his own company in the highest degree burdensome. It was a terrible thing to have no one to talk to. He shook his head despondently and began to reflect on his melancholy situation. He knew of no one in the entire world who had his interest at heart or even cared what became of him. He doubted if even Maeve cared. Did her thoughts ever stray back to those days when they had first known one another? It had been in her father's cottage at the edge of a mountain lake not very far from the spot where he now sat. For three glittering weeks they had walked and chatted, scrambling over the boulders at the lake's edge, until Fursey had been caught in the web of her kindness and had lost his heart utterly. But had she ever loved him? He doubted it. He knew little of women and less of the emotions that inform their actions, but he suspected that what had been a glorious companionship for him had been for her no more than humdrum daily existence. It was true that at a moment's notice she had run away with him from the very steps of the altar; but, he asked himself bitterly, was it not the case that in so acting her motive had been to avoid an unwelcome marriage? He could not believe that she had ever really cared for a boastful bully like Magnus. Her father had forced the marriage upon her; and, acting on a sudden impulse, she had seized the opportunity of escaping from it. It was not love for Fursey that had motivated her actions at any time. On her own admission to the Abbot Marcus her only feeling for Fursey had been pity because he was helpless and without friends. Fursey's spirit twisted and turned inside his frame under the torture of those remembered words. He found himself grinding his teeth angrily. He was rather surprised at the sudden vision he had of himself sitting crouched at the edge of the track, grating his teeth horribly in anger at the thought of his wrongs. The picture pleased him. It made him see himself in an unaccustomed light—as a very formidable fellow, intent on the satisfaction of his injuries, so he crunched his teeth again with greater vehemence.

"I'll get even with them both," he said darkly. "First I'll quench Magnus, and then I'll brew Maeve such a powerful love potion that she must needs worship me for evermore."

But instead of being ravished with delectable visions of the future, Fursey began to brood gloomily on his imminent apprenticing to the master sorcerer Cuthbert, a man with whom he was already acquainted and whose proximity had always filled him with fear. The prospect of spending some weeks, or even months, in the company of such a formidable wizard caused Fursey the liveliest apprehension.

"It will be a dark and dirty business," he muttered, and began to think bitterly of the forlornness of his situation. His thoughts wandered back to his lack of someone in whom to confide. He thought of Albert, but he hesitated a long time before summoning his lugubrious familiar. At last he sighed despondently and whispered the name.

"Albert!"

The two bear's paws came slowly into being, followed by the rest of Albert's unlovely anatomy. The familiar was squatting on his hunkers on the path, his head bent forward as he contemplated his master balefully.

"You don't seem very pleased to see me," said Fursey. "Your face is a veritable map of sorrow."

Albert's smoky red eyes flashed fire. He bared his teeth.

"Just look," he ejaculated. He gripped the ground firmly with his front paws and shook himself like a dog. He was immediately enveloped in a cloud of white dust.

"What's that?" asked Fursey in surprise.

"Dandruff," snarled Albert. "My coat is falling out in chunks."

Fursey ran his eye over the rusty black hair which covered his familiar.

"How is that?" he asked innocently.

"How is that!" howled Albert indignantly. "Because you're deliberately starving me. I'm almost completely dehydrated."

"Oh," said Fursey with distaste. "I suppose you're looking for more of my blood."

"More!" screeched Albert. "What did I ever get out of you except a thimbleful? Didn't I tell you the last time you summoned me that I needed feeding at least every second day? God be with the days when I had a master with some sense of his responsibilities! I didn't know how lucky I was. You'd never think to look at me now that I was once a nimble and lively elemental. Your meanness and neglect has me completely destroyed and punctured."

"See here," said Fursey. "I'm not going to stand impertinent backchat from you. I've enough troubles of my own without, every time that I see you, having to concede to your selfish demands."

"Selfish demands!" Further words failed Albert. He rose and padded back and forward on the road for a few moments, throwing his snout despairingly to the sky as if to call

all creation to witness that never had an elemental been so tortured. At last he came to rest opposite Fursey, and bent his gaze upon his master with hatred flickering in his eyes.

"I only wish," he choked, "that in your recent several perambulations a brace of lusty wolves had fastened on you with their paws."

"To feed you constantly with my blood," said Fursey coldly, "would seem to me curious and dreadful conduct."

"You're a man of perverse intelligence," yelped Albert. "Who better than I can advise you as to what things will tend to your profit and welfare? But you are determined to maltreat me and make an enemy of me."

"I'm tired of your company and your bad temper," replied Fursey. "Kindly vanish."

"I'll thwart you in your designs," screeched Albert as he began to disappear in spite of himself. "I'll frustrate you. I'll tell every spirit and demon I know that you're nothing but a hard-fisted curmudgeon."

As he faded into nothingness Fursey shook his head sorrowfullly. He sat for a time in gloomy meditation, then he rose with a sigh and continued his way along the mountain track He had not travelled very far when he came to the edge of a small moorland lake. A man in grey stood on the brink. He held a fishing rod in his hand and was carefully coiling up his line. When he saw Fursey, he walked over to join him.

"Any luck?"asked Fursey, nervously wondering who the stranger was.

"No luck," replied the angler, "though I tumbled one or two."

Fursey recognised in the stranger's eye the mad glint of the fanatical fisherman.

"Is the fishing any good around here?" he asked soothingly.

"No," said the stranger. "Limestone bottoms."

"I beg your pardon," said Fursey.

"It's a very serious thing for an angler to have a limestone bottom," explained the man in grey.

"I suppose so," said Fursey, looking at his companion curiously.

"Ground feeding," said the angler.

"I see," said Fursey.

"Maybe you're going my way," said the man in grey. "Up the hill? My name is Turko."

Fursey bowed his head politely, but did not otherwise reply, as he deemed it unwise to tell in turn his name to the stranger. The omission did not pass unnoticed by Turko, and he eyed Fursey suspiciously as they mounted the track. They had not walked very far when he suddenly stopped and turned about.

"I trust that you're not a spy from Cashel," he said menacingly, "because if you are, it would be better for you that you had never been born."

Fursey hastily assured him that nothing was further from his thoughts than to spy on anyone.

"What are you doing then in this gloomy and inhospitable region? I warn you not to attempt to dissemble. You're in a very sorcerous neighbourhood, and we refugees in the hills are men of irritable temper."

Fursey did not like the turn the conversation had taken, but he thought it wiser to speak the truth. "My name is Fursey," he replied. "I'm seeking an old acquaintance named Cuthbert, who, I have been told, has taken up residence in the hills."

"Oh," said Turko, "so you know Cuthbert. He lives in a cavern some distance from this spot."

"Being in the neighbourhood," volunteered Fursey cautiously, "I thought it would be but courteous to call on him and pay my respects."

Turko shot a quick glance at him and then began to lead the way up the hillside in silence. They had progressed a considerable distance before he stopped again and spoke.

"You know that Cuthbert is a sorcerer?" he asked, looking Fursey straight in the face.

Fursey hesitated. "Yes," he replied at last "in fact, I have some slight acquaintance with sorcery myself, but I'm in a very small way of business."

Turko seemed at last convinced of Fursey's *bona fides*. His face cleared and he took Fursey by the arm. When he again spoke, his voice was shot through with friendliness.

"I see by your dress," he said, "that you are a stranger in these parts, but if you are a displaced person like ourselves you are heartily welcome to our community. A couple of months ago the Bishop of Cashel launched a pogrom against the men of intellect resident in his diocese. Many of us met our end at the stake, which is an unlucky way to die and very inconvenient. Others did not even get that far, but died uncomfortably during the preliminary examination, in which the racks, thumbscrews, knotted cords and ingenious wheels were brought to bear in order to drive home the authorities' point of view. Fortunately, some of us escaped by timely flight to the hills, and we now dwell in rather loose community in sundry caves and foxholes which we have rented from Festus Wisenuts, who is the landlord and sole owner of this area of mountain. You will find us interesting and distinguished company. I myself am a crytallomancer—I read the future in a crystal. I possess a very potent stone, which I brought with me in my flight. Our community does not lack scryers and astrologers; we have an abundance of sorcerers, a couple of mathematicians, a ventriloquist, two conjurers, three clairvoyants and one reciter of poetry."

"One cannot but be at home," murmured Fursey courteously, "among such polite society."

"We are fortunate in having an enlightened and sympathetic landlord," explained Turko. "He's a man of ineffable ambitions, who for many years devoted himself to the mysteries of occult mathematics, a subject which is enveloped in a chaos of cloud and darkness. To tell you the truth, I doubt if Festus Wisenuts came out any wiser than he went in. But he is a man with a raging thirst for knowledge, and for some years past he has been treading the crooked paths of sorcery. He began his studies by taking up residence among the tombs, but I don't think he learnt much there either. He now lives a little distance from here in a dreary cavern and does magic all day long. He rarely emerges except to climb the mountain to a plateau of abominable repute, where he spends a couple of hours trying to coax the demons from their marshy haunts."

"He must be a man of interesting and elegant mind," said Fursey nervously. "It will be a great pleasure to make his acquaintance."

"Yes," said the crystallomancer slowly, seeming to weigh his words. "I have no doubt but that you will find him interesting. He is a man of most distinguished appearance, tall, grave and handsome. His face is ornamented with a narrow, silvery beard, which is the envy of many. He affects a black cloak covered with the signs of the zodiac, which imparts to him a priestly appearance. But I'll let you in on a secret," added Turko confidentially. "He's not any good as a wizard. A man like Cuthbert could make rings around him. But naturally none of us ever dares to let him suspect our opinion of his efforts and achievements. After all, he's our landlord; and if he took it into his head, he could turn us all out of our caves with a notice to quit. Of course, he's not likely to do so. I suspect that he's secretly glad of the proximity of so many wizards. You see, he's not at all above picking up magical tricks from his tenants and pretending that they were always part of his own repertoire. But I'll say this for him, he's a man devoted to his profession. He works hard. As I passed his cave on my way down here, he was standing in the entrance essaying some magical sleight-of-hand with the remnants of a goat."

"Is it not the case," enquired Fursey, "that these interesting experiments are not always performed with complete immunity from danger to those who undertake them?"

Turko lowered his voice. "I'll be quite frank with you," he said. "I'm glad that I'm not a wizard. The gift of sorcery is frequently an embarrassing profession; in fact, it's apt to prove in the highest degree perilous."

"There's no need to tell me that," replied Fursey with conviction. "I know from my own experience that a sorcerer needs the utmost subtlety to continue alive at all."

"That is so," conceded Turko; "but I wasn't referring to outside interference by busybodies, who can only think in terms of flaming pyres and torture chambers. I was referring rather to the perils to which even a cunning wizard exposes himself when actuated by an insatiable and base curiosity. Too frequently he will essay untravelled fields of experiment and will unloose potent forces which he lacks the knowledge to control. The end is disaster."

"Crystal gazing seems a much safer profession," remarked Fursey sadly.

"It is," agreed the crystallomancer, "though the authorities burn you for that, too; but there's no use worrying about such things, as they'll burn you for almost anything. In the eyes of established authority the one unforgivable sin is to have an original and enquiring mind. Ideas—that's what they're afraid of."

"Life is very peculiar," commented Fursey.

"But to come back to what I was saying," continued Turko, "Festus Wisenuts as a wizard labours under a feeling of inferiority. He knows in his heart that he's a negligible sorcerer, but he daren't admit it to himself or to anyone else. The result is that to convince himself and others of his great abilities he's always attempting the most extravagant experiments. At one time he had a young cockatrice chained in the depths of his cave, and he spent a fortnight trying by magic to teach it to play the bagpipes. As you may well imagine, the cockatrice didn't like it; and it strained at its chain and behaved in a most formidable manner, menacing destruction to all who approached. We were all of us afraid to enter the cave to pay the rent, and Festus Wisenuts became quite nasty about it. Then, unlike other sorcerers, he will not rest content with a dun dog or a speckled cat as his familiar, but must needs have nothing less than a tawny Moor. Well, tawny Moors are hard to come by, and for a long time past he's been trying to conjure one into existence. He spent a week going around in circles with his face awry, breathing to left and right, and sprinkling powdered load-stone; but all he succeeded in conjuring up was a young hippogruff suckling its supernatural children."

"Was there no sign of the tawny Moor?" asked Fursey, interested in spite of himself.

"Not a sign," answered Turko shortly. "He tried it again, lost his head in the middle of the spell, forgot the words, and all but turned himself into a frog."

Before Fursey could comment there was a sudden clap of thunder overhead and a comet shot across the sky. Turko flung himself on his face and Fursey immediately followed suit.

"There he is again," said Turko savagely. "Another experiment gone wrong."

When the crystallomancer was satisfied that the danger was past, he got slowly to his feet and brushed the dust from his clothing.

"I have little sympathy with such apish antics," he commented bitterly. "I don't mind a man becoming learned in runes or spending his time compounding salves. I don't deny that magic may be useful sometimes; for instance, in enabling one to tie up an enemy's guts. But there should be a law against a man releasing infernal powers when he doesn't know how to control them. What are you standing there for? Why don't you come on?"

"Do you not think," enquired Fursey, "that it might be wiser to retrace our steps?"

"Nonsense," replied Turko shortly. "You'll have to get used to the perils inherent in close residence to Festus Wisenuts. Not," he muttered, "that there isn't a certain amount of wisdom in what you suggest. I've told the others again and again that Festus is a danger to us all; but what can we do? If we descend into the plain the Bishop will have us burnt."

Turko continued along the track for some time with set brows, while Fursey trailed along behind him. When the crystallomancer spoke again, he prefaced his remarks with a gloomy shake of the head.

"The experiments of Festus," he said, "have been playing havoc with the weather, too, during the past week. If you come out of your cave for a breath of air, and go for a ramble, you're lucky if you succeed in covering a hundred paces without hearing an explosion, and before you can race back and gain the shelter of your cave you're deluged by a shower of rain. God knows our caves are damp enough without the addition of artificially induced thunder showers. To tell you the honest truth, I'm sick and tired of living in this locality. Apart from the danger of having as neighbours a bunch of short-tempered wizards, my digestion is ruined by witch's broth."

"It does not appear to be a suitable locality in which to set up residence," commented Fursey; "at least not for a man who hopes for quiet and longevity."

Turko turned his head and stared at Fursey earnestly.

"Life here," he said, "is in the highest degree a hazardous business. I strongly advise you as long as you're here to keep on the best of terms with everyone. That's what I do, and in addition, just for safety, I keep in my cave a heated plough-share, which is well-known to be a powerful antidote against the spells of wizards."

"You don't happen to have a second one to spare?" enquired Fursey.

"I'm sorry, I haven't. If I had, you'd be welcome to it."

They breasted the rise and paused for a moment to re-gain their breath. A narrow area of moorland stretched from where they stood to the base of a high cliff.

"You have uttered your mind to me very openly," said Fur-sey with feeling, "and I want you to know that I'm grateful, and that I'll respect your confidence. I hope that during my stay here we'll be friends."

The crystallomancer's face softened suddenly and he flashed a smile at his companion.

"Of course we will," he answered. "I've taken quite a fancy to you."

They made their way across the broken ground towards the cliff. Fursey noted with a sinking heart the awful desolation of the place. The bracken through which they had to pass was nearly waist-high and the ground underfoot so broken and treacherous that he stumbled several times over rocks hidden in the waste of fern. When they emerged from the bracken and began to skirt the base of the cliff, Fursey glanced up at the soaring wall of fissured stone overhanging their path and hoped earnestly that nothing would fall on him. As they made their way around a giant boulder they came suddenly on an old man of venerable appearance sitting cross-legged on the ground in the lips of a narrow cleft. His nose was sunk in his extensive white beard, and he sat so motionless that at first Fursey thought that he was either asleep or dead.

"He's a mathematician," whispered Turko. "We mustn't disturb him. He sits there all day, his daring spirit essaying untravelled realms of speculation."

Fursey tiptoed past. A few moments later they passed the opening of a vast cavern.

"That's where Festus Wisenuts lives," said Turko. "It's too late in the evening to bring you in to introduce you. In any case he's probably busy doing magic."

Fursey was not sorry to defer his visit to the erratic Festus, especially as he noticed that there was a corporal's guard of moles standing at the entrance to the cavern. Of the landlord himself he could see nothing: no doubt he was busy pondering magic in the dark depths within. As he hurried past, Fursey's gaze made a quick circuit of the cave mouth, from the row of sentinel moles, over the jagged sides and ceiling. He shuddered: the opening was like a giant mouth yawning wide to snap and swallow him. He was glad when they left the cave behind. He was grateful, too, for Turko's comforting presence.

"I'll tell you what we'll do," said the crystallomancer suddenly. "My cave is close at hand. We'll go there, and I'll let you search the future in my crystal. This is the very best hour for using the crystal, the hour of sunset."

This suggestion was very agreeable to Fursey, who was by no means averse to deferring his visit to the sorcerer Cuthbert as long as possible. He quickened his pace instinctively, and Turko fell into step beside him, so that before long they arrived at the hollow cavity in which the crystallomancer dwelt. It was a pleasant, open place, with a neat bed of mugwort growing at the entrance. At the rear of the cave stood a small table. The crystallomancer lifted it and, bringing it towards the entrance, placed it before a low rock, on which he told Fursey to sit. Fursey seated himself and watched Turko's further preparations with considerable interest. First, Turko covered the table with a white linen cloth. Then he took a black, ebony wand and traced on the ground a circle seven feet in diameter so as to include in its circumference the table and rock on which Fursey was sitting. He placed a small brazier in the vicinity and drawing some handfuls of grains from a series of silken bags which hung on the wall, he cast them on to the glowing coals. A fine smoke arose, struck the rugged ceiling and spread throughout the cave. Fursey sneezed once or twice as the aromatic perfumes crept up his nostrils.

"You will soon accustom yourself to the vision-inducing incense," said Turko, appearing suddenly through the smoke. Fursey wiped his streaming eyes and nodded his head bleakly.

Turko disappeared once more into the depths of the cave and emerged a moment later loaded down with the paraphernalia of his profession. Carefully he drew from its black cloth a crystal of pale, water-green beryl and placed it on the table. Then he added a sword, a length of twine, a new knife, a pair of scissors and a piece of stick.

"What's that?" asked Fursey, alarmed at the production of lethal weapons.

"It's a wand of hazelwood of twelve months' growth and three feet in length," explained Turko, "and this is a magic sword."

"I see," said Fursey. "What do we do next?"

Turko placed two tapers on the floor on either side of the circle. He lit the tapers before he replied.

"You mustn't move," he said. "You must keep your face towards the east and your eyes fixed upon the crystal. I am now about to charge the potent stone. When you observe a mist gathering in its depths, the interior faculties of your being will expand like a flower. Then when you are thoroughly entranced, the globe itself will vanish from your sight, the mist in its depths will part and you will be ravished by a vision of the radiant being who is the abiding spirit of the stone."

"I see," said Fursey nervously.

"I must warn you," continued the crystallomancer, "that if your purpose is evil the crystal will avenge itself on you sooner or later with awful effect."

"I have no purpose," said Fursey hastily, "other than to learn what the future may hold for me."

"That's all right," said Turko soothingly. "For your information, you may as well know that the basis of this operation is magnetism, which accumulates in the crystal by reason of the iron with which its constitution is infused. In the cerebellum," he said, tapping Fursey on the back of the head, "there is a reservoir of magnetism, which streams forth from the eyes when the gaze is concentrated on the crystal. We must establish contact between the magnetism projected from your skull and the magnetism trembling in the stone. "Now," he added briskly, "do you wish to observe events taking place at a great distance in time or space, or do you prefer rather to be made aware of events which will occur in the near vicinity and before very long?"

Fursey thought of Maeve, who was no doubt resident at no great distance.

"Events near at hand," he replied, "and which will happen soon."

"Very good," said Turko, and he began to make passes with his hands back and forward over the crystal. "What are you doing?" asked Fursey.

"I'm magnetising the stone," replied Turko shortly. "Don't talk. Concentrate."

Fursey found it hard to concentrate with the crystallomancer's hands waving back and forward within two feet of his nose, but he continued to stare at the globe. At long last Turko, with a final languid wave of his hand, withdrew on tiptoe and cast another few handfuls of grains into the brazier. A cloud of white smoke billowed up and obliterated everything.

"What do you see?" hissed the crystallomancer in Fursey's ear.

"Nothing," said Fursey.

"It's a good sign," came the answer. "If the crystal at first is hazy, it means that one is likely to see an image."

"But I can't see the crystal," said Fursey. "I can't see anything with the smoke."

"Keep looking at it," came the angry reply. "The smoke will clear in a moment."

As the smoke thinned, the crystal swam slowly into Fursey's view.

"Do you see black clouds?" enquired the crystallomancer, anxiously.

"No," replied Fursey.

"Good thing," muttered Turko. "Black clouds are inauspicious. By the way, I should have told you that anything you see on the right-hand side is merely symbolical. Keep concentrating."

Fursey was becoming dizzy, but he continued to stare at the crystal for a seemingly interminable length of time. The veins stood out on his forehead.

"What do you see?" came the sibilant voice of the crystallomancer.

"Nothing," gasped Fursey.

"Keep concentrating," said Turko savagely.

Fursey's two eyes protruded like bullets. Turko was making frantic passes over the crystal.

"The crystal is darkening," cried Fursey suddenly.

"Good," exulted the crystallomancer. The sweat ran down his forehead as his hands waved wildly back and forward over the stone.

"The crystal is becoming blindingly bright," shouted Fursey. "It dazzles me."

"The effulgence proceeds from its interior," replied Turko. "Keep staring at it. Don't mind your eyesight. Is a form or vision becoming manifest?"

"Something is becoming manifest," said Fursey, lowering his voice suddenly.

"Do you see a radiant being, the abiding spirit of the stone?"

"No. I see a cow."

"A what?"

"A cow's head."

"What's she doing?"

"She's looking at me."

"What do you mean 'looking at you'?"

"Just looking at me."

"Well, you keep looking at her. Don't let your gaze waver."

Fursey and the cow continued to stare at one another for a long time without either party making a move.

"What's happening now?" came the crystallomancer's voice.

"She's waggling her ears at me."

"Remarkable," muttered Turko.

"There are shadows beginning to move across the crystal from right to left," announced Fursey. "The cow is fading."

"The operation is at an end," declared Turko. "You will see no more."

Fursey rose to his feet and felt suddenly very tired. They walked together into the fresh air outside the cave.

"Remarkable," repeated Turko. "Have you ever had dealings with a cow?"

Fursey thought for a moment. "No," he answered.

"Then there's a cow coming into your life," declared Turko with finality. "We will try the experiment again before the moon becomes full. In the meantime you would be well advised to take an infusion of the herb mugwort from time to time during the moon's increase. It has valuable anti-bilious properties and will aid your power of vision. I shall not charge you my usual fee for to-day's session."

"That's very generous of you," responded Fursey, "but you must at least let me stand you a drink. I'm sorely in need of one myself."

Turko watched suspiciously as Fursey manipulated his rope and produced two flagons of ale.

"I had forgotten that you are something of a wizard," he muttered as he took the proffered flagon gingerly. "I trust that I did not offend you earlier in the evening by my remarks about the profession."

"Not at all," replied Fursey. "You have earned my gratitude by being so frank. I'm glad to know the nature of the people amongst whom I must dwell."

"Do you intend prolonged residence?" enquired the crystallomancer politely.

Fursey stirred uncomfortably. "Some weeks at least. I shall probably stay with Cuthbert or in his neighbourhood."

"Is it long since you have seen Cuthbert?" asked Turko.

"About three months."

"I'm afraid that you will find him sadly changed. The poor fellow has become a martyr to drink."

"Indeed," commented Fursey.

"He made his way here in a tattered and deplorable state. His cottage had been burnt by a furious mob during the witch hunt inspired by the Bishop, and Cuthbert barely escaped with his life. His sorrows are many, but most of all he deplores the loss of his store of magical books and his collection of horrible rarities, moles' feet, murderers' knucklebones and the like."

"Yes," said Fursey, "he had a considerable collection. I saw it once."

"When he came here first," continued Turko, "there was no consoling him. 'What use is a sorcerer to anyone without his stock-in-trade?' was the burden of his complaint. Poor fellow, he's scarcely to be blamed that he took to smothering his sorrows in alcohol. Like you, he has a rope, so that the means to intoxication are unfortunately always ready to hand. However, he keeps a plenteous board, due to that same rope, and he is able to produce the most delectable dishes, a fact which renders him highly popular in the community. I'm sure that you will be happy with him."

"I hope so," replied Fursey, without conviction.

"It grows late," said Turko. "It is time for us to go. At least a mile of rough mountain country lies between us and the cave in which Cuthbert dwells."

Fursey rose unwillingly to his feet and they set out across the soggy moorland.

"I'm still exercised about that cow," remarked Turko. "Are you certain that your vision was not due to the delusions of a bewildered fancy?"

"I saw a cow," replied Fursey obstinately.

Turko shook his head, and they continued the rest of their way in silence. From time to time Fursey glanced apprehensively at the black shadows oozing from the crevices of the awful heights which reared themselves above the stretch of bogland. In the twilight the outline of the hills was harsh and threatening, and their mass overwhelmed whatever little spirit he possessed. He felt against his face the small, damp wind which came across the moors. It stroked his face mockingly and slid away, smoothing a path for itself across the tips of the heather. In the failing light the entire upland had assumed an ominous character. The familiar material things, rock, bogland, shimmering pool and hill, seemed charged with malice. They seemed to Fursey to be watching him closely, waiting for the appropriate moment to rise up and destroy him. His fears were by no means diminished when there suddenly came to his ears from the heights above the lonely howling of some distant wizard chanting his way carefully through the intricacies of a conjuration. Fursey gasped and quickened his pace so as to keep abreast of his companion. At last they came to a tumble of great rocks sprawled in the shadow of the hill.

"This is the place," whispered Turko. "I'll leave you now. Unless I regain my cave before nightfall I'm likely to break a limb in crossing this unfriendly stretch of country."

Without another word he turned and hurried back along the way they had come. It came into Fursey's mind that the crystallomancer also was afraid of Cuthbert; then he forgot Turko and looked anxiously about him. He was at the entrance to a slender cleft in the rocks from which emerged a negligible trickle of water, formed probably by the continual gathering of moisture on the roof of the cave into which the crevice opened. As Fursey peered nervously into the orifice he became aware of a dim light in the interior. All at once it was obliterated. Someone had come between it and Fursey. He could see the outline of a human being standing before him.

"Who's there?" asked a hollow voice.

Fursey mastered a sudden impulse to turn and take to his heels.

"Fursey," he quavered, "your old friend, Fursey."

A tall man with stooping shoulders emerged from the cave. He was clad in a tight-fitting suit of black, sadly dilapidated. He bent his wan face on his visitor and examined him with sharp, glittering eyes. He had a puckered, rabbit's mouth and a long lock of black hair hung down over his forehead. His appearance was far from prepossessing. He was the sort of creature one might reasonably expect to meet about midnight on a lonely country road in the neighbourhood of a graveyard. Fursey shuddered under the steady gaze.

"I'm Fursey," he squeaked. "Don't you remember me?"

Cuthbert raised a meagre hand and rubbed his cheek. A sly and furtive look came into his eyes, but he said nothing.

"I met you last spring when you were sexton of Kilcock Churchyard," continued Fursey. "I enjoyed for one night the hospitality of your cottage."

"Yes," answered Cuthbert at last, "I remember you. You're the little laybrother whom they expelled from the monastery because the demons began to play tricks on him. I remember you well. Come in."

He turned and re-entered the cave. Fursey with a quaking heart stumbled in after him. Inside it was more light. From a flat rock, which evidently served as a table, a long taper flickered oddly, casting shadows that advanced and retreated up and down the walls. On the floor at the back of the cave was spread a heap of rushes. There was a large number of empty flagons scattered here and there, but there were no furnishings. Cuthbert seated himself on a stone and motioned Fursey to a similar one where the taper light would play on his face. They looked across at one another in silence. In the half-light Cuthbert's visage seemed demoniacal.

"Will you have a drink?" he asked suddenly.

Fursey was conscious of a sudden relaxation of tension. "No, thank you," he gasped, remembering even in his frightened state that he would be wise to keep his mind clear so as to be able to grapple with whatever might ensue.

Cuthbert raised a flagon from the ground at his feet and took a deep draught. Fursey realised suddenly that he was half drunk.

"You see before you," declared Cuthbert, "the ruins of a great sorcerer."

With a grandiose gesture he replaced the flagon on the floor at his feet. Fursey murmured deprecatingly, but Cuthbert raised a silencing hand.

"Yes," he said, "I have lost everything. I have lost my magic books. I have lost my store of insidious poisons, powders and philtres, my menagerie of toads, moles, bats and vipers, my beautiful garden of noxious herbs and plants—the collection and care of a lifetime, all gone! Not even the marrows of a murderer or the thumb of a suicide is left."

As he sank back, resting his spare frame against the wall of the cave, he presented a most rueful spectacle, a living example of the condition to which sorcery and alcohol can bring a respectable sexton.

"A man of your abilities—" began Fursey soothingly.

Cuthbert shook his head despondently. "How can I start again?" he asked. "A sorcerer without the tools of his trade is lamed and helpless. It would have been better if they had apprehended me and immolated me in the fire which consumed my possessions."

"We must never lose heart," muttered Fursey.

"Such an affliction as I have undergone," answered Cuthbert, "undermines the spirit. There is no medicine for a cankered heart. I am an outlaw who may never abide for long in the one place. Soon the authorities will search out this refuge, and I shall have to take to the roads. I may make an ignoble living amongst sportsmen and peasants, charming cocks for cock fighting or the like. I have no other future."

Listening to this dolorous discourse, Fursey began to wonder whether his long journey and the manifold dangers which he had encountered had all been to no purpose.

"But you still retain your knowledge," he argued anxiously "You know how to manufacture love philtres, for instance?"

Cuthbert appeared to observe the note of anxiety in Fursey's voice. He raised his head suddenly. "What do you want of me?" he asked.

"I was advised by Satan to seek you out," began Fursey.

"A very upstanding gentleman," commented Cuthbert with a respectful bow of his head, "but one with whom I have only a slight acquaintance. How is His Highness keeping?"

"When I last saw him," replied Fursey, "I regret to say that he was not in the best condition."

"Indeed," replied Cuthbert solicitously.

"He presented a very battered appearance," replied Fursey. "He was generally soiled and seemed very rickety as to his legs. Moreover, he had lost the tip of an ear."

"I'm sorry to hear that," commented Cuthbert. "Did he have the misfortune to meet with an accident?"

"He had the misfortune to meet with a gentleman of the anchorite class," explained Fursey, "and the affair had an unfavourable outcome."

"These religious have the country ruined," remarked Cuthbert acidly. "Things have come to a nice pass when the Prince of Darkness himself is not safe from their depredations."

"He advised me to apprentice myself to you."

"With what object?"

"Well, chiefly so as to learn the manufacture and use of love philtres."

Cuthbert turned on Fursey a disapproving eye.

"I'm surprised at you," he said. "I would never have suspected you of gallantry. I hope that your ultimate intentions in the matter are honourable."

"Most honourable," Fursey hastened to assure him. "I merely wish to deprive an unpleasant fellow of his life and contract a union with his spouse."

Cuthbert's brow cleared. "That's all right," he said. "I feared at first that more than one female was involved and that the matter wasn't respectable."

He sat for some time in silent thought, staring at the floor of the cave. When he raised his head to look at Fursey once more there was a brittle glint in his eye.

"Am I to understand that you are fully resolved in your purpose?"

"Yes," replied Fursey stoutly. "I'm ensnared in the love of a woman whose natural perfections are such that I'm determined to stop at nought to gain her regard. To begin with, I want to learn how best to murder an audacious villain named Magnus, against whom I am implacably incensed. My hatred of mankind is such that I shall stop at nothing. Already I have become a man of the most pernicious principles. I've sold my soul to the Devil, and my rogueries are being spoken of far and near. I've led a band of Viking pirates against

Clonmacnoise and burnt the holy settlement to the ground. I'm determined to become a menace to humanity, and I beg of you to take me as your apprentice and use your utmost endeavour to instil into me all the wickedness you know."

Fursey paused from lack of breath and anxiously studied Cuthbert's face to ascertain if he could whether or not the sorcerer believed him. Cuthbert was leaning forward with his elbows on the table watching him closely. As Fursey finished his peroration, Cuthbert slapped one hand into the other enthusiastically.

"There's a catching oratory in your words," he declared. "I'm glad you came to me. Maybe your companionship will serve to free me from my present morbid melancholy. We'll begin your instruction to-morrow. We'll go down to the graveyard and raise a wraith or two, for there's much to be learnt from the souls of the lost."

Fursey heard this speech with considerable trepidation, but he smiled bravely and assured the sorcerer that there was nothing he would like better. Cuthbert rose smiling and laid a skinny hand on the shoulder of his apprentice.

"Take some of the heather," he said, "and make yourself a comfortable couch. The taper is flickering out. It's time for all good people to be in bed."

CHAPTER VI

Notwithstanding Cuthbert's apparent enthusiasm on the night of Fursey's arrival, he manifested no inclination on the morrow to commence the instruction of his apprentice in the sinuous mysteries of witchcraft. A great lethargy possessed him, and during the ensuing weeks he lazed about the cave, sometimes drinking moodily, at other times sitting for long hours with a twisted smile on his face as if his mind was busy with curious and serpentine designs. He roused himself from time to time to deal with customers, besotted peasants who came with offerings of rough wooden bowls or ill-made pottery, requesting him to cure warts or whooping cough. Except for these folk cures he did no magic; and Fursey, secretly glad of the respite, performed the menial tasks of the cave, drew water from a nearby brook and brought in sticks and gorse to burn, for it was already winter. The only other duty laid upon him was the collection of herbs and venomous plants, which he soon learnt to identify. Besides their use in the making of drugs and medicines, Cuthbert spoke constantly of the necessity for building up a large stock of magical armament in keeping with his position as a major sorcerer. Fursey was a docile and assiduous servant, and came back from each excursion bowed beneath a load of poisonous fungi, foxgloves, hemlock or the dreaded deadly nightshade. He even went beyond his instructions and brought in plants that looked to him tolerably venomous. Some of these Cuthbert discarded,

127

others he put aside to try by way of experiment on the next peasant who should call seeking his assistance. Fursey was kept busy. Some herbs had to be gathered at certain phases of the moon, and he spent a week hunting for a stone which it was indispensable to find in a peewit's nest. A brisk trade developed with the other warlocks scattered throughout the hills. On Cuthbert's instructions, Fursey carried loads of dogwood, hawkweed and henbane to their caverns and bargained with them for elf-shots, murderers' knucklebones and the fingers of unbaptised babes. Cuthbert spoke vaguely of making magic brews and performing rituals but his lassitude was such that he never made a start.

At first Fursey was nigh overcome by the demoniacal character of his surroundings. The weather was of a very irregular character. Patches of druidical fog floated against the wind, and the neighbourhood was subject to sudden storms and hail. One heard strange voices on the breeze, and at times the air would be filled with a kind of twittering or chirping, which Fursey knew to be the voices of spirits. It was not unusual to meet some initiate toiling up the track with a load of assorted stones collected from four parishes, or to see a wizard coursing back and forward on the hillside in the form of a greyhound. The night was often hideous with tumults and strange bawlings, and from the mouth of the cave wandering fires were visible. At first Fursey could not sleep at night through fear of being suddenly embraced by the spectral arms of some visitant. He felt that if he were to experience such a foul caress he would surely breathe forth the vital spark. But soon the fatigues of the day, his journeyings hither and thither, guaranteed his night's rest, and he was asleep as soon as he laid his head on its rustling pillow. He accustomed himself also to the less alarming of the magical manifestations. He could look on a griffin rampant in a green field without feeling an overmastering desire to take to his heels. He came to appreciate that these projections and appearances, not being directed at himself, were in nowise likely to injure him. He knew that no one on the mountain had reason to bear him malice, so that he no longer took cover if he saw a pale young gentleman floating by him on the wind or beheld high overhead in the grey cloud drift of the sky a boat of shining crystal rowed by a faery on his way to The Land of Youth. He even accustomed himself to the scratching and mewing of enchanted cats at night and their hideous caterwauling. There was, however, one mountain slope which he avoided, a place where chimeras, spoorns, calcars and sylens slouched among the rocks leering at the passers-by. Turko the crystallomancer had told him that on the summit of the mountain itself dwelt belated worshippers of Ogma and Segomos and the other weird, cruel and bloody divinities of the Gael. Their devotees adored holy wells and the elements, and their crude shrines were tended by loathsome and malignant witch-hags. They were the last worshippers of the old native faith, which had been supplanted everywhere else by the foreign religion that the blessed Patrick had brought from Britain. Fursey knew that wherever there was strong religious conviction there was blood-letting and oppression, so he avoided the hill where the pillar stones of paganism still stood. Once when he was on his way to a piece of soggy ground well known to him as a place where all classes of vegetable wickedness grew in hideous luxuriance, he essayed a short cut, which brought him within the shadow of the mountain of ill-repute. All at once he found himself on the edge of a crevasse across which a bridge had been flung. A woman stood on the bridge and, as Fursey stopped to stare at her, she held out her hand, offering him a cluster of nuts. He immediately turned and retraced his steps, and as he glanced fearfully over his shoulder he saw that both bridge and woman had vanished. In this neighbourhood on All Hallows Eve the nature spirits of paganism fore-gathered, lingering for a while as if in sadness by the cairn on the mountain top and beside the dolmen which Christian iconoclasts had overthrown. Fursey saw their great shadows against the sky at sunset and fled to the safety of the sorcerer's cave.

Before a couple of months had run, Fursey had come to know, at least by sight, most of the mountain dwellers who lived nearby. The mathematicians rarely spoke to anyone and had no interest in Fursey's bundles of herbs or venomous plants. All day they sat in the openings of their caves working out problems far exceeding all numbers in arithmetic. The sorcerers were in general cross-grained and snappy, and were always asking Fursey to undertake little jobs for them, such as the kidnapping and murdering of small boys, from whose boiled bones a powerful ointment could be made. Fursey invariably declined with his best regrets, pleading that he was articled to Cuthbert and was precluded from performing such tasks for others, however anxious he might be to accommodate them. The wizards would mutter in their beards and become very testy in their subsequent conversation, so that Fursey as soon as courtesy permitted would bid them good day, hoist his wares on his back and proceed on his way.

Some fifty paces from Cuthbert's cave dwelt an alchemist, a person of the human species, but lame and crooked, squat and bandy-legged. As one might expect of a man whose only desire was to assemble wealth, he was in the highest degree hard-visaged. His efforts to turn into gold the flint arrowheads and horseshoes with which his cave was littered, appeared to meet with little success. Clad in base and servile weeds, he seemed an impoverished and benighted creature. From time to time, when he wearied of treating his flints and horseshoes with balm of mercury and putting them through the various methods of alchemical confection, he would revert for a week or so to a search for the Elixir of Life. He would sit for days almost completely immersed in a herbal stew over a slow fire, striving to renew his youth by saturating his body with certain potent juices, of which sugar of mercury and celestial slime were important ingredients. The preparation of this bath was a slow affair, a lengthy process of congealation and distillation was necessary before the advent of a divine sparkle in the mixture indicated to the alchemist that it was time for him to peel off his clothes and get in. He was an unfriendly fellow, who held intercourse with no one. He was suspicious of all who approached his cave, imagining that they were intent on prying into his alchemical secrets.

Fursey met the cow while he was on one of his excursions collecting sowthistle, nipplewort and buckbean and similar herbs of a soothing nature. Although the snow had fallen in thousands during the preceding night, he found the constant bending and tugging at obstinate roots very warming, so he had taken off his cloak and flung it on a nearby hedge. When his basket was full, and he turned to resume the garment, he saw the last shred of it disappearing down a cow's gullet. Fursey's first thought was that the cow was apparently hungry. There was snow on the ground and the poor beast's bones were apparent through its hide. Then it was borne in on him that he had seen that particular cow somewhere before. When she slowly stirred her ears, he remembered Turko's crystal. For a long time he stood staring at the cow, while she returned his gaze with impassive melancholy. It was apparent that no thoughts were stirring in her brain, she was just looking at Fursey because she couldn't think of anything better to look at.

"She's lost her way," he thought, "and she's suffering grievously from malnutrition."

He put down his basket and scraped away a square yard of snow from the ground. Then he directed her attention to the grass growing underneath. The cow seemed unimpressed.

"I don't wonder that you're dejected," said Fursey. "You look as if you hadn't eaten anything for a month. If only I had my rope with me I'd produce some bodybuilding food for you. The best thing you can do is to come along with me and we'll find you something to eat."

He walked around the cow and gave her a smart slap on the buttock. As she did not seem to have anywhere in particular to go, she permitted Fursey to drive her before him up the track to the cavern. Cuthbert, who was sitting inside drinking a flagon of mead, sprang to his feet when the cow walked into the cave and stood staring at him, flicking her tail.

"Where did you get her?" he demanded hoarsely. "Did you steal her?"

"Certainly not," replied Fursey primly. "I just brought her along for a square meal."

Cuthbert muffled a curse, and began hastily to move his most cherished possessions out of the cow's reach.

"You better get her out," he said meaningly.

"You surely wouldn't begrudge her a bite to eat," retorted Fursey. "The poor thing is almost hollow."

Taking up his rope he cast it over a projecting ledge of rock and pulled. Immediately a load of hay fell from the ceiling. The cow bowed her head and began to munch contentedly. There was a string of blasphemy from the back of the cave, and a moment later Cuthbert came clambering across the hay.

"If you haven't that animal and the haystack out of this cave by the time I come back," he snarled, "I'll have your life."

He stamped out into the open air and disappeared from view. When the cow had eaten her fill, watched by the admiring Fursey, he led her out and tethered her in a hollow in the cliff, where she would be assured of some protection from the elements. Then he started to carry out the hay in armfuls and pile it about her. The cow watched him contentedly. Then she brought up Fursey's cloak from her stomach by way of cud and Fursey shook his head at her in smiling disapproval, and returned to the cave to sweep out the last traces of the hay. As he finished the task, Cuthbert re-appeared and stood in the cavern mouth watching him approvingly.

"I'm glad this happened," declared Cuthbert. "The incident has thrown a flood of light into the recesses of your soul. As it happens, I am a profound psychologist as well as a considerable sorcerer. When I saw the care you bestowed upon that ruminant I read your spirit like an open book. Your soul stood naked before me."

"What did you see?" asked Fursey, leaning on the broom.

Cuthbert nodded his head sagely. "Your affections have welled over the dam of your resolution. Your brimming heart craves an object to love and cherish. We must win the woman Maeve for you at once. We have delayed too long."

"Oh, thank you," said Fursey delightedly.

"Don't thank me," replied the sorcerer in businesslike tones. "To a considerable degree I am consulting my own convenience and comfort in the matter. Unless we provide you with a proper object for your affections, I don't doubt but that before long you will have the cave so full of feathered and four-legged pets that there will be no living here at all. Not that I blame you," he added kindly. "It's your nature, and no man can slip away from his nature. Now, what was it I undertook to do for you?"

"First we have to rid the world of an objectionable oaf called Magnus," prompted Fursey; "a man who has done grievous wrong to me and mine."

"Exactly," said Cuthbert. "I clearly remember the circumstances. We shall slay him to-night."

"How?" asked Fursey breathlessly.

"Such a matter is a mere bagatelle to a man like me," replied Cuthbert. "I'll riddle him with magic. Let me see."

He seated himself on his favourite rock and absently conjured up a flagon of black ale to help him in his cogitations.

"How would you like him to die?" he asked at length.

"Roaring," replied Fursey without hesitation. "Roaring and wallowing in a horrible manner."

"Let me see," repeated Cuthbert. "We could overthrow him by cold and heat, but that would require a spot free from observation, a napkin of unblemished whiteness and a chafing dish. We have the first named, but we lack the other two; so we'll have to think of something else."

He took a long pull at the flagon of ale and ruminated.

"Will you be satisfied," he said at last, "if I afflict him with a lingering and painful disease, so that his speech and hearing become benumbed, his toes and fingers fall off, and he finally be bereft of every sense?"

"No," declared Fursey fiercely. "I will not be talked into a persuasion that anything less than his total demise will suffice."

"But it's a lovely spell," said Cuthbert coaxingly. "Its first effect would be to afflict him with a baldness; and all we would need for it would be the toenails of an unbaptised male child, the entrails of a sacrificed cock and the molars of a glutton."

"I respect your artistic instincts," said Fursey firmly, "but I will not be satisfied unless you pierce the fluidic envelope of his soul."

"Very well," sighed Cuthbert, "have it your own way. We shall drown all his faculties at once if you so desire. We could waste him by burying a taper, but that's a slow and tedious business. The surest and speediest method of inducing death is to get your familiar to wear a pair of the victim's drawers while a certain potent spell is woven. The drawers are then dipped in boiling water mixed with blood, and buried. Death follows within an hour."

Fursey's fancy was for a moment beguiled at the thought of Albert in the unaccustomed garment, but he shook his head sadly.

"I haven't got a pair of his drawers," he admitted reluctantly.

"You're not much help to me," muttered Cuthbert. "There's only one thing for it. We must have a parricide's skull. Go over to Festus Wisenuts and borrow the one he has. Tell him I sent you and he won't hesitate to lend it."

"Is it essential?" asked Fursey in dismay.

Cuthbert turned on him a glittering eye. "Yes," he answered, "if you want the job done to-night. In the meantime I'll prepare the ingredients, and we can start the spell the moment you return."

Fursey set out reluctantly. Although he had been more than four months resident in the cave in the Knockmealdown Mountains he had not yet seen the erratic landlord whose sub-tenant he was. He dreaded, however, that unless Magnus was quenched to-night, long months might elapse before Cuthbert would again be in the mood to weave the necessary spell. He knew the exact location of Festus' dwelling and began to hurry his steps, remembering that he had left Cuthbert with almost a full flagon of ale in his fist. It would be a heartbreaking disappointment if on his return he were to find the sorcerer, as was so frequently his wont, lying on the floor of the cave snoring.

As Fursey approached the rocky place where Festus lived, there was a crack of thunder overhead and there fell from the sky suddenly an abundance of white pullets. On striking the ground they shook their tails and scampered away in all directions, watched by Fursey with eyes as round as saucers. He halted in miserable indecision, and it was a long time before he succeeded in forcing himself to go on. As he dragged his feet after him towards the yawning mouth of the cave he saw with relief that there were no sentinel moles. A single green cat sat in the entrance washing her face. She looked up as Fursey approached and contemplated him inquisitively, with one green forepaw suspended in mid-air. Fursey eyed her suspiciously and walked in a wide circle around her. As he did so, he came suddenly on Festus Wisenuts himself in the opening of the cave.

Festus was exactly as Fursey had heard him described, a tall, grim-visaged man with a long, slender, silvery beard, clad in an imposing black gown ornamented with the signs of the zodiac. He did not observe Fursey's approach, being apparently intent on the spell which he was weaving. Fursey watched with horror as the old man in hideous ecstasy capered around a copper tripod, sprinkling ground glass and powdered spurge. Beyond the tripod stood a virgin kid crowned with vervain. Suddenly Festus began whirling himself around in a magical manner. Faster and faster he whirled, while the air became full of a sound like the plaining of damned souls. All at once, Festus stopped and tearing a stone of red enamel from the folds of his flowing black gown, flung it into the tripod. An inky cloud billowed forth and enveloped Fursey. Half-blinded, Fursey retreated backwards until he bumped into the wall of the cave, where he stood with coal-black hands and face, coughing and rubbing his smarting eyes.

"Success at last!" came an exultant voice. "I have created a tawny Moor."

Fursey, his eyes still streaming, stood gaping at Festus.

"Approach," commanded the magician, "and henceforth do my bidding."

"I assure you, sir, that you're making a mistake," choked Fursey.

"What?" thundered the magician. "Can it be that, like the others, you are nought but a false seeming and that my suffumigation has once more gone awry? That is soon proved."

He picked up a blade and tested the point with his thumb while Fursey looked desperately to left and right.

"You have nought to fear," declared Festus. "This is a new and unused knife. It cannot hurt an elemental essence, as I judge you to be; but if you are a mere figment, your natural antagonism to new steel will cause you to disappear, probably in a thin smoke."

"Such action as you contemplate can only have tragic consequences," said Fursey faintly. "I'm human. I beg you to believe me, sir."

"Human! Nonsense" snapped the magician. "I've just conjured you into existence. I admit that you're not my idea of a sooty Moor, but in these hard times we have to be content with what we can get. Approach until I test your quality."

"Honest to God, sir, I'm human. To stab me would be a great mistake."

"How can you be human?" cried Festus in a sharp, shrieking voice. "You're standing within a circle fortified with mysterious characters of which the import is known to me alone. There was no one within the circle when I began the spell. If you are human and have since crossed it you would have received a shock which would have killed you."

Fursey desperately rubbed some of the black from his face with his sleeve.

"Can't you see I'm not a tawny Moor?" he said imploringly. "I'm Cuthbert's apprentice, and I came to you to borrow a parricide's skull."

Festus stood in the centre of the cave breathing angrily through his nostrils.

"If you're deceiving me," he declared menacingly, "I'll inflict you with violent fits."

"I never deceived anyone in my life," said Fursey pitifully. "I haven't it in my nature. I'm only a simple country boy. I beg you to believe me, sir."

Festus flung his knife suddenly on the ground and turned aside with a gesture of angry impatience. Fursey saw his chance and, darting from the cave, fled down the hillside as if all the powers of darkness were in close pursuit. He did not slacken in his flight until he was once more climbing the rise to Cuthbert's cave. Even then he was afraid to stop to recover his breath, but continued to stagger forward with one hand pressed hard over his heart in an attempt to stay its frenzied beating. As he re-entered the cavern, Cuthbert cocked a lively eye in his direction. Fursey sank on to a stone and breathlessly told his story.

"Never mind," grinned Cuthbert, putting down the empty flagon. "We'll do without the parricide's skull. I've since thought of another way of annihilating your enemy Magnus. We'll damp him out by the antagonism of fire and water."

"I wish you had thought of that before you sent me near Festus," complained Fursey.

"Never mind," said Cuthbert soothingly. "At least it was an experience for you, and your life is the richer for it."

It was fully half-an-hour later before Fursey felt himself capable of rising to his feet preparatory to taking his part in the black ceremony which was trembling in Cuthbert's well-stocked mind. Even then he only dragged himself to his feet because he noticed that his companion was advancing steadily in inebriation, and he feared that if the weaving of the spell were any longer delayed, Cuthbert would become completely incapacitated. As it was, the master sorcerer was rather unsteady on his legs and very talkative. He began by making Fursey kneel down while he crowned him with a wreath of wild parsley and vervain. Then he spent some time rooting in a corner amongst a heap of elf-shots, rowan twigs and holed stones. At last he found what he was looking for, a flint pebble, which he handed to Fursey; instructing him to go outside into the open air and cast it over his left shoulder. When Fursey had done as he was bid, he returned and found Cuthbert standing in the centre of the cave with one hand resting on the rock table. The sorcerer's pallid countenance was overcast by a film of thought.

"It won't work," he said. "I forgot completely that four black cats are required and a bat who has been killed by lightning, as well as the nails from a murderer's coffin; and that all must be set up at a crossroads on a suicide's grave. Moreover, the proper time is during the waning of the moon. The still hours of the night are best, and it doesn't do at all to select a spot where spectres are addicted to appearing."

"It seems to me," said Fursey impatiently, "that we won't get anything at all done to-night."

"Trust me," said Cuthbert with a drunken hiccup. He disappeared once more into the recesses of the cave and reappeared with a fresh wax taper.

"Over there on the shelf of rock," he said, "you will find a box containing sticks which I have gathered at midnight from four points equidistant from a suicide's grave. Yes, that's it. Now we must kindle a fire."

The sorcerer chatted amiably while Fursey wearily heaped the sticks in the cave mouth and struck fire from a flint. Soon the sticks were crackling merrily.

"The fire must be periodically renewed in proportion to the length of the business," declared Cuthbert. "That will be your duty. In addition you must cast on the flames from time to time a handful from this bag of calcined bones, but not so much as to put out the fire. And above all, don't let that vervain crown fall off your head."

Fursey re-adjusted his wreath and took the bag which Cuthbert handed him. Then he squatted on the floor beside the fire. Cuthbert held the wax taper towards the flames until it slowly softened in his hands and he was able to knead it into the rough image of a man.

"Does that look like Magnus?" he asked.

"Not very," admitted Fursey.

"Not a bad likeness all the same," remarked Cuthbert blithely, "when one takes into consideration the fact that I have never seen him. Well, we'll trace his name on it so that there'll be no mistake." He produced a needle and with its point carefully lettered the image. "Now," he continued, "you must concentrate your will power on Magnus. Concentrate on him with every faculty of your being."

Fursey's countenance assumed a dogged, far-away expression as he strove to carry out the sorcerer's instruction. Cuthbert, in the meantime, retired to the back of the cave and began to chant an incantation. It was a lonely sound, and Fursey was glad to see him re-appearing from the shadows with the image still held in his hand. He advanced slowly towards the fire, mouthing foul and baleful jargon. Then he knelt and traced a circle around the fire with his finger. Further muttering and mumbling followed until Fursey began to feel the air thickening and becoming greasy with wickedness. At last Cuthbert stopped. He made a few mysterious passes in the air as if he were milking an imaginary cow, then he turned his face to his apprentice.

"Now," he whispered, "I have charged the element. Hand me that needle and keep concentrating on your enemy."

He took the needle from Fursey's trembling hand and, heating it in the fire until it was red-hot, he jabbed it viciously into the stomach of the waxen image. There was a sudden screech from outside the cave. Fursey and Cuthbert straightened and looked at one another.

"What was that?" enquired Cuthbert.

"I don't know," replied Fursey.

They listened for a few moments, but the uncouth sound was not repeated.

"An animal I suppose," remarked Cuthbert, and, bending forward once more, he heated the needle in the flame. When the steel had again reddened he withdrew it and carefully stabbed the image a few times, finally drawing the needle out at its back. There immediately burst upon their ears a series of the most fearful howlings. Cuthbert paused and once more looked at Fursey.

"There it is again. It seems to proceed from the alchemist's cave. Maybe you ought to go and see what it is. Perchance there is something amiss."

Fursey scrambled to his feet and trotted the intervening fifty paces to their neighbour's dwelling. When he peered in he was astonished to see the alchemist, his face ashen, lying doubled up on the floor, with his two hands pressed against his stomach.

"What's wrong?" enquired Fursey.

The alchemist turned on him a pair of bloodshot eyes.

"Sudden, strange, unheralded pains," he gasped.

"Oh, is that all?" said Fursey, and he turned and trotted back, anxious not to miss any part of the quenching of Magnus. Cuthbert was busy turning a poker in the fire, bringing it to a red-hot condition.

"Indigestion," he commented when Fursey told him what he had seen. "If it were a mental malady, we could perhaps cure it with soft music; but there's nothing to be done about indigestion."

He withdrew the glowing poker from the flames, blew on it once, and thrust it into the stomach of the image. From the direction of the alchemist's cave the most pitiful lamentation smote the air. Cuthbert paid no attention; but, uttering a baleful verse, cast a handful of calcined bone dust on the now mangled image and worked the dust into its stomach with the poker. Suddenly there appeared at the mouth of the cave a distraught figure raving and cursing in a most fearful manner. It was the alchemist, and as Fursey and Cuthbert rose to their feet in astonishment, he fell on his back and rolled about on the ground.

"He appears to be in great sweat and agony," remarked Cuthbert. "Go and see what's wrong with him."

"He's ill all right," replied Fursey, trying to hold the alchemist in the one place by pressing his shoulders against the ground.

"Great nuisance," commented Cuthbert. "Just when we were getting on so well too."

"He won't stay still," shouted Fursey as he struggled with the wallowing alchemist, "and he's vomiting a marvellous diversity of objects. Already he has brought up four pieces of coal, a brass mirror and two hilted knives."

"Indeed?" replied Cuthbert admiringly, and he approached to view the phenomenon. The alchemist seemed in evil case: he had broken out in so great a sweat that the very fat seemed to be running off his body. Cuthbert glanced at the wretched man and his face at once fell. He rushed back to the cave and grabbed the waxen image, which he laid down before the fire and which was slowly melting away.

"I shall try to disenchant him," he shouted. "Keep a tight hold on him."

Fursey wrestled manfully, one knee on the alchemist's chest and the other on his forehead.

"He's retching in a most formidable manner," he cried. "He has just brought up a handful of human bones varying greatly in size and character. Do you think they're his ribs?" he added anxiously.

"Keep holding him," shouted Cuthbert. "I'll try to turn off the magic, but I fear that I may be unable to prevent the spell taking its ordained course."

The alchemist's struggles grew less violent as Cuthbert hastily kneaded the wax image into shape again, stamped out the fire and started enunciating the spell backwards. When the disenchanting formulary was at last completed and he emerged again from the cave, his unfortunate victim had ceased to struggle altogether and lay on the ground looking up at the sky with glassy eyes.

"Poor fellow," commented the sorcerer. "You better help him to his feet and bring him in for a drink. It's the least we can do for him."

The alchemist allowed Fursey to assist him to rise and seemed to be glad to have someone to hold on to, as he was hardly able to keep his legs under him; but when he realised that he was being led towards Cuthbert's cave his eyes became round with horror. He was incapable of speech, but he resisted Fursey desperately. He broke away at last and made off staggering across country with only one apparent wish, to put as great a distance as possible between himself and the cave of the master sorcerer.

"A strange affair," remarked Fursey; "but to return to matters of greater moment, do you think that we have successfully annihilated Magnus?"

Cuthbert had sobered considerably. "I do not," he replied solemnly, "and I'm not going to try it again."

It was some hours later, when he was turning restlessly on his heather bed, that Fursey realised what had happened. He lay still for a while listening bitterly to Cuthbert's alcoholic snoring; then he turned and buried his face in the pillow.

On the following day the alchemist was found in an exhausted condition in a distant boghole. He was conveyed back to his cave by some of his acquaintance and carefully put to bed. Cuthbert did not fail to do the gentlemanly thing. He made a formal call and offered his apologies. The alchemist listened to his explanation with a wan smile.

During the ensuing weeks Cuthbert avoided the subject of Magnus, and when Fursey at last summoned up courage to ask him to make another attempt, he replied coldly:

"You must learn to do these things for yourself and cease relying on me for everything. When you are a fully qualified sorcerer you can set the matter in train yourself."

"But when will I be fully qualified?" asked Fursey despairingly. "I seem to be learning nothing."

"You're too impatient," answered Cuthbert. "Why, as yet you're merely a novice. I'll see about having you initiated at the Sabbath on May Eve. In the meantime you should devote yourself to a life of wickedness. As far as I can see, you don't seem to be doing any wickedness at all. A man in your position should perform at least one evil deed every day."

While Fursey was most anxious to do everything proper to a novice in the Black Art, his difficulty was that he couldn't think of anything wicked to do. Such things as uncharitable conversation about his fellow sorcerers or theft of their goods were out of the question, for he was in mortal terror of the possible reaction of his victims. He had a wholesome fear of exciting their malice, having no wish to find himself suddenly transfixed by a spell and perhaps turned into a toad or something equally loathsome. The mathematicians seemed the least dangerous, and he spent a whole day making a circuit of their caves, searching for the smallest and weakest of their number so as to pick a quarrel with him, and then suddenly fall upon, kick and otherwise belabour him. But they all looked so grandfatherly with their flowing white beards that he hadn't the heart to interrupt their calculations; and so ended by doing nothing. He experienced a certain satisfaction from the fact that he was slowly starving the lugubrious Albert, but he was very much in doubt as to whether or not this would be in his favour when he had to make confession of his wickedness at the forthcoming Sabbath. He had not summoned Albert for many months, and he often wondered whether his familiar had by this time faded away altogether through inanition. He doubted it; after all, Albert was pure elemental spirit; and Fursey had a shrewd suspicion that he couldn't fade away, however shadowy and intangible he might become.

One of Fursey's regrets was that he very rarely saw Turko the crystallomancer, who spent all his spare time on angling expeditions. The promised second sitting before the crystal had never materialised. When Fursey met the cow, he had gone over on the following day to tell Turko all about it, but the crystallomancer had manifested no interest whatsoever. Fursey had left the cave very hurt and had not sought his company since. He realised that Turko's was a mercurial disposition, sometimes he was glad to see a visitor, but at other times, especially if he was working, he greeted with a scowl anyone who approached him. A man as shy and tender-hearted as Fursey was grievously hurt by an unfriendly reception, and after experiencing Turko's uncertain temper once or twice, he was unwilling to seek the crystallomancer's company again without positive invitation.

Fursey's main pleasure now was feeding the cow, who had grown so fat that she could hardly walk. She didn't want to walk anyway. She seemed content to spend her life eating the wall of hay with which Fursey kept her provided and reflecting about it afterwards. She even slept standing up with her chin resting on the rampart of hay, while she contentedly inhaled its aromatic sweetness.

Spring came late to the mountains, but padding rains and fitful sunshine brought it at last. The flaming yellow gorse ran in thin columns up and across the hillsides, and birds made their appearance, fluttering from bush to tree. The air was dry and sweet, and the constant breeze heady like new wine. The exiles in the hills emerged from their caves rubbing and scratching their beards, and perambulated blinking in the sunshine and smiling affably at everyone they met.

"It wants but a week until the Witches' Sabbath on May Eve, when you will be formally initiated as a sorcerer and become a recognised member of a coven," said Cuthbert to Fursey. "It would be a good thing for you to become socially acquainted with the more influential members of our community before that date, therefore I have decided to give a party."

Fursey was deeply moved by this evidence of his master's kind interest in his welfare and, as he was himself very fond of human society, he lent a willing hand in the preparations. First the invitations had to be issued. Cuthbert, after careful thought, decided on twenty guests, and writing the invitations on small pieces of sheepskin, he despatched Fursey with them to various caves and holes in the mountain. The invitations indicated that Cuthbert would be "At Home" at sunset on the following Saturday night and that formal dress should be worn. Then master and apprentice hung up their ropes in the cave and set to with a will producing delectable foodstuffs and an adequate supply of drink.

"We have no pottery," said Fursey suddenly. "What will they drink out of?"

"My dear Fursey," smiled Cuthbert, "we are going to do this thing in style. We shall borrow from an old warlock friend of mine his much-prized set of robbers' skulls."

On the morning of the party Fursey took a besom and swept the cave, while Cuthbert nailed a forked branch of wild hazel over the entrance. Then the master sorcerer tastefully arranged a few feathers from the wing of a black cock and some belladonna in a small bowl, which he placed in the centre of the rock table.

"What do you think of that?" he asked, stepping back to admire his handiwork.

Fursey, with his head on one side, contemplated the bowl in its circle of robbers' skulls.

"It's very genteel," he replied.

Cuthbert rubbed his meagre hands with satisfaction and allowed his eyes to travel back and forward through the cave.

"All in the best of taste," he remarked. "Now all we have to do is to place the brazier where it won't be knocked over and leave beside it an adequate supply of soothing perfumes for burning."

As the sun shot its last beams from the distant horizon, the first of the guests arrived, a small, swarthy warlock from a cave near at hand.

"An ill-bred fellow," muttered Cuthbert to Fursey; "he would be the first to arrive. His father was a tradesman, so I suppose we can't expect anything else."

The warlock shook hands with his hosts in a perfunctory manner and, not noticing Cuthbert's slight hauteur, immediately began to talk shop. He drew from his capacious pocket a rope plaited the wrong way and a handful of weasel's teeth, and began to extol their magical properties. Cuthbert escaped from him as the other guests began to arrive and took his stand in the opening of the cave, shaking hands with each newcomer and introducing Fursey to those who did not already know him. Although most of the guests had perforce left their wardrobes behind in their flight from the authorities, they each had made an attempt at formal or festive attire. There was a considerable display of black gowns ornamented with stars, pentagrams and crescents, and many wore wreaths of wild parsley around their necks. Fursey had never seen so many long beards assembled together before, and he blushed when affable notice was taken of him. Most of the guests were wizards, but Turko the crystallomancer had also been invited, as well as a mathematician, a scryer and a clairvoyant. The reciter of poetry was not amongst those asked, as he was not considered good class. There was one gate-crasher, the alchemist, who came wandering in, pretending that he did not know that a party was in progress. He was loud in his offers to retire, but Cuthbert, very tight-lipped, insisted that he should remain. The guests stood around in genteel conversation, wondering when the eating and drinking was going to begin. At last the atmosphere became so charged with impatience that Cuthbert turned to apologise, saying that he was waiting for the arrival of the last guest, Festus Wisenuts.

"I know that no one would wish to sit down to table," he said smilingly, "without our revered landlord."

The company hastily deprecated the very idea of starting supper without Festus, but their eyes continued to wander longingly towards the row of flagons in the corner. At last Festus arrived in a cloak flashing silver and golden stars, the very latest thing in sorcerer's dress. As he paused to speak a few rich man's words to Cuthbert, complaining of his worries and the present state of the bullock market, Fursey withdrew towards the back of the cave and hoped that he would not be seen; but as they all seated themselves at the table and addressed themselves to the first course, a porridge of eel's meat and winkles, Festus fixed Fursey with a terrible eye. Fursey rose nervously and busied himself in helping to fill the robbers' skulls with ale, mead or metheglin according to each consumer's taste.

"Who's that fellow?" Festus asked Turko, who was sitting beside him.

"Which fellow?"

"That small, tubby man with the shock of white hair and the round, moonlike face?"

"Oh, that's Fursey, Cuthbert's apprentice. A nice fellow, but somewhat thin-minded. Why do you ask?"

Festus blew hard through his nostrils. "I am doubtful and suspicious of his origin. I don't know that I didn't create him."

The small, swarthy warlock, whose father was a tradesman, was talking loudly with his elbows on the table. To the disgust of everyone present he was spearing his food with the point of a hunting knife and so conveying it to his mouth, instead of eating it in a genteel fashion with his fingers like everyone else.

"I do think Cuthbert should be more selective in whom he invites," muttered the scryer to the mathematician. The mathematician nodded rapidly. He had never seen so much food on a table in his life and he hadn't time to reply in words. Turko raised his skull of ale and bowed smilingly to Fursey, who experienced a rush of happiness at this renewal of their friendship. At the head of the table, Festus Wisenuts was denouncing the government of King Cormac.

"We're taxed out of existence," he complained. "I had to surrender twenty head of cattle this year to meet the cost of the war with Thomond. Politicians are all the same. They hate the rich. They crush us with taxes, but they never think of taxing the poor."

The four of his tenants who were within earshot, nodded their heads sympathetically and waited in respectful silence for his next utterance.

It was a most successful banquet. Cuthbert knew that the secret of a successful party is a never-empty beaker and a judicious mixing of the drinks of those who tend to be abstemious. The good humour increased as course followed course of the most delectable viands, smelts, lampreys, mussels, fowl, edible roots, mountain berries, honeycomb and acorn pie. As the black, yellow and golden liquor flowed in an unending stream, Festus Wisenuts sat back on his lump of rock and tolerantly allowed those near him to speak as well as himself. Esoteric jests with a strong Black Art flavour were bandied from one bearded mouth to another, and even the mathematician was heard to emit a hoarse laugh. The small, swarthy warlock started an intense argument with the scryer about divination from the flight of birds, a subject about which he knew nothing; but the company's good humour was by now such that they regarded his ill-breeding with greater tolerance. Fursey spent most of his time swilling mead and laughing at nothing in particular. He laughed at every sentence addressed to him, thinking it was a joke; and he even began to laugh whenever he caught anyone's eye. Cuthbert, who knew his responsibilities as a host, drank moderately and unobtrusively watched everything and everyone. When he judged that his guests were replete and in sufficiently good humour, he gave the signal to rise. He then drew everyone's attention to himself by a slight but penetrating cough. When all eyes were focused on him, he gently enunciated a few un-recognised words and waved his right hand. Immediately all traces of the meal vanished from the table, leaving the rock bare. Even a piece of acorn pie which Fursey was stuffing into his mouth disappeared from between his fingers. After a moment's initial surprise, there was a burst of polite applause from the company. Very neat, was the comment, a great labour-saving device which must ultimately do away altogether with the necessity for domestic help. The only one who looked at all anxious was the wizard, who had lent Cuthbert his unique and valuable set of robbers' skulls; but Cuthbert allayed his anxiety a moment later by producing them undamaged from the rock shelf and re-filling them for his guests. The company then disposed itself in comfortable positions on rocks and boulders, and waited for the next part of the entertainment.

Cuthbert constituted himself master of ceremonies in vir-tue of his position as host, and began by inviting a sprightly, young wizard to perform a piece of magic. The young man came forward, blushing shyly. He was a trifle nervous, but the benevolent interest apparent on every face seemed to give him courage. He began to speak in cultured tones, carefully enunciating a spell which he had apparently learnt by heart for the occasion. Then he made some circles in the air over the rock table. A water dog came slowly into being, squat-ting on its hunkers. It looked around the circle of approving faces with its wise dog's eyes and carefully wagged its tail. The young wizard reversed the circles in the air, spoke some further magical words, and successfully re-conducted the animal into nothingness. There was a round of polite applause and he retired, bowing gracefully.

"Encore!" shouted the swarthy warlock, who was by this time half drunk.

The nostrils of the assembled wizards quivered slightly in disdain of the vulgarian. Those in his vicinity turned their backs and engaged in learned conversation. Cuthbert's eye had fallen on the alchemist, who had spoken to no one since his arrival uninvited, but had guzzled everything within his reach during supper. He was now sitting in the front row, leering delightedly at the free entertainment.

"Maybe our friend the alchemist will oblige," suggested Cuthbert. "I'm sure we should be all interested to see him manufacturing a few bars of gold."

Every face lit expectantly, but faded again as the alchemist began to protest that most unfortunately he had left all his machinery at home. Cuthbert turned from him, the shadow of a supercilious smile playing about his mouth, and immediately fixed his gaze on a tall sorcerer, who, notwithstanding his flowing white beard, retained still the lively and audacious eyes of youth. Cuthbert nodded slightly.

"Our friend Gustavo?" he queried.

Gustavo came forward at once and laying a phial of mercury on the table, began to conjure by air, fire, water and earth. Then he withdrew a mouse from his sleeve and tossed it into the air. Some weird gestures followed and the enunciation of rugged verses. Then with elaborate ceremony he poured a few drops of mercury from the phial. A cool breeze brushed the faces of those present, there was a sensation of throbbing in the cave, and seven young eagles fell from the ceiling into the alchemist's lap. There was a titter from the wizards as they saw the alchemist's face. The moment that the manifestation was over, the disconcerted alchemist rose and pleaded to be excused. He explained that he had just remembered a valuable herbal stew left simmering on the fire in his cave, and that he would really have to return and attend to it. He shook Cuthbert hastily by the hand and thanked him for a very pleasant evening.

When the gate-crasher was gone, Cuthbert called upon the mathematician. The old man explained that his subject was excessively curious; and spreading some sand on the table, he traced a triangle with his forefinger. Then he prolonged two of the sides and proceeded to demonstrate that the angles at the base of an isosceles triangle are equal. The company listened intently; and when the demonstration was over, sat back somewhat exhausted by the mental wrestlings involved. Then a mild-featured wizard advanced and laying himself on the ground, called on the spirit of darkness. As the spirit troubled him, he tore and wallowed, and his howls and yells were truly terrific. At length there appeared a weird form which emitted a curious kind of light. It seemed to be some class of serpent with a cock's head, but it vanished again before its nature could be properly studied. As the wizard rose to his feet and dusted himself down, the company applauded politely, but there was a general feeling that the demonstration was not altogether in good taste.

Then the scryer delivered a short discourse on divination by observation of the heavens and the planetary courses, by the interpretation of dreams, from sneezing or from the voices of birds. Having burnt some laurel, he produced a raven from beneath his cloak, and from its croaking divined that there would be an increase in taxation in the ensuing year.

Cuthbert, observing that interest was flagging, sent Fursey around the cave to renew the drinks. The guests brightened somewhat, and Cuthbert called on Turko the Crystallomancer to give a demonstration of his art. The swarthy warlock volunteered himself as subject, and Turko went through the ceremony already familiar to Fursey. But when the clouds in the crystal divided, the warlock became suddenly wan. He announced in trembling tones that all he could see was the leaping flames of a pyre and a circle of grim-visaged clerics standing around it, apparently chanting a requiem. When the vision faded he rose with a white face and made his way unsteadily back to his corner where he remained for a long time taking no apparent interest in the subsequent proceedings and seemingly plunged in gloomy foreboding. The other guests too seemed affected and became very silent. Turko explained in an apologetic whisper to his host that the phenomena in the crystal were altogether outside his control. Cuthbert reassured him in kindly tones that no one would think of blaming him, and with his hand on his shoulder conducted him back to his seat.

Many other interesting demonstrations followed. Severed hands phenomenized, a banshee came into being screaming and sobbing, and a swarm of flies as big as nuts flew in circles about the cave. Each won its meed of applause, and the company had begun to tell one another that this was one of the best parties they had ever attended, when Cuthbert turned to Festus Wisenuts and asked him would he deign to give a demonstration of his magical skill. The landlord signified his willingness and rose rather importantly. He took his stand by the table in the centre and bending down to the floor, drew a circle, which he examined carefully to satisfy himself that there was no break however small in its circumference. From his pompous bearing it was borne in on everyone present that a magical operation of a major character was imminent. With one accord the guests moved in closer to the circle so as to miss nothing.

"Gentlemen," began Festus, "after much labour I have perfected a conjuration for the creation of a tawny Moor. I am now about to bring him into existence."

The wizards shifted in their seats and looked at one another doubtfully, but no one said anything. Festus planted the brazier in the centre of the circle and began to feed the flames with bruised herbs. Then he made a circuit of the circumference breathing to left and right. In spite of their doubts as to his ability, the interest of the onlookers increased as he produced a mole from a bag and immolated it. They watched with bated breath as he began to sway gently from side to side and chant an incantation in a low melodious voice. Before long the air became brittle. The assembled magicians manifested a certain uneasiness when they found themselves suddenly involved in a hollow cloud, but it was not until a thick darkness supervened that they began to whisper to one another nervously. The atmosphere had become foul, portending that something extraordinary was about to happen. Their confidence returned somewhat as the darkness cleared, and Festus was seen to be standing calmly by the brazier heaping on odiferous herbs. As they bent forward so as to watch his every gesture, there was a sudden blinding flash of flame, which burnt the beards off everyone present. So intent, however, were the wizards on not missing any part of the experiment, that at first few noticed their loss.

"That Festus is a real hard ticket," commented Turko to Fursey as he picked up a handful of singed hair from his lap.

" 'Twill be well if nothing worse ensues," replied Fursey nervously.

He had no sooner spoken than it was observed that a hare had appeared from nowhere and was coursing in circles around the interior of the cave. It sprang and tumbled over rocks and other obstacles, its antics watched with the greatest interest by all present.

"There can be no doubt," whispered Turko admiringly as the hare ran along the ceiling, "but that Festus Wisenuts is a remarkable man. Nothing could be more beautiful than his ideas, but I cannot acquit him of being a trifle precious . . . "

Before he could finish his sentence, the hare sprang from the ceiling on to the table in the centre, and there vanished before their eyes. A sickly green light illuminated the cavern, there was a crackle of thunder overhead, and the rafters of the sky began to shake. Outside the rain fell in torrents. All at once there appeared suspended in the air over the heads of the company, two-thirds of a horrific monster vomiting flames. A shower of fire and blood descended. The assembled magicians retreated precipitately to the back of the cave.

It was obvious to everyone that something had gone amiss. One had but to look at the hideous and appalling specimen overhead struggling furiously to bring its missing one-third into existence, while Festus Wisenuts sweated as he strove with magical gesture and conjuration to wipe out the two-thirds which he didn't want.

"It's a kraken," muttered Cuthbert in awe stricken tones.

"I adjure thee, thou old serpent," Festus was shouting, while outside a terrible tempest raged, with lightnings, thunder and fireballs. The magicians cowered against the back wall, while Festus who to gain greater freedom of movement had stripped off his cloak and stood in a star-spangled singlet and drawers, waved his arms frantically, doing all the magic he knew. At last he succeeded, and the kraken faded slowly out of existence snorting sparks and bellowing indignantly. But it was apparent that things had been upset in the world of shadows. A series of ghastly illusions followed one another with great rapidity, evil-favoured spectra in divers and horrible forms and with much din. The crouching magicians saw Festus struggling manfully to explode these painful phenomena, but no sooner had he banished one than there was another gnashing its teeth in its predecessor's place. They followed one another with bewildering rapidity while the quaking sorcerers at the back of the cave shouted frenzied advice. At length the succession of manifestations slackened. They appeared and vanished more slowly, and began to present an increasingly watery appearance. The last of them was little more than a shadow, and when Festus banished him, he went with a querulous croak which was scarcely audible. Festus stood leaning against the table completely exhausted, but with the light of victory deep down in his eyes. He did not enjoy his triumph long; for as the guests rose from their haunches and ventured a wary return to the centre of the cave, there was a flash of blue light, and when the pungent smoke had cleared, there was nothing left of Festus Wisenuts but a small circle of grease on the floor. The company stood for a moment staring at the circular patch, then those of them who were wearing hats, removed them reverently. Cuthbert did his best to reanimate the party, but a general gloom prevailed; and one by one his guests took their leave with silent handshaking.

CHAPTER VII

When Fursey awoke on the ensuing morning he found the cave cluttered with magical stores, horrible rarities and incantatory equipment of every description. Cuthbert was standing in the midst haggard but satisfied.

"I have not slept," he explained. "I spent the night travelling back and forward to the cave of our late, lamented friend, Festus Wisenuts. Poor Festus! He had a great regard for me, and I know that he would have wished me to have his personal effects. Moreover there was much in his cave that was exquisite and dangerous, and it would not do at all if it were to fall into unskilled or unworthy hands. Many of our acquaintance, I regret to say, are of an acquisitive disposition; and I'm afraid that when they awake this morning and shuffle their thoughts together, there will be a most indecent rush towards the cave of the deceased. How do you feel yourself? Every time that I looked at you last night, you had a flagon of mead balanced on your nose."

"I feel as if countless men were hitting me on the head with hammers," replied Fursey dolefully. "They strike with extraordinary regularity, and never miss a stroke. In addition, I feel as if there was a forest growing on my tongue."

"Go out and dip your head in the stream, while I snatch a few hours' slumber. We have now an excellent and varied stock of magical armament at our disposal. When you come back, we'll talk about that love philtre which you have set your heart on. You've been a good boy, and it's only fitting that I should reward you."

Fursey wandered out into the lazy morning sunshine. Still only half awake, he made no attempt to assemble his scattered wits. "Drink is a curse," he kept telling himself as he stumped with loosened knee-joints through the rocks and heather to where a small stream fell like a sheet of shivering glass into the excited pool below. He paused uncertainly on the brink; then he lay on his stomach and immersed his head in the pool. Oh, the pleasure of cold water on heated, throbbing temples! He scooped a handful of water on to the back of his neck, and raising himself slightly, let it run down the length of his spine. He shivered deliciously and immersed his head again. Then he lay for a long time on his stomach unwilling to move. It seemed to him that nothing was so excellent as the neighbourhood of water. He listened delightedly to the never-ceasing tinnient roar of the cascade and marvelled at the beauty of the silver drops which oozed from the peaty bank and fell to be lost in the mad, scintillant rush of waters below. "If only man were absent," he said to himself, "how beautiful the world would be!" When he had drunk his fill, he rolled over on his back letting the points of the rushes tickle and prick his ears and cheeks. Slowly his wayward wits came home to roost.

He had been painfully impressed on the preceding evening by the unexpected dissolution of Festus Wisenuts. It had been perturbing to see a well set-up, haughty gentleman, apparently the master of his fate, suddenly taking his departure without leaving as much as a souvenir; and as Fursey had crept on his hands and knees into bed, he had drunkenly resolved to abandon the profession of witchcraft before something equally deplorable happened to himself. But now, lying beside the stream in the timid morning sunlight, with an early bird on a nearby bush warbling for his delight, he was inclined to take a less pessimistic view of his situation. For one thing, he had been strangely pleased by Cuthbert's reference to him as "a boy". Although it had never occurred to Fursey to worry about the shame of middle-age, there is no man of forty but is gratified at being reminded that he is still only a young fellow. Then, Cuthbert had practically promised to compound a love philtre for him at last. This had been tidings most grateful to his ear. He closed his eyes and smiled at the sky, his thoughts straying away to fasten on the image which was so frequently in the forefront of his mind, an image, not of the Maeve who stood in front of the fire stirring something, or looking worried because she could not lay her hand on the right pot at the right time, but of a Maeve who turned on him a gaze that was sweet, kind and understanding, a woman who spoke but little (and then only when spoken to), but who stood slender and graceful, her face demurely aglow with love for her lord and master.

The bird, trilling on the bush, nearly burst himself in a final bravura crescendo, and deciding that he had had enough of it, fluttered off in search of worms. Fursey rolled over, gathered himself together, and getting to his feet, sauntered off among the rocks and the gorse, whistling blithely to himself. He did not return to the cave until it was early afternoon.

"So you've untethered the cow," remarked Cuthbert. "About an hour ago she had her head around the corner looking in at me."

"Yes," replied Fursey, "I thought that on such a nice morning she might care to take a walk. I don't imagine that there's any danger of her getting herself lost: she'll stay in the neighbourhood of the food supply."

The master sorcerer was busy at the back of the cave packing away the last of his new acquisitions.

"Sit down, Fursey," he said, "and give your best attention to what I have to say."

Fursey seated himself on a lump of rock and fixed his eyes expectantly on the pallid countenance of his master. Cuthbert paced for a few moments back and forward, his hands clasped behind his back and the black lock of hair nodding on his forehead. He paused at last and faced his apprentice.

"Are you still desirous of magically influencing this woman so that she will love you?"

Fursey nodded vigorously.

"Very well. I now possess the ingredients for the composition of a most powerful philtre. The process is very concealed and recondite, and the manufacture of the potion will take three days. It is necessary that a man for whom a love philtre is made, should spend three days fasting, fed only on an occasional hair from the magician's head. You must partake of no food other than one of my hairs, which I shall deliver to you on a plate of unblemished whiteness three times a day, at sunrise, at midday and at sunset. Are you prepared to do as I say and abstain from solid food?"

Fursey nodded again, but with less enthusiasm.

"There are vulgar methods of inducing love in a woman," continued Cuthbert, "such as the placing under her pillow of a few flocks of wool soaked in bat's blood, but such a method would scarcely be appropriate to the case."

"It would not," said Fursey decidedly. "If Magnus saw me approaching her pillow, he'd have my life."

"Exactly," replied the master sorcerer, "therefore a love philtre is best. I shall proceed at once to the manufacture of a bucketful; and when the process is complete, we shall bottle the mixture. You may take a bottle with you, and you must find some means of introducing the contents into her food. All that will then be necessary, is that you should be the first person on whom her eyes alight, after she has consumed the potion. I shall keep the remaining bottles myself for disposal at a fair price to possible customers harrowed by the pangs of unrequited love."

Fursey arose very satisfied, while Cuthbert placed a bucket in the corner and got immediately to work. During the three days which followed, Fursey lay outside in the open air or on his bed striving not to let his mind dwell on his emptiness. Three times a day Cuthbert plucked a hair from his head in a businesslike manner and laid it on a plate, which he presented to his apprentice. Fursey experienced considerable difficulty in swallowing the hair until he hit on the expedient of washing it down with a flagon of mead. Meanwhile, the cave was murmurous with soft-spoken incantations and perfumed with healthful herbs and incense. The sorcerer had begun by placing, by way of sympathetic magic, two twisted straws at the bottom of the bucket. To these he added an apple shot through and through with magic, and the hearts of two pigeons. He sat by the bucket for hours on end stirring the mixture while he invoked Venus and other beings of loose reputation. Each morning a fresh confection of powders was added, and the resultant paste subjected to heat and reinforced by another atmosphere. On the third afternoon Cuthbert announced that the philtre was ready, and the joyful Fursey sat down to a gargantuan meal while Cuthbert stood alongside in friendly chat.

"We shall leave it to settle for a few days," he said, "and then we shall proceed to bottle it. I advise you to give it to the lady in small doses. It is an exceptionally potent philtre, and it seems to me that your state of love is such that you are likely to succumb to anything in the nature of an impassioned embrace."

"Could we not bottle it now?" asked Fursey looking longingly at the bucket.

"No," replied Cuthbert shortly. "It must remain exposed to the airs for a few days so that it may acquire a certain consistency. As it is at present, it's too watery. Its only effect would be to make the lady giggly and flirtatious. When we come back from the Sabbath it will be almost ready for use."

161

"The Sabbath!" exclaimed Fursey in sudden dismay.

"Yes," replied his master sternly. "To-morrow is May Eve. Surely you haven't forgotten the Witches' Sabbath at which you are to be initiated as a fully-fledged sorcerer."

Fursey had indeed forgotten about the Sabbath, his mind in the previous few days had been so occupied with thoughts of love. He knew nothing of what happened at a Sabbath: he only knew that it was an orgy of wickedness at which no honest man would care to find himself. When he remembered that he was no longer an honest man, but one sworn to wickedness, he groaned aloud.

"Where is it to be held?" he asked.

"On the enchanted mountain of Slieve Daeane in the territory of Sligo."

"Is that far from here?"

"About a hundred miles from here, in the north."

"And how do we get there, on horseback?"

"No," snapped Cuthbert, "we fly. Here is a box of magical ointment. You will find a broomstick at the back of the cave. You'd better start anointing it."

There was considerable bustle on the hillside the following morning as the wizards made their preparations. Some sat in the sun outside their caves anointing besoms and staves, while others indulged in short trial flights to and fro. Every now and then some elderly sorcerer who was stiff in the joints and out of practice, had to be extricated from a tree. Familiars had been summoned to assist in the preparations, and they ran back and forward between the rocks shouting encouragement and directing their masters to suitable landing grounds. They were a motley crew, foals, toads, rats and giant fowl; and there was one horse-faced creature whom Fursey didn't fancy at all. Cuthbert's own familiar, a monstrous cat called Tibbikins, sidled in and out of the cave leering obscenely at Fursey as he sat in the entrance putting an extra thick coating of ointment on the flimsy broom allotted to him, which seemed to him totally inadequate to bear his weight. The younger wizards gambolled and capered through the air at great speed, essaying every type of dangerous trick, looping the loop, victory rolls and even flying upside down. One fell off in mid-air, but his cloak spread wide as he fell, and he made a successful parachute landing. Fursey, sitting outside the cave, viewed the whole proceedings with misgiving.

The wizards did not begin to take off until dusk. The date of the great quarterly assemblies of witches, Candlemas, May Day, Lammas and Hallowtide, were widely known; and at these times it was usual for the sturdier members of the clergy to prowl about the roads armed with slings and with their pockets full of stones. It was accounted a considerable feat to bring down a flying wizard; and many a cleric, otherwise undistinguished, owed his advancement to his good marksmanship. The wilier wizards, therefore, never began their airy journey until nightfall, and they sought to attain altitude as soon as possible. Cuthbert stood outside the cave watching admiringly as his fellows one after another took off and shot into the air.

"Hurry up," he said impatiently as the wretched Fursey emerged trailing his broom behind him.

"Supposing I fall off?" said Fursey miserably.

"If you fall off, it'll serve you right," snapped Cuthbert. "Throw your leg across and come on."

"The handle is very slippery," complained Fursey, "and it's not at all broad enough to support my person."

"I'll leave you behind," hissed Cuthbert, "unless you start at once. It's only a matter of balance. You know what to do. You have only to wish the broom to take you to Slieve Daeane."

Fursey threw his leg tremblingly across the broomstick. As he did so, Cuthbert left the earth and shot into the sky. Fursey closed his eyes, mentally enunciated the direction, and was immediately precipitated into the aether. Fursey had made one long flight before, when he had carried off the comely Maeve to Britain, but night flying was quite new to him. It was by no means dark for there was an expansive moon overhead, and there was little danger of collision with other sorcerers as there was plenty of room in the sky. He could see them to left and right of him at varying altitudes, their black cloaks flapping in the breeze and their faces intent as they leaned over their broomhandles. Not all rode on broomsticks; some favoured stout polished staves, and there were a couple of warlocks of distinguished appearance on buck goats. The riding of goats was accounted a difficult art, because when travelling at high speed one's face was subjected to the constant whipping of their beards, with consequent reduction of visibility and increased danger of accident. Moreover, while they provided a more comfortable seat than a broomhandle, they were far less maneuverable in the air, and being of an obstinate and wanton disposition, they were quite capable, if annoyed, of turning their heads and trying to unseat their masters with their horns.

Fursey had no time to watch the other members of the black armada, all his thoughts being devoted to the importance of not falling off. But gradually he acquired confidence. He had some moments' anxiety when a wild goose joined him and flew alongside, turning her head from time to time to look at him and emit a squawk as if challenging him to race her. He was relieved when she fell behind, as he had feared that she might either collide with him or attempt to alight on his broom and so upset his balance. He increased his speed and soon caught up with Cuthbert, who was flying in a most peculiar fashion leaning over sideways so as not to miss the scenery below.

"A lovely night," shouted the master sorcerer above the rushing of the wind. "Do you see the River Shannon unwinding like a silver ribbon?"

Fursey glanced down at the countryside far below. Dimly he discerned field, forest and lake beneath a blue moonlight web.

"Isn't it lovely?" shouted Cuthbert.

"Wonderful," gasped Fursey, "I wish I was down there."

"We must strive to gain altitude," cried Cuthbert. "We have soon to hop our first line of mountains."

He rose steeply, and the terrified Fursey saw him disappearing into the blue. He followed suit wondering would he ever feel the kindly earth beneath his feet again. For three long hours they travelled until Fursey became so stiff with the cold that even his brain became benumbed. Mountain chain and lake uncurled themselves below. Again and again Cuthbert was lost in the darkness ahead when the moon gathered the straying clouds over her face. Fursey ceased to care whether Cuthbert was in sight or not. He knew that the broomstick, throbbing like a live thing between his knees, would bring him inevitably to his destination. He clung tightly with his knees and with his benumbed hands, and ceased to think. The intense cold induced drowsiness, and he must have fallen asleep; for he was startled suddenly by a hubbub of screams and shouts. When he opened his eyes he found that he was mounting a hillside at a height of about ten feet from the ground while four lank shepherds and a flock of sheep fled hell-for-leather before him. The sheep scattered, and the shepherds precipitated themselves over hedges and into bog-holes. Fursey reared the handle of the broom sharply and rose again into the sky.

"That was a near one," he muttered to himself. "I very nearly crashed."

He remained awake after that and soon was flying across the stone-studded pass between the Ox and Curlew Mountains. In the half-light he discerned ahead a great lake littered with wooded islands. The broomstick banked sharply and began to circle slowly as if seeking a landing place. Fursey peered down and saw below him a sprawling mountain of naked rock. It crept back from the lakeside into the darkness, a tumbled mass of low, rounded heights, glittering grey-blue as the bare schist caught the straggling moonlight. If ever a mountain looked enchanted, this one did. Fursey's heart began to hammer as he beheld the great, hungry clefts, bespattered with patches of tawny grass, which ran hither and thither into the interior. As the broom circled lower and lower his eye caught the flash of water, and beside the water a wide circle of flaming torches. It was the landing ground. His broomstick drifted gracefully down into the shadow of the bare cliffs, and he found himself on the earth once more.

"Broomsticks to be parked by the lakeside on the left," shouted a tall man in black.

Fursey's legs were so stiff that he could scarcely stand, but he succeeded in staggering painfully in the direction indicated, and left his broom against a great crag by the water's edge. He gazed fearfully over the small, black lake. It was a forlorn and isolated spot. The tarn lay still and dead. There was none of the usual small movement of wind or water amongst the reeds or grasses at the edge. Fursey turned a white, frightened face and looked up at the bare, blue-grey cliff.

"This way," cried the man in black. "Familiars to be summoned, and stabled under the blasted oak fifty paces to the right."

Fursey moved as in a nightmare. The circle of torches shed little light where he now stood, but he was vaguely aware of shadowy figures moving and tumbling in the background beyond the fatal oaktree. Slowly he wound his way between the rocks. The word "familiar" was still vibrating in his mind, and he suddenly realised that he would have to summon Albert. The thought afforded him a moment's relief from his fright. It would be good to see someone he knew, even if it was only Albert. He stopped and whispered the name. The bear's paws appeared resting on a boulder. They were followed slowly by the rusty hair of Albert's person until finally the jaws and smoky red eyes of the familiar came into view.

"Hullo," said Albert.

Fursey gazed at his familiar with amazement. He had expected to see a shadowy figure more like a wisp of smoke than a lusty elemental spirit, but here was a broad, plump Albert with an impertinent smile upon his snout. There was no evidence whatever of many months' starvation.

"You've been up to something," said Fursey indignantly.

Albert did not reply, but looked at his master roguishly.

"I know what you've been doing," said Fursey with a sudden flash of inspiration. "You've been knocking around with vampires. That's what you've been at."

Albert shifted on to one fat ham, raised a leisurely paw and began to scratch his ear, still looking at Fursey over his shoulder with a self-satisfied smile. Before Fursey could express himself as to this seemingly insubordinate conduct, a thin hand was laid on his shoulder.

"Why are you loitering here?" asked the black-clad attendant. "I said that familiars were to be stabled under the tree."

"Yes, sir," said Fursey hurriedly. "Come on, Albert."

Albert clambered off the rock and ambled up the incline in Fursey's wake. There was a curious collection of freaks sitting in a circle under the oaktree. Monstrous cats were washing their faces, or spreading their formidable claws and smiling at them. There were moles, hares, rats in great abundance, ferrets and greyhounds. The horse-faced familiar was there, and there were several imps with ears like elephants, and a brace of dwarfs. Albert walked into the circle and sat down demurely. Fursey observed Cuthbert's familiar Tibbikins leering at him from a branch overhead. So Cuthbert had arrived. Fursey wondered where he was.

"This way," said the man in black. Fursey followed him with foreboding. They had not far to go, and as they approached the place where the torches threw a fitful glare, Fursey beheld with trepidation a man clothed so as to resemble a giant goat, sitting on a solitary rock in the centre of the circle. He wore a headdress ornamented with curling horns and to his hands were affixed a pair of alarming claws. Around him circled in a wild dance a horde of the most hideous witches and wizards, each one whirling a cat by the tail.

"Why do you hang back?" asked the attendant suspiciously.

"I'm not hanging back," squeaked Fursey. "What do I have to do?"

The man in black produced a sack from which there proceeded the most uncouth squawking. He drew out a cat by the tail and handed it to Fursey.

"Join the circle and dance."

A moment later Fursey was on the ground wrestling with the cat.

"What are you doing?" asked the attendant impatiently. He recaptured the animal and deposited her in the sack once more while Fursey mopped the blood from his face.

"You saw it yourself," he answered indignantly. "She nearly tore the clothes off me. I'm lucky she didn't take out one of my eyes."

"You should hold her taut and keep her at arm's length," explained the black attendant. "Thus you will escape injury. Try it now."

Fursey took the cat's tail gingerly, tightened his grip, pulled her suddenly from the bag and swung her around his head.

"That's right," said the attendant, "keep her taut. Go on now, join the circle."

Fursey capered across the sward trying to imitate the weird cavorting and prancing of an aged witch-hag in front of him. Around and around the central figure they danced, while the goatman looked down on them from his rock throne. Fursey, as he capered past, desperately whirling the cat over his head,

168

threw one terrified glance at the sneering mask which covered the goatman's face. It was an awe-inspiring scene, hideous with evil and contorted faces appearing and vanishing in the glare of the torches as the dancers twisted and twirled this way and that in the ungainly measure. The air was full of a horrid hubbub, the wild cries of the dancers grating on the screeching of the cats, who seemed to be all of one mind in disliking the part which they were called upon to play in the business. Before Fursey had completed the circle once, he was quite convinced that he had lost the greater part of his scalp: but when on completion of the second circuit, the attendant deftly took the cat from him, he was amazed to see that there were only a few handfuls of his hair adhering to her claws. The sable attendant dropped her quickly back into the sack among the other cats, where, to judge from the sounds proceeding therefrom, she continued to express her indignation.

"Supper is served one hundred and fifty paces to the left," said the man in black, and Fursey stumbled in the direction indicated wondering miserably what fresh horror awaited him. As he approached the table he recognised some of the wizards from the mountain, but with difficulty. Men whom he had known as courteous, dapper sorcerers were guzzling food with an air of frenzy, their beards and hair awry, their faces scratched and their clothes torn to shreds. Horrific witches sat at the table screeching stupid feminine jests across at one another, hags whose ugliness was of such a revolting character that one glance at their visages was enough to convince the most passionate man that, when all was said and done, celibacy was best. Fursey had never before found himself in such alarming company. On his arrival at the table a one-eyed wizard whose hair hung about his shoulders like a wreath of snakes, raised a shout: "The meat course has arrived!" It would not have surprised Fursey to have found himself suddenly seized and dragged on to the table, but his momentary panic was allayed when an incredible hag made room for him beside her with a kindly "Don't be frightened, lovey". He seated himself smiling wanly.

Fursey was a man who enjoyed food, and his eyes nearly fell from his head when he saw what he was expected to eat. There were huge dishes on the table loaded with strings of entrails, carrion and putrid garbage. The black-clad attendant had set up a brazier beside the table, and when anyone seemed diffident about consumption of the food placed before him, he was immediately threatened with red-hot iron plates. To convince the delinquent that he was in earnest, the attendant directed attention to a leg-crushing machine in the background. Fursey ate with difficulty as the hag beside him had apparently taken a fancy to him and retained one of his hands in her lank claw all during the meal. Between courses she made love to him cackling girlishly. Fursey wished earnestly that he was elsewhere, as smiling politely, he gently repulsed her advances with an affectation of boyish shyness. He could see no sign of Cuthbert anywhere.

When at long last the unappetising meal was over, he managed to slip away from the amorous witch. She followed him a little way cooing seductively, but her chase of him was considerably slowed down by the necessity she was under of proceeding with the aid of two sticks on account of a fallen hip. No sooner had he removed himself to a safe distance than he found the ubiquitous black attendant standing at his elbow.

"You do not act wisely in rejecting the advances of Arabella," he said meaningly. "She is a most powerful witch, and she could easily deprive you of your life by shooting a flint arrowhead from the nail of her thumb."

Fursey took one look at the appalling specimen of womanhood in his rear.

"I prefer death," he said simply.

The attendant shrugged his shoulders and turned away.

"Take your places for the homage," he announced.

They lined up, and one by one paid homage to the great goatman, still sitting seemingly indifferent and immovable on his great stone seat. Fursey, when his turn came, did as the others: he went on his knees, bowed his head to the earth and swore allegiance. When this ceremony was over, there seemed to be a pause in the proceedings, and Fursey had time to look about him. There appeared to be about a hundred people present. It was hard to estimate the number as there was an incessant scurrying to and fro of shadowy figures in and out of the wavering light shed by the torches. He knew that a coven consisted ordinarily of thirteen persons, and he guessed that there were nine or ten covens present, perhaps not all in full force. Covens were rarely complete on such occasions, due to illness, some untoward accident such as had befallen Festus Wisenuts, or the activity of the authorities in sending the less agile wizards up in smoke. If the sorcerers and witches would only have remained still for a few moments, Fursey would have essayed a count, if only to keep his mind from occupying itself wholly with his fears, but the lakeside was a veritable bedlam: men and women skipped and tumbled with no apparent object, distorted faces emerged suddenly from the darkness and as quickly disappeared; witches sprang from rock to rock their faces intent, while others rolled in the heather, and a coven from the County Cork paraded back and forward walking on their hands. The screaming and the shouting united into a clamorous din, as if a hundred cats were being trodden on simultaneously. Several sorcerers, their eyes wide with excitement, spoke loudly to Fursey, boasting of their malice and the extent of their wickedness. Before he could answer they had run off to find other listeners. A torch in his vicinity spat a shower of sparks, and in the sudden glare he detected a small man leaning dejectedly against a rock. He looked reasonably harmless, so Fursey moved over in his direction.

171

"Very fine Sabbath," remarked Fursey ingratiatingly. The stranger raised a pair of melancholy eyes.

"Yes, but I'm in no mood to enjoy it."

"Dear me," said Fursey, "that's too bad."

"Domestic trouble," sighed the little man. "In the course of an experiment this afternoon I accidently exploded the wife. She was a very good cook."

"This world is a vale of tears," said Fursey shaking his head sympathetically. "I've a little worry on my mind myself."

"Is that so? Maybe I could be of help."

"Well, as yet I'm merely an apprentice, but to-night I'm to be initiated as a fully-fledged sorcerer. I'm completely in the dark about the ceremony of initiation. Could you tell me whether it involves much pain or discomfort?"

"Not much," answered his companion. "You will be required to take your stand before the goat-man and place one hand upon your pate and the other on the sole of your left foot, and you must vow all between, that is your whole person, to his service. You will be required to swear complete obedience to the master of your coven and renounce the Christian and all other faiths. He will initiate you by baptising you with a new name, perhaps your own name spelt backwards, and by pricking you twice with a needle on the wrist. It is usual for him also to place his seal on the candidate by giving him a sharp nip on some part of his body. The resultant bruise will never disappear, and the spot will ever afterwards be insensitive to pain. The ceremony will probably conclude with a sermon by the goat-man on Evil's age-long struggle for empire."

"It could be worse," said Fursey with a sigh of relief.

"I beg your pardon," replied the wizard suspiciously.

"What I mean," said Fursey hastily, "is that while I'm quite prepared to surrender life or limb in the service of Evil, I'm naturally glad that neither is yet demanded of me."

"Hm! You know, of course, that if the candidate is adjudged unworthy of the honour to which he aspires, he is simply thrown into the lake."

"Thrown into the lake?"

"Yes, it removes all traces, and there are no embarrassing questions afterwards. The lake by which we are standing, is the terrible Lough Dagea. Anything which breaks its waters, is never seen again."

Fursey smiled nervously and moved nonchalantly a pace or two, so as to place his companion between himself and the brink.

"Why has this long pause occurred in the ceremonies of the night?" he asked by way of changing the subject.

"A pause has not occurred. The goat-man is making a circuit of the revellers requiring of each a recital of his wicked deeds. In any case in which the amount of evil done since the last Sabbath, is not satisfactory, he scourges the delinquent with a wire whip. I observe that he's coming in your direction now."

Fursey started and moved back against a crag as he saw the great horned figure striding towards him. The melancholy wizard slipped away unobtrusively and was lost in the darkness. Fursey shook in every limb as one part of his mind remembered the proximity of the fatal lake, and the other part strove to assemble his little share of wit so as to confront the danger. The goat-man had taken his stand some paces distant. He was of normal height, but his goat mask and formidable horns conferred on him a terrible majesty. He held in his hand a most efficient-looking whip of woven wire, with which he carelessly flicked the tips off the heather. Fursey was dimly aware of a semi-circle of white faces, as other sorcerers and witches pressed around watching breathlessly.

"State your name and rank."

"Fursey, apprentice sorcerer."

"Your address?"

"Knockmealdown Mountains."

"To what extent have you established your claim to be one of this noble company?"

"I'm a man given to all manner of wickedness, sir."

"For example?"

"Church burning, calumny, detraction, uncharitable conversation, envy of my betters, sloth, gluttony, drunkenness and the telling of lies."

"What churches have you burnt?"

"The whole monastery of Clonmacnoise."

"You're a liar," said the goat-man coldly. "It was Vikings who burnt Clonmacnoise. All you did was to run around making a fool of yourself."

"That just goes to prove," gasped Fursey, "that as a teller of lies I'm at the top of the profession. I can't myself believe a single word I say."

The goat-man raised his whip alarmingly and cut a gorse bush in two with a sudden flick of his wrist.

"Why have you so scandalously denied your familiar his proper meed of blood from your person?"

Fursey's limbs had turned to water, and he would certainly have fallen only for the rock against which his back was pressed. The sweat coursed down his face as he strove desperately to think of an answer, but relief came from an unexpected quarter. The dark-robed attendant stepped suddenly into the circle.

"I have viewed the familiar in question," he said. "He's certainly not suffering from malnutrition. In fact, he presents every appearance of being not only well-fed, but even pampered. Our information on that point must have been unreliable, my lord."

The goat-man paused uncertainly. Fursey passed his tongue over his lips and strove desperately to bring his knocking knees under control. When the goat-man had first spoken, Fursey had recognised the voice of Cuthbert, but with the goat mask Cuthbert seemed to have assumed another personality. Fursey felt that he had no reason to expect mercy on account of mere acquaintance.

"What's that I see on your face?" demanded the horned figure. "Brackish tears?"

There was a gasp of horror from the onlookers.

"Yes," squeaked Fursey with a break in his voice.

"What has caused them?" thundered the goat-man.

"Fright," whimpered Fursey.

"It's a well-authenticated fact," announced the goat-man in a terrible voice, "that no witch or wizard can weep. You're not all that you would have us believe," and raising his whip he cut at Fursey. Fursey yelled and tried to escape, but there was no getting out of the circle. He capered madly as the whip was dexterously wielded, inflicting on him many a sore stroke. His howls were truly terrific, and when the goat-man desisted, it was not through any sympathy for his victim, but because of a sudden counter-clamour which attracted general attention. All hell seemed to have broken loose under the blasted oak-tree. One could see, even in the dim light, fur and feathers flying in all directions, while yelping and gruff barks pierced the night. With one accord the company, led by the goat-man, hurried towards the tree, while Fursey aching in every limb scrambled after them, making a circuit however, so as to lose himself somewhere in the crowd. When he reached the vicinity of the oaktree, a remarkable sight met his eyes. The monstrous cat stood against the bole, her back arched, spitting fire. Albert was tumbling on the ground fighting with the horse-faced familiar, while the two dwarfs clung to his back kicking him wherever they could. Smaller familiars scurried back and forward barking shrilly. A hare and a mole were up on their hind-legs squaring up to one another, while rats ran in and out of the fighting, nipping everyone they encountered.

"This is unprecedented," shouted the goat-man. "Stop it at once, the whole of you."

There was an immediate lull in the fighting. Albert made use of the unexpected armistice to turn suddenly and aim a swipe at one of the dwarfs, knocking him sideways. In a moment they were all at it again. Various witches and wizards now intervened, ordering their respective familiars to vanish according as they became involved, until at length only Albert remained, squatting on a carpet of fur and broken claws. He swung his eyes intently left and right watching for the possible re-appearance of an enemy.

"Whose is this ungainly monster?" demanded the goat-man, choking with rage.

"Fursey's," cried a dozen voices.

"Where's Fursey?"

For a few moments there was silence. Then a thin voice came quavering from the fringe of the crowd.

"I'm here, sir."

"Come forward and take possession of this wild beast of yours."

The crowd parted, and Fursey crept halteringly through the passage.

"Someone will pay for this sacrilegious disturbance of our Sabbath," said the goat-man grimly.

"Yes, sir," said Fursey.

By the goat-man's directions the other familiars were summoned by their masters. The air trembled and condensed as they came one by one into existence. Albert, his head leaning forward from his bull-neck, fixed his red, smoky eyes threateningly on one of the dwarfs, who after the manner of small men, had his tongue out and was making faces at him.

"Keep them separated," commanded the goat-man. "Now, who began it?"

"He did," squalled the brindled cat glaring balefully at Albert.

"Yes, it was Albert," cried a dozen of the familiars.

"What did he do?"

"Making nasty remarks about everyone," shrilled the cat. "Putting on superior airs; looking for fight, that's what he was. He trod on one of the dwarfs."

There was a chorus of assent. Albert had assumed a hang-dog look. "It was an accident," he said sheepishly.

"No accident," screamed the horse-faced familiar. "He's been elbowing us all and goading us ever since he arrived."

"He said his bear's claws were superior to mine," snarled the cat.

"Feminine envy," muttered Albert.

"Hold your tongue," snapped the goat-man. "Fursey, order this monster of yours to disappear."

Fursey did as he was bid.

"Now," proclaimed the goat-man, "you may get your broomstick and take yourself home. You're expelled from the Sabbath. A man who cannot keep his familiar under control, cannot hope to be initiated as a fully-fledged sorcerer."

There was a murmur of approval. Fursey went without a word. He found his broom beside the lake where he had left it, and in a few minutes he was winging his way across the mountain. As he flew southwards his emotions were of a very mixed character. He was relieved to be away from such an abominable spot, and he was strangely pleased that he had escaped initiation. It left him as he was before, a sort of half-sorcerer. He did not doubt but that Albert's behaviour had been deliberate, and that its object had been to embarrass him. Had not his familiar threatened to thwart and annoy him? But it might well be that Albert had unsuspectingly done him a very good service. Fursey was sick of the company of magicians, which seemed to him to be not only unpleasant, but in the highest degree dangerous. He was tempted to turn the broom handle in another direction and wing his way to some territory where he was unknown, but he remembered the love philtre now ready for use. At all costs he must secure possession of it. Then, if Cuthbert permitted him to do so, he would take his departure. "I must really get rid of Albert," he told himself, "if I don't, he'll get me into serious trouble."

When he alighted on the hillside before the cave, the light was creeping into the sky in the east, and in their nests the birds were stirring their wings. As he entered the cave the first thing he saw was the broad buttocks and twitching tail of the cow.

"What are you doing here?" he asked, giving her an affectionate slap on the flank.

The cow raised her head and swung it around to look at him. Then she turned away and buried her muzzle once more in the bucket which contained the love potion. There was a loud, sucking noise.

"Come away," shouted Fursey, realising suddenly what was happening; but by the time he had dashed to her head and snatched away the bucket, it was empty. For a moment he felt like striking her, but a wave of misery swept away his anger, and walking to a rock in the cave mouth, he sat down in bitter despondency. He was recalled to present events by a gentle nuzzling on the shoulder. He looked up. The cow was beside him. She extended her broad, rough tongue and licked his ear. He sprang to his feet. There could be no doubt about it: the light in her eye was an amorous one.

Two hours later, as the returning sorcerers circled the hillside on their broomsticks, they marvelled exceedingly to see Fursey scuttling in and out among the rocks with a cow loping close behind him. From time to time he turned and beat her about the head with an empty bucket; but when he resumed his flight, she followed once more at a steady trot, mooing pathetically.

When Cuthbert returned to the cave he had shed altogether his character as goat-man. He was once more the friendly, though sometimes snappish, master whom Fursey had previously known. When he was told of the loss of the philtre, he gave vent to a sudden outburst of rage, but he recovered quickly and acted towards Fursey much as he had acted before. Fursey noticed however that the line of his mouth was more tightly drawn, as if his patience was almost exhausted. He helped to secure the cow and tie her once more in her stall, but her heartbroken mooing got on his nerves to such an extent that after two days he obtained Fursey's consent to destroy her.

A deep depression settled on Fursey. He was unwilling to leave the hillside as he still nourished a hope that Cuthbert might yet consent to help him either in the matter of removing Magnus or by preparing another philtre, but he felt himself to be in such disgrace that he did not dare to raise either matter with his master. He knew too that his stock stood very low on the mountain. The other wizards when they passed him on the hillside, averted their heads and plainly indicated that they were not on speaking terms with him. It was a week before Cuthbert summoned him to the back of the cave and spoke to him about his affairs.

"I hear," began the sorcerer smoothly, "that you did not show up at all well at the Sabbath. It's evident that you will never graduate as a wizard."

Fursey nodded his head in sorrowful assent.

"You will really have to go away," declared Cuthbert with a sudden burst of impatience. "You were useful to me as a servant, but the sight of your doleful countenance is having a most depressing effect upon me; and if I have to endure it much longer, it will certainly drive me back to drink. Nor can I risk the spoiling of important experiments through your incompetence. That love philtre would still be here only for that cow you had mooching around the place."

"I'll go," replied Fursey, "but first I have three requests to make."

"Three!" shouted Cuthbert. "I must say that I admire your audacity."

"Yes," replied Fursey determinedly, "first I want you to help me to rid myself of Albert."

Cuthbert had looked as if he was going to fly into an uncontrollable rage, but when Albert was mentioned, his countenance underwent a sudden change.

"That's the first wise thing I've ever heard you say," he conceded. "It's high time that a stop was put to that fellow's proceedings. We'll auction him off this evening."

"I give you a present of him," replied Fursey. "It will be a little acknowledgement of my debt to you. You auction him and keep the proceeds."

Cuthbert looked pleased. "Thank you," he said with a courteous bow. "I've no doubt but that we shall find a purchaser. A spare familiar is always useful."

"All I want," said Fursey heavily, "is to be assured that I shall never see his ugly face again. I want to be entirely rid of him."

"You're right," said the sorcerer. "It's obvious that you don't know how to control a familiar, and a desperate character like Albert is apt to get a man into trouble."

"I have two other requests."

"What are they?" asked Cuthbert shortly.

"I want you to annihilate Magnus and win for me the love of his beautiful spouse."

Cuthbert sprang from his seat and raged up and down the cavern.

"We're back where we were when you came here last October," he stormed. "Why I have neglected to turn you into a toad long since, is something which I shall never be able to explain to myself."

"Satan would have wished you to help me," replied Fursey quietly.

Cuthbert paused at the sound of that great name.

"The fact that you are well-connected," he said acidly, "doesn't justify you in imposing on everyone you meet. I refuse absolutely to do any more magic on your behalf. I shall not manufacture one drop of love potion while you are still within the territory. As for Magnus—well, I'll do this much for you: I'll give you some advice before you depart from here to-morrow."

Albert was auctioned that evening. Fursey summoned him, and he squatted on the central table, his snout wreathed in a self-satisfied smile. There was a good attendance, and the wizards whispered to one another and nodded their heads gravely as they felt his hocks and his haunches, and examined his teeth. The bidding was brisk and rose quickly from a set of moles' paws to a wraith in an enchanted bottle. There the bidding ceased, and Albert was knocked down to an earnest, young wizard who was known to be a coming man. Fursey made a declaration solemnly handing over the familiar; and at his new master's bidding, Albert gracefully disappeared with a smug smile upon his face.

On the following morning Fursey coiled his rope and slung it over his shoulder. As he stood in the mouth of the cave ready to depart, he looked down sorrowfully at his tattered clothes and broken shoes.

"Will you not even give me a small phial of water," he asked, "to pour on Magnus' doorstep, so that by its latent magic, he may fall grievously and haply kill himself?"

"I'm determined to give you nothing of a magical nature," replied Cuthbert firmly. "I'm convinced that if I did, you would inevitably misuse it and injure yourself. Your wit is too thin. I advise you strongly never to attempt to practise the fatal arts. You're a man whose brain moves round and rattles in his head. I'm persuaded that dire effects will attend any magical operation in which you have a hand."

Fursey looked at him glumly. "You promised me advice. How will I proceed to destroy my enemy and win the affections of Maeve?"

"You must overcome Magnus by natural means."

"How?"

"You must challenge him to fight."

"But," protested Fursey, "he's a very considerable muscle-man."

"I'm not sending you away empty-handed. I've composed a letter for you. When you come within sight of Magnus' dwelling, pause in your travels and take up your abode in some convenient thicket. Then send this letter to him by trusty messenger."

"What's written in the letter?"

Cuthbert unrolled a small parchment and read:

"Deliver up at once, perverse monster, the woman of whom you have robbed me, before my just rage brings about your deserved destruction.

Your implacable enemy, Fursey.

If he has any manhood at all, he will react violently to such a challenge, and will come forth at once to meet you."

"And suppose he kills me?"

"Why will you always insist on looking on the dark side of things?" asked Cuthbert impatiently. "Even if he does, your troubles will then be over. But there's no need for you to let yourself be killed. All you have to do is exchange a few lusty knocks with him, and then when he's not looking, stab him with a bodkin."

Fursey looked gloomily at the piece of parchment and stowed it away in his pocket.

"Here is a poisoned bodkin. It's in a sheath, so that you won't kill yourself with it. A single scratch will encompass Magnus' death. Now are you satisfied?"

"It's all very fine to talk," whimpered Fursey as he took the bodkin, "but this Magnus is a man of the most unexampled fierceness. He's a most savage character as well as being a regular Hercules. It's in the highest degree unlikely that I'll survive his initial blow."

"Then why let him have the first blow?" said the exasperated Cuthbert. "All you have to do is get in the first buffet yourself; and when he's on the ground, you can finish him off with the poisoned bodkin."

"I see," said Fursey.

"When he's slain," continued Cuthbert, "keep your head about you: don't fall into a swoon through exceeding joy. Remember you still have to win the woman."

"Could you not give me a small bit of magic," pleaded Fursey, "just enough to take away his bodily strength before I fight him."

"No," snapped Cuthbert, "it concerns my honour. If I gave you anything magical, you would surely transfix yourself. Goodbye now, and don't come back."

"Goodbye," said Fursey, and he turned and made his way slowly down the hillside towards the plains and the world of men.

CHAPTER VIII

Fursey made his way along the shoulder of the mountain, knowing that on the windswept ridge the ground
would be dry and firm underfoot. He continued as
far as he could on the higher levels, descending slowly in
a sweeping curve towards the plain. When at last a direct
descent of the mountain flank became necessary, he picked
his way carefully around the patches of soggy grassland, often
turning to retrace his steps so as to avoid the treacherous peat
swamps which lay across his path. He had a wholesome fear
of the sodden bogs, so deceptively covered with fine grass.
He knew that a single false step in those areas would result
in a sucking sound and his total disappearance. But he made
his way down the hillside without mishap, and in the early
afternoon came to a long line of hedge, bright with hawthorn
blossoms. He soon found a gap and clambered through into
a bed of nettles. A moment later he was on the road. He
seated himself on the bank amid the daisies and the but-
tercups, and sighed with satisfaction. It was good to have
left the mystery-riddled mountains behind and to feel one's
feet on the solid highway once more. He sat for a long time
in quiet contentment. It was a still, bright afternoon. The
air was soaked through and through with sunshine. It oozed
like honey from a comb, spreading itself on the thick, green
tangle of the hedgerows, and slipping down to surround and
embrace the dandelions and the primroses and all the other
white and yellow flowers which brightened the borders of the

184

road. He glanced down the highway and over the plain. As far as his eye could see, the countryside was alight with the graceful gaiety of May. Some trees sported buds which resembled brussels sprouts, the chestnuts were laden with their usual white pyramids: indeed, every tree had something fresh to show, for over all lay the delicate, green web of spring. He smiled, rubbed his chin and began to plot his course.

It was not difficult. He did not know the exact site of Magnus' dwelling, but he believed it to be in the vicinity of The Gap, the great pass separating the Knockmealdown Mountains from the neighbouring range. All that he had to do, was to follow the road until he had made a half-circuit of the mountains: probably a day's travelling would bring him to his objective. He was so pleased at having escaped unscathed from sorcerers' territory that he did not worry as to how he should encompass Magnus' dissolution and win the affection of Maeve. The sheathed bodkin in his pocket gave him confidence, and he determined not to occupy his mind with future events until it was necessary for him to do so. He sat for a long time in dreamy vacancy, dimly aware of the minute sounds about him, the careful stirring of a bird in the hedge and the slight rustle of the long grasses as they captured a straying wind, held it for a moment and let it go. He lacked the will to proceed further, and a long time elapsed before he rose to his feet, hitched his rope over his shoulder and made his way down the road. With the renewal of physical activity his mental lethargy departed, and soon he was whistling blithely. After the manifold dangers through which he had passed, the possibility of being recognised, denounced and burnt as a sorcerer scarcely bothered him. It was nearly a year since he had been in the hands of the authorities at Cashel, and he felt that the passage of time must have made him less readily recognisable—at least, he would not still be in the forefront of men's minds. So he went on his way, passing without fear the mud and wickerwork cottages before which naked children played and tumbled, while dogs ran around importantly. He even shouted a greeting to the women sitting in the doorways polishing cheap ornaments of bone and bronze. He looked with affection on the evidences of human activity, the carefully woven thorn fence enclosing the field, the wooden plank across the stream, and the heaped peat won from a neighbouring bog. He stopped for a while to watch from a distance a group of men by the side of a lake busy at work on the framework on a coracle, bending the strong wattles and covering them with hide. Evening came as he proceeded, and with it came rustling showers of rain. Mists drifted across the plain, parting from time to time to let the weakened evening sunlight pick out some scene of faeryland unreality. The road was stony, and he began to become very footsore. He halted at sunset, and seated himself in the shelter of the ditch. His rope quickly procured him his supper, and he began to eat with relish. He had finished his meal and had a beaker balanced on his nose draining the dregs of the ale when he heard a lonely sound some distance down the road. A quavering voice was raised in lamentation, and the words came clearly to his ears:

"Woe to Fursey!"

He dropped the beaker and sat paralysed. He listened to the pad of approaching footsteps, and heard the voice once more. It began with a series of staccato groans, then rose in a melancholy wail until it attained a high pitch, where it remained.

"Woe to Fursey!" it announced. "There is a chattering in the sky, and when I listen I hear voices. I hear voices in the earth and voices in the winds. And all the voices that I hear, have but the one burden: 'Woe to Fursey!' "

Fursey blinked incredulously, then he dropped on his hands and knees and, crawling forward a couple of paces, raised his head over the edge of the ditch. He peered cautiously in the direction from which these alarming words proceeded. A strange-looking character in fluttering rags was approaching with a lengthy stride down the centre of the road. His head was bare, and he was plentifully supplied with grizzled whiskers. As he came by Fursey's hiding place, he raised a skinny arm high over his head and gave vent to another moan.

"Woe to Fursey!" he repeated in heartbroken tones.

As he passed by and continued down the road, Fursey watched him from over the edge of the ditch like a rabbit looking out of a burrow. When he had gone some distance, Fursey scrambled to his feet and ran down the road after him. The stranger proceeded with a long, springy stride, but Fursey caught up before long and patiently trotted alongside. It was some minutes before the old gentleman noticed his presence. When he did become aware of the small man running beside him, anxiously attempting to attract his attention, he halted and looked at Fursey enquiringly. Although the stranger was big-framed, he was meagre and bony. His watery blue eyes were benevolent, but they wandered across Fursey's face without apparent interest.

"Have you come that I may hollow out a grave for you?" he asked.

"I have not," answered Fursey, more alarmed than ever. "What put that thought into your head?"

"I beg your pardon," replied the stranger. "I am a Christian man, and one of the corporal works of mercy in which I habitually engage, is the burial of the dead. I thought for a moment that you were a client."

"I'm very far from dead," retorted Fursey. "I merely wish to enquire what you were shouting as you came along the road."

"I have no recollection."

"But it was only just now. You were calling out 'Woe to Fursey' or words to that effect."

"Was I? The name Fursey is quite unknown to me. I must have been prophesying. No doubt I was in a state of angelic possession."

"Angelic possession?"

"I'm a rustic prophet," explained the stranger mildly. "I'm frequently moved to prophecy, particularly on Fridays and Saturdays."

"Do you think that you'll feel moved any more this evening, sir?"

"I imagine that it's worn off now, but I can't say for certain. Why?"

"Because my name is Fursey."

"Indeed. That's very interesting. Well, I mustn't detain you any longer. Good evening to you."

"I'm accompanying you," declared Fursey determinedly.

"Why?"

"In the hope of hearing something more. After all, it's very alarming to hear a gentleman of your apparent piety shouting one's name on the breeze and coupling it with woe and destruction."

The old man meditated for a moment. "That never occurred to me before," he said at last. "I suppose that it may well be alarming if one has something on one's conscience. I'm sorry if I distressed you. The best thing you can do, is repent of whatever you have to repent of. Then you'll be safe."

"I can't repent just yet," Fursey blurted out. "I've an important murder on hands."

"Oh, dear me," said the rustic prophet in shocked tones, "you shouldn't do that. Don't you know it's wrong?"

Fursey stirred uncomfortably. "I can't help it," he faltered. "A murder is necessary to enable me to put my affairs in order. After that I expect to be happily married. Maybe I'll repent when that joyful event has taken place."

The old man shook his head disapprovingly. "I'm afraid that you are in evil case, and stand sorely in need of spiritual treatment. I'll stay with you for a little while. It may be that the spirit of prophecy will seize on me again, though I really think that it's gone for the night."

He seated himself on a bank by the wayside and allowed his pale blue eyes to travel over Fursey's person. Fursey stood stock still in front of him until the scrutiny was complete.

"Your shoes are sadly broken," remarked the prophet at last. "Oblige me by accepting mine."

"Oh no," protested Fursey, "I can't do that."

The old man removed his sandals without a word and laid them at Fursey's feet.

"Please do not deprive me of the merit I shall gain in Heaven by my charitable act," he pleaded.

Fursey stared at him, not knowing what to say. In the face of such insistence it seemed discourteous to refuse. He seated himself on the bank and taking off his broken shoes, shame-facedly assumed the stranger's footwear.

"You are most generous," he muttered.

"You have little understanding," replied the prophet mildly. "I am in fact most selfish. I have merely exchanged the perishable goods of this world for a sure reward in the next. To be unselfish in these matters one would have to give without hope of recompense. Only those who do not believe in an after-life, can be truly unselfish."

"Do you always act like this?"

"Certainly. I have been addicted to the practice of charity ever since as a small boy I learnt that whatever I gave away, would be repaid to me in the next world a thousand-fold. Only last week a wandering bandit held me up at the sword's point and robbed me of my cloak. I ran beside him for an hour-and-a-half offering him my drawers as well. He persisted in refusing them, saying that he had a pair already. At length in exasperation he turned on me and beat me sorely."

"I'm not surprised," commented Fursey. "Why do you do these things?"

"Because I am a Christian."

"I beg your pardon, sir, but is it not the case that everyone in this country is a Christian, barring those who have adopted the professions of banditry and sorcery?"

"No," replied the stranger. "I've walked the roads of this country for well-nigh fifty years doing good, but I've never met a Christian man other than myself."

"I've a suspicion that it's not healthy to be unique. One of these days the authorities will burn you."

The prophet shrugged his shoulders. "What's that to me? The stake would be merely the antechamber to Heaven, where a vast reward awaits me."

Fursey pondered in silence. It seemed to him that for the first time in his life he had met a really good man, and moreover a man who might be prepared to help him.

"Sir," he said at length, "if you wish to do good, you have here a Heaven-sent opportunity. You see before you a man whose misfortunes and miseries are such, that they have become an everyday part of his existence."

The rustic prophet rubbed his hands with gratification.

"Tell me more," he said. "Anything that I can do to relieve you of your misfortunes and make them my own, will fill me with the greatest satisfaction. Hold nothing back. I am afire with Christian charity."

Fursey hesitated for some moments wondering how he would begin his marvellous tale. At length, encouraged by the eager old man, he commenced in a faltering voice to relate his story. He told of his years of happy ignorance as a laybrother in the monastery of Clonmacnoise, and of how a year previously the forces of Hell had invaded the holy settlement and made his cell their headquarters, from which to sally forth to tempt the good monks from their duty. He related how every wicked wile had failed. The obstinate sanctity of the monks had been such that showers of gold, offers of kingdom, and visions of the most lively and engaging females had left them unmoved, but the discipline and good order of the monastery had been sadly disturbed; and to rid the settlement of its unwelcome visitants, it had been deemed necessary to expel Fursey, to whose person the devils had particularly attached themselves. The rustic prophet listened round-eyed, interrupting only with an occasional pious ejaculation, as he heard how Fursey, relieved of his vows, had been forced into marriage with a witch, and how, as she lay dying, she had, before he knew what was happening, breathed into him her sorcerous spirit.

"So you're a wizard," he exclaimed in horrified accents.

"Yes, but an extremely unwilling one. I'm able to fly on a broomstick and produce food by pulling on a rope. I know no other sorcery whatever. Tell me, sir, is there no way of curing a sorcerer of his affliction other than by burning him to a cinder? You're a man who has travelled the roads of the world, and are no doubt learned in these things."

The prophet raised a claw-like hand and stroked his grizzled whiskers meditatively.

"I've never heard of any other method of treating sorcery," he said at last, "but we could try reversing the process by which you became a wizard. You could try breathing your sorcerous spirit into someone else."

Fursey shook his head despondently.

"There are few who would wish to accept such a legacy."

"Nonsense, I'll accept it. It will be a most charitable act and will put me in the very front row in Heaven."

Fursey looked at the mild-featured old man with astonishment.

191

"Are you not afraid that it may put you down into the other place?"

"I've no reason to believe so, as I'll never make any use of the sorcerous powers which I'll obtain from you. All my life I've been a powerful drawer of souls. I've endowed many monasteries with the gifts acquired by my sanctity. It's unlikely that in my old age, now that passion and desire have long since ceased to trouble me, I shall be tempted to make use of such unholy powers as may attach themselves to my person. Let us lose no time, but proceed at once to the experiment."

Fursey rose joyfully to his feet and stood facing his benefactor.

"How exactly did the old witch pass her spirit to you?" enquired the prophet.

"She simply breathed suddenly and violently into my mouth when I was not expecting such action on her part."

The old man rose to his feet and took his stand squarely on the roadway. He opened his mouth and closed his eyes tightly. Fursey, his heart beating excitedly, filled his lungs to bursting point, so anxious was he to make a good job of it and leave no trace of the sorcerous spirit in his system. Then he exhaled violently down the old man's throat. The prophet reeled and placed a trembling hand over his heart.

"How do you feel?" Fursey enquired anxiously as he helped his companion to sit down. The old man seemed to find difficulty in speech. Tears oozed from his eyes and made a wayward course down his corrugated cheeks. His mouth remained open, and he gasped once or twice.

"I feel queer," he said at last. "My stomach seems to be on fire, and I'm conscious of turmoil in my chest, as if certain of my organs were fighting one another."

Fursey could contain his impatience no longer. He ran to a nearby tree to put the experiment to the test. He uncoiled his rope with trembling fingers and flung it over a branch. "Bread," he whispered in an agonised voice and pulled the rope. It ran over the bough and fell to the ground at his feet, but no foodstuffs of any kind materialised.

"Hurrah!" he shouted, "I'm cured."

"I hope it's all for the best," gasped the old man, who had risen to his feet and tottered after him.

"Of course it is," cried Fursey giving the prophet a slap on the back that nearly put him forward on his face. "Here, take this rope and throw it over one of the branches. Now, ask for wine."

The old man seemed upset, but he did as he was bid. He showed surprising agility a moment later in skipping out of the way when a gigantic beaker came crashing through the foliage. Fursey danced and capered for joy, but his benefactor, far from sharing in his good spirits, had seated himself once more on the bank, the picture of doleful foreboding. Fursey looked at him in amazement.

"What's wrong?" he enquired. "Why don't you take the wine? Surely you're not a teetotaller?"

"This is a dark and sordid business," replied the prophet. "I fear that ill may come of it."

"Nonsense," rejoined Fursey. "A few more years in this wild world of sin and wrong, and then you're off to Heaven to claim your glittering reward. I don't know what you're looking so miserable about."

"I don't know what I've swallowed," groaned the old man, "but whatever it is, it has affected my system powerfully. I'm conscious of heartburn and something akin to palpitations. But apart altogether from that, I fear that I have acted somewhat precipitately in the matter. Already my rashness has betrayed me into mortal sin. I have produced alcohol by witchcraft. Oblige me by taking back your terrible gift."

"Not on your life," rejoined Fursey. "It's far safer in the keeping of a man of sterling piety like you. Drink the contents of the beaker and forget your worries."

"I'm afraid to move," whimpered the prophet, "lest perchance I fall down and die before I have confessed my sin. It is the teaching of the infallible church that a lifetime of austerity and prayer is obliterated by a final grievous sin and that nothing awaits the offender but the Pit."

"I've been walking on a tight rope over the Pit so long," replied Fursey, "that I exude brimstone through every pore. I have to leave you now as I have an important murder on hands. The best thing you can do, is trot down to the nearest monastery and devote the rest of your life to doing penance. I'm very obliged to you for your kindly act. Goodbye."

He turned and stepped out gaily along the road, his heart lighter than it had been for many a long day. He reminded himself that in future he would have to work or beg for his bread, but he felt that to be a small price to pay for his relief from the incubus of sorcery. After all, you could not pay too high a price for normality. So he continued lightly on his way until the road bent suddenly towards the mountains, and he saw high above him the great cleft which was known locally as The Gap. He hastened his steps, happy in the thought that the greater part of his journey was over. He soon came to a crossroads and realised that the road which intersected his own, was the one which led to The Gap. As he turned the corner he became suddenly aware of a hideous and unwieldy demon sitting on a stile at the side of the road. The creature was of extraordinary aspect and stature, at least ten feet in height and built in proportion. He was coal-black in hue and covered with a rough, hairy hide. His deformed head was made remarkable by a pair of eyes like burning saucers and ears that hung down nearly to the ground. He had a pair of feathered legs and was very sordid as to his habiliments. He was in every way a most deformed monster, most dreadful to behold, and the fact that he was breathing forth flaming sulphur, did not add to his attractions. Fursey was most unfavourably impressed.

194

"Good evening," he said hurriedly, and hastened his steps along the road.

"Just a minute, boss," said the monster hoarsely, sliding his loathsome carcase from the stile and lumbering across the road. Fursey knew that it was unlucky to encounter such apparitions, and unluckier still if they chose to follow you. He quickened his pace, but the cacodemon joined him and kept walking alongside.

"Did you hear me talking to you?" he growled, looking down at Fursey menacingly. "I desire some conversation with you."

"I'm busy," replied Fursey nervously. "It'll have to be some other time. Go away now like a good man."

The cacodemon parted his hairy lips and disclosed a mouthful of teeth that gleamed and champed.

"I have my orders," he said doggedly. "If you won't wait to hear what I have to say to you, I'll just have to break one of your legs to prevent you proceeding further."

Fursey came to a halt and looked up at his terrible companion with foreboding.

"What is it?" he asked faintly.

"Life is a loathsome business," said the cacodemon. "Why not end it?"

"What's that?" squeaked Fursey.

"Self-destruction. Why not escape from your worries and your troubles by suicide? It's very easy."

Fursey moistened his lips, but was unable to reply.

"About thirty paces to the left," cooed the monster ingratiatingly, "there's a lovely precipice. Why not fling yourself over?"

"Because I don't want to," gasped Fursey. "Please go away."

"Oh no," leered the cacodemon rolling a flaming eye at his victim. "I'm never going to leave you as long as you live."

He fastened a huge claw on Fursey's arm and gave him a friendly squeeze as if to emphasise his words. Fursey staggered and just managed to gain the grassy bank beside the road before his legs gave away. He seated himself quaking in every limb. The demon took his stand facing him and wagged his head roguishly.

"Don't you understand?" he said persuasively. "I'm tempting you."

Fursey took a look at the monster's flaming jowls, shuddered and turned away his face.

"Consider your situation," continued the cacodemon quite unabashed. "You're a sorcerer whose powers benefit him nought, but are on the contrary an intolerable burden. Sooner or later you must fall into the hands of authority, from whom you can expect nothing but an uncomfortable end by fire. You have found life empty and unprofitable. Man has been unkind to you and will continue so, because you are weak and unfitted by nature for the struggle of life. Your birth into a world inhabited by the hard and the strong, was a mistake and a misfortune. You have nothing to hope for in this world, and in the next only the flaming pit of Hell awaits you. Let me lead you to the accommodating precipice to which I have already referred, and show you how easy it is."

"It would seem the height of foolishness," faltered Fursey, "to precipitate myself into Hell prematurely."

"Maybe Hell doesn't exist," was the smooth reply. "It's certain that this world is a miserable abode. Why hesitate to barter your present tangible misery for the possible miseries of another world which may not exist? Perchance the end of all is dreamless sleep."

"All matter clings to its present existence," argued Fursey, "That's true even of a lifeless stone. It resists destruction. One has to pick up another stone to smash it."

The monster looked at Fursey with disgust and spat a sheet of flame into the hedge.

"If you think you can blind me with science," he said stiffly, "you're very much mistaken."

"Anyway," continued Fursey gaining courage, "you have your facts all wrong. I'm no longer a sorcerer, but a normal country lad. What makes you think that I'm so miserable? I have my hopes to sustain me."

The demon opened his jaws and beat his teeth together so alarmingly that the resultant sound was like the strokes of a hammer on an anvil.

"You're an obstinate man," he said gratingly. "Don't you realise that I'm talking for your own good. If you're not miserable now, you're at least going to be miserable henceforth. I shall never forsake you as long as you live. How do you like that prospect?"

"I don't like it at all," admitted Fursey.

"Well, self-destruction is the only means you have of escaping me."

"Look here," said Fursey determinedly. "I know that it's the object of demons to persecute and delude mankind. Do not imagine that you can fascinate my imagination with your apish threats. You may think that you're putting up a great show with your eyes like burning saucers and your hide like a doormat, but I'm accustomed to such manifestations. You needn't think to impress me with your monstrous proportions or with threats to rend me in pieces. I have suffered so much terror and affrightment from your like during the past year that I can gaze on the worst that Hell can produce, quite unappalled. Oblige me by loping away now in a rapid canter. Any negotiations that I care to enter into with the powers of darkness, will be with the Prince of that dreadful territory from which you have escaped. He's an old friend of mine. Be on your way now, and don't bother me any more."

The demon seemed considerably taken aback. A stream of black smoke issuing from either nostril, gave the impression that he was entirely deflated.

"Is it that you want to see the Boss?" he asked in astonishment.

"I don't discuss my affairs with underlings and callboys," said Fursey haughtily. "What are you in Hell anyway? A scullion or a stoker, I suppose."

"All right," muttered the cacodemon as he passed rapidly into a state of condensation. "I'll call the Boss."

The outline of his giant form shivered for a moment in the air before it disappeared.

"I've not time to wait," shouted Fursey to the empty air, and began to march down the road. He was conscious of a warm glow of confidence as he continued on his way. He told himself that in order to dispel fear, all that was necessary was to downface the danger. "I've become a man at last," he said to himself wonderingly, but he had not gone more than a hundred paces when he heard a small explosion behind him. He glanced over his shoulder and saw that Satan had appeared on the spot where the cacodemon had stood. The Devil looked to left and right as if searching for Fursey; then seeing him in the distance, came running down the road after him.

"You might have the good manners to wait for me," he complained as he came alongside.

"I didn't send for you," replied Fursey coldly. "I want to have nothing to do with you or your ilk."

"We'll soon see about that," said the Devil grimly. "One of my ilk has just complained that you insulted him."

"That's right," said Fursey belligerently. "Do you want to make anything of it?"

The Archfiend looked surprised. His crafty eyes examined Fursey's moonlike face for some moments. When he spoke again, he seemed to choose his words carefully.

"So at last you have rid yourself of your sorcery."

"Yes. How did you find that out?"

"An old gentleman has just arrived in Hell. He states that his occupation was that of rustic prophet. According to what I can make out, he is of opinion that you played a very doubtful trick on him."

"Dear me, is he deceased already?"

"He died as a result of shock shortly after you left him."

"That's too bad," commented Fursey. "I formed the opinion that he was a man of sweet and amiable nature."

"I hope you're right," said the Devil eyeing Fursey narrowly. "He created a considerable furore when he recognised his surroundings. He was still giving vent to the most uncouth language when I left. He's shouting something about filing a petition."

Fursey shook his head sadly. "He was, perhaps, a trifle too precipitate. The golden rule in life is to think twice and do nothing."

"You seem to have become suddenly endowed with wisdom," said the Devil carefully. "I observe that you are able to twist most things so that they serve your interest."

"I'm no fool," replied Fursey, sticking out his chest. "I'm well able to look after myself."

"No one suggests anything else," said the Archfiend soothingly. "I understand that you're contemplating suicide."

"I am not," said Fursey heatedly. "It seems to me that you're in an indecent hurry to get hold of me."

There was a brittle glint in the Devil's eye as he fixed his gaze on Fursey's face.

"It would be well for you to fall in with my wishes," he answered coldly. "Do you not realise that it is my intention, if you oppose me, to make your life miserable with hideous apparitions and manifestations of the most abominable character?"

"Call them up in their dozens. I'm ready for them."

The Devil looked at him in wondrous amaze. He raised a hooked claw and thoughtfully pulled one of his pointed ears.

"Your senses are obviously in decay. How long do you think that your sanity could endure the proximity of infectious dragons and the never-ceasing bustle of demons? Moreover, you do not seem to appreciate that it's in my power to molest you with loathsome diseases, such as involuntary twitching of the legs, for I am never without my machinery and subtle contrivances."

"Why must you always be such an unpleasant fellow?" enquired Fursey. "No one has ever a good word to say for you. Does popularity mean nothing to you, and the good opinion of your acquaintance?"

"It is my business to undo mankind."

"I don't care a snap of my fingers for your snares. I'm not going to commit suicide to please you or anyone else."

"Then," said the Devil grimly as he rolled up his sleeves, "I shall have to throw you over the precipice myself."

Fursey regarded him coldly.

"That would be the height of foolishness. You'll never get me then. I'll die a blessed martyr, and be carried off to Heaven to the sound of lutes."

The Devil paused and savagely shot his cuffs back into position.

"You're very glib," he snarled, "but it's only a matter of time. I'll have you in the end of all."

"I wouldn't be too certain. I've abandoned my life of wickedness. I'm no longer a man of pernicious principles."

"What's that?" asked the Devil incredulously.

"You heard what I said. Evil is a very overrated pursuit. I never got anything out of it except kicks and beatings. I'm not going to indulge in wickedness any more. I'm going in for virtue in future."

"What you tell me causes me the greatest inquietude and alarm. Next thing you'll be trying to denounce the pact you made with me."

"What pact?" asked Fursey.

The Devil emitted a howl, and his eyes flashed lightning. "The pact which you signed in your blood selling me your soul. You swallowed the duplicate copy in my presence."

"I haven't the faintest notion what you're talking about. It's true that after I last saw you I was violently sick. Certainly, I retain no such pact about my person."

"Ah," said the Devil, "you're very clever, but the original is filed in my cabinet in Hell."

"Are you certain that you're not mixing me up with someone else? A robber captain from the County Cork, for instance."

"Look here," said the Devil violently. "Who's the Father of Lies, you or me?"

"You are," replied Fursey innocently.

"Well, kindly remember it; and don't be trying to oust me from my office. I hold an agreement for the sale of the soul of one, Fursey, in consideration of two pieces of advice."

"There's a mistake somewhere. I signed no agreement. I can neither read nor write."

"You made your mark at the bottom of it," howled the Devil indignantly.

Fursey looked at the darkening sky and the cloud drift overhead. He pursed his lips and whistled a few bars from a sprightly tune. Then he let his roving eyes return and rest carelessly on the swarthy face of the Archfiend.

"I trust," he said sweetly, "that my mark to the document in question was duly witnessed by a third party. I'm afraid that otherwise it can have no validity. Without the signature of a witness no court on earth or in Heaven would accept it as genuine in the face of my denial."

For a moment the Devil stared at Fursey, then he turned completely black. He no longer bore the slightest resemblance to a gentleman, decayed or otherwise. He stood crouched there in all his hideousness, a hunchbacked figure with pointed ears, hooves and a forked tail. Pitchy clouds rolled overhead, and darkness began to overspread the earth.

"We don't want you here," said Fursey quietly. "You would be wise to take your departure before I call a handful of children to stone you."

The Devil's countenance became contorted with a paroxysm of fury. He gave one whisk of his fork tail so that it wound for a moment around Fursey's middle, almost persuading Fursey that he was cut in half. Then in a blinding flash the Enemy of Mankind disappeared. Fursey waved a languid hand to dispel the reluctant cloud of sulphurous smoke, then he turned and began to amble down the road, his hands behind his back, whistling "The Haymaker's Jig". But his confidence did not last very long; he became sad and tired. He realised that great labours still lay ahead of him. As he climbed the rugged track that wound towards the pass, he appreciated that he might soon have hunger to contend with as well. It began to rain. Night came down, and he had to search long before he found a convenient overhanging crag, under which he crept, and rolling himself into a ball, composed himself for sleep.

Sleep did not come easily. It was cold, and there was a surprising amount of rustling and stirring on the hillside. The moon came in and out with irritating regularity as clouds scurried across the sky before the high wind which had sprung up. Fursey tossed and turned, rolling over on to his hands and knees from time to time to remove a piece of stone from the small of his back. It was past understanding how there could be so many hard, round stones in such a confined space. He grunted and wallowed and asked himself how the wind managed to blow from every quarter at the same time. No sooner had he settled himself into what promised to be a comfortable position, than the chill breeze began to play about his ankles or his neck. Then the long grasses began to tickle his ears. He hammered them flat and lying down again, slowly drifted into an uncertain sleep.

He dreamt that he was standing in a waste spot, hideous with malformed boulders and stunted bushes. It was forlorn territory, and Fursey looked about with sick apprehension.

As his eyes accustomed themselves to the fitful light, he saw that the blasted countryside, stretched away from where he stood, in all directions but one; and on that one side there was an awful precipice. He realised that he was standing on the very brink. Far below him a dense pall of smoke rolled about in the abyss. In its depths thin slivers of flame, seemingly hundreds of feet in height, wavered and stabbed the surrounding gloom, lighting for a moment the grey, billowing clouds of smoke. A sickening smell of brimstone and burning flesh assailed his nostrils. From the pit arose a continuous, despairing cry, which was not one cry, but the woven screams of a myriad human beings in unspeakable agony. As Fursey listened shuddering, he discerned behind and beyond this awful plaint, the never-ending crackling of human bones and bodies, ablaze with a fire that tortured but did not consume. He swayed, sick with terror, for he realised that he was standing on the edge of Hell. He tore away his eyes and cast them upwards. Worlds and universes coursed through the heavens; and as he gazed, he saw a host of beings like himself as thick as snowflakes falling, ever falling from above into the abyss.

He started from beneath the boulder fully awake. The sky was grey in the east, and a mournful wind blew, held its breath and sighed again, so that the tufted reeds about him, shook their heads despairingly. He struggled to his feet choking with terror, and made for the road. The familiar world was about him once again, and he stared at it as if he could never gaze his fill. He sat down by the track and covered his face with his hands. The horror of his dream took possession of him once more. He sat hour after hour, alternately hiding his eyes and uncovering them to gaze at the reality about him. What if after all he ended up in the eternal torments of Hell? He told himself again and again that it could not be the case that a merciful divinity would so torture His creatures. But he knew that as long as he lived he would never rid himself of the beliefs and fears hammered into his head by his teachers in his childhood. He might forget or put aside such terrors for a little while, but he knew that they would persist in coming back from time to time to plague his sleep and waking hours, and he knew that inevitably they would forgather to press around his bed in the last awful hour when it was time for him to die.

He tried to pray, but it was no use. He realised that it would be the merest hypocrisy. He had changed. He had lost his simple faith, and he knew that it was gone for ever. Moreover, his future course of action was determined. No matter what punishment might await him, he would kill Magnus and have Maeve.

CHAPTER IX

He stood on the ditch and peered down at the beehive hut, two hundred paces away, a hut in no way remarkable, but just like any other hut which one might find in a spot where the woods or the overhanging mountains provided shelter. Fursey fixed his eyes on it, telling himself that humble as it was, it held the woman who was superior to all other women in comeliness and kindness. It was of wickerwork, the twigs cunningly interwoven and the crevices filled with hardened mud. The conical roof was thatched with grass and rushes. Peat smoke drifted gently from the doorway: the pleasant smell came to him where he stood. In a field behind the cottage two cows moved, peacefully cropping the grass. He heard the crowing of a cock.

He looked down at his clothes. He was a sorry sight. He had torn his trousers and vest crossing a thick fence of woven thorns, and he had slipped and fallen at the edge of a bog pool.

He was conscious of the brown peat mud caked in his hair. He climbed down from the ditch and began to consider a plan of action.

A small boy came along the track whistling shrilly. He was an unpleasant, grubby little fellow, who kicked the stones along the road as he walked, and occasionally bent quickly to pick one up and fling it at an unwary bird hopping in the hedge. When he came to where Fursey was standing, he halted and began to stare rudely.

"How are you, my little man?" said Fursey, "and isn't it a glorious afternoon?"

The boy gaped at Fursey and spat contemptuously on to the road; but he did not deign to reply.

"Tell me," continued Fursey soothingly, "does a man called Magnus live in the little house beyond the trees?"

The boy regarded Fursey critically.

"What will you give me if I tell you?"

"A poor man like me has little to give except his blessing."

The boy stared at Fursey. It was obvious that he did not regard a blessing as a marketable commodity.

"Ay, he does," he admitted grudgingly.

"I want you to do something for me," continued Fursey producing the little roll of parchment on which Cuthbert had inscribed the letter of challenge. "Take this down to Magnus and hand it to him."

"What will you give me if I do?" repeated the youth. Fursey felt in his pockets. They were empty except for the sheathed bodkin.

"I shan't give you anything for doing it," he replied sweetly, "but if you don't do it, I'll knock your head off."

"Garn!" exclaimed the boy contemptuously. "An old fellow like you!"

Fursey made a move in the objectionable youth's direction. The small boy did not retreat, but bent and picked up a heavy stone. Fursey halted and the two eyed one another in silence for some moments. Then Fursey stepped back a pace.

"When you have performed the errand, I shall reward you handsomely."

The boy hesitated. "You promise?"

"I promise."

The small boy held out his hand for the parchment, and when he had secured it, started at a run in the direction of the cottage. With the consciousness that great events had been put in train, Fursey scrambled over the ditch and ducked down behind a bush. Trembling, he took the poisoned bodkin from his pocket and drew the blade from its sheath. It glittered wickedly in the slanting sunlight. He shuddered, pushed it back into its cover, and slipped it into his pocket. Then he raised his head and watched with an anxious eye the devious course which the small boy was taking. He grunted indignantly as the youth stopped for some moments to paddle his feet in a stream and then set off across a field in pursuit of a rabbit; but the urchin returned at last and circled the fence of sharp stakes with which the hut was surrounded as a protection against wild beasts. There was an opening through which he could have passed with no inconvenience to himself, but he chose rather to climb across the fence at what seemed to be the most difficult part for such an operation. Fursey sighed with relief as he saw the boy at last entering the doorway of the hut.

Inside was a scene of domestic bliss. A fire blazed in the centre of the earthen floor, and the resultant smoke filled the interior of the hut, circulating slowly as it drifted towards the doorway and slipped through the opening. The boy's sharp eyes picked out at once the woman of the house standing at a table with her sleeves rolled up as she pounded a shapeless slab of dough into a condition more shapeless still, lifted it up, flung it on its back, and began to beat it with her fists. Magnus lay in a chair before the fire, his long legs stretched out on either side as if to embrace it, his jowl on his chest, fast asleep. The boy stood on one leg and fixed his eyes with interest on the sword and shield which rested in a corner beside a formidable spear.

"What do you want, Benignus?" asked the woman kindly.

"A message for Magnus."

"Well, you had better awaken him."

Magnus awoke with a muffled oath as he felt himself suddenly pushed. The brat was standing in front of him tendering the tiny roll of parchment. The man yawned, rubbed his eyes and took it from him. He examined it from every angle, finally opened it, and looked at the writing and at the back.

"This is not much good to me," he remarked. "I can't read. Where did you get it "

"From a queer-looking fellow up the road."

"What sort of a queer-looking fellow?"

The boy shrugged his shoulders impatiently. "A queer-looking fellow with white hair."

"What did he look like?"

"He looked like something that had fallen off the back of a tinker's cart," replied the boy acidly.

Magnus rubbed his head. "I better go and see," he muttered.

He rose, stretched himself, went out through the doorway and stood blinking in the sunlight. His roving eye rested at last on a small, plump figure peering at him from behind a bush. With a puzzled frown he strode in the stranger's direction. As he approached, the small man skipped from the shelter of the bush and hid behind another one. Magnus stopped to consider this unusual behaviour. He could see the stranger's head around the edge of the foliage and a pair of round eyes still staring at him.

"Who are you?" he called out. "Come forth and declare yourself."

After a moment's hesitation the stranger emerged and stood in the open, one hand behind his back.

"Fursey!" gasped Magnus. "Are you really still alive?" and he bounded in Fursey's direction.

Fursey had expected at least a blow, and he was considerably taken aback to find his hand seized and shaken heartily. He slipped the naked bodkin into his pocket as Magnus slapped him on the back and assured him how delighted he was to see him.

"The whole countryside thinks you're dead," he exclaimed. "On the day on which the Vikings sacked Clonmacnoise, a glorious apparition of you in shining armour was seen on the hillside giving warning of the impending danger to the holy settlement. The timely vision enabled the pious inmates to seek the shelter of the round towers, and thus they were preserved from slaughter."

Fursey was too dumbfounded to reply.

"Why man," continued Magnus, scarcely pausing for breath, "you have been publicly rehabilitated, an image of you has been erected in Clonmacnoise, and the cause for your canonisation is well under way."

He seated himself on a stone and grinned at Fursey delightedly. Fursey stood opposite him, his mouth fallen open as he strove to collect his scattered wits.

"So you're not dead?" said Magnus at last.

"No," admitted Fursey, "I'm alive."

"And what are you doing in this part of the country?"

"I was passing by," stuttered Fursey, "and I thought it but courteous to call and pay my respects."

"Maeve will be delighted to see you," Magnus went on. "She told me all about you, what a harmless, poor fellow you are, and that you're a man more to be pitied than blamed; so that the bad opinion I once had of you, is entirely dispelled."

Fursey conjured up a polite smile, but from behind the smile he looked at Magnus with distaste. Magnus had become stout, his face was puffy from good cooking and a fond wife's care, his stomach pressed hard against his breeches' belt. Fursey fingered the bodkin in his pocket and thought how pleasant it would be to rip Magnus to the midriff and see his entrails fall out. But in the hard school of danger Fursey had learnt how to dissemble. Black as were his thoughts, they cast no shadow across his blandly smiling countenance.

"Do you ever do an odd bit of sorcery now?" enquired Magnus giving him a fat wink, "not that your powers in that regard were ever very formidable."

"No," replied Fursey, "I'm entirely cured. I'm glad to say that I'm a normal, decent Tipperaryman once more."

"I suppose you're going back to the monastery?"

Fursey looked at him in astonishment. "I never thought of that," he said slowly.

"It can be easily arranged," continued the soldier. "As a matter of fact I have a bit of influence with the abbot myself. We became great friends on the journey back from Britain. Come on down to the house, and we'll talk it over with Maeve. You must stay to supper anyway."

As Magnus strode ahead of him, Fursey stared at the ruddy bull-neck and broad shoulders of his host, and marvelled at the man's self-confidence. Apparently the prime necessity for success in life was a firm foundation of insensitiveness mortared well in by stupidity. Magnus entered the cottage first and stridently announced Fursey's arrival. She dropped her work at once and advanced to greet him with both hands extended.

"Is there something wrong with your eyes?" asked Magnus solicitously.

"The peat smoke affects them," muttered Fursey, brushing away with the back of his hand the moisture which had gathered.

Maeve glanced away and dragged a stool from a corner. Fursey went stumblingly forward and seated himself. For a long time the cottage was loud with Magnus' raucous joviality, Fursey's timid replies and Maeve's silence. Once or twice when Fursey ventured to look at her, he saw that she was observing him steadily; but when she met his eyes, she turned away her own and began to busy herself about her work. When they sat down to supper, Fursey gave a cautious account of his good fortune in encountering a man of great piety and being cured of sorcery by him. He admitted that he had been at Clonmacnoise in the flesh. He had disguised himself in a Viking's helmet and armour, and had hurried ahead of the raiders to apprise the settlement of its danger. He said nought of his sojourn among the refugee wizards in the hills.

"And what have you been doing these last ten months since the affair at Clonmacnoise?"

"Working with a farmer here and there, making pilgrimages, and in general mending my soul."

"You must have become a man of great piety," exclaimed Magnus with admiration.

"Well, I'm better than I was," admitted Fursey modestly.

"We must really get you back to the monastery," declared Magnus.

"Yes," put in Maeve. "It will be the best place for you."

Fursey raised his eyes to her face.

"You will be happiest there," she added quietly and turned away her head.

When the meal was over, Magnus drew two flagons of ale, and handing one to Fursey, led him out-of-doors into the mild evening sunlight. They sat down at the base of a tree. The dreaming hills which surrounded them, the drifting smoke from distant cottages and the muttering of a nearby stream among the stones induced in them a quiet in keeping with that breathless hour of evening. From time to time Magnus spoke, random and unfinished sentences; occasionally he sighed for no apparent reason. There was war in the north. It promised good and bloody fighting, and much booty. He would like to go. He felt that he was growing too comfortable and soft. Sitting at home watching a woman work and eating the food which she prepared, was no life for a man. He would like to go. When he was old he would have plenty of time to sit warming his knees before the fire. A homesickness came on him at times, a longing to face a fierce and bitter enemy, and to return blow for blow. But Maeve thought that he should stay at home. Warfare is all right for single men, she said; a married man has his responsibilities.

Magnus heaved great sighs and buried his face in his ale-mug. He spoke another few random words. Fursey scarcely listened. He was thinking of the strangeness of things, of his own hatred of adventure and his longing for the quiet and safety that went with marriage and a little piece of land. He sighed too, but more gently than the windy Magnus. Then he remembered that he had sat like this under a tree in Britain and looked about him at a scene in which everything was in harmony except himself. In those days he had possessed woman and house and land, and such share of wealth as he needed. Yet he had felt himself an outsider. He had not been content: he had been a man of property sitting under a tree aware of his possessions and of the beauty of the world in which he moved; but he had not been content. His friend the molecatcher was a philosopher and might have been able to explain these things; but they had taken the molecatcher and hanged him from his own roof-tree.

It waxed late. Magnus rose with a grunt and led the way back to the cottage. It seemed to be accepted that Fursey would remain in the hut for the night, and after a feeble protest he consented. A bed of rushes was spread for him on the floor, and he crawled on to it muttering his thanks. Magnus and Maeve stood in the doorway of the hut until a late hour conversing in undertones. Fursey, lying on the couch, wondered what they were whispering about. He suspected that it was about himself; and at first he strained his ears to hear, but their speech was too low, and he soon gave over the attempt. He stretched his neck on his soft pillow and reflected on the strange turn which matters had taken. Instead of quenching Magnus as he had intended, he had permitted lassitude to creep over him. His instinct now was to allow events to take whatever course they would. He told himself that he was indifferent.

He was awakened early on the following morning by a busy stir in the cottage. He was surprised that breakfast should be so early—it did not seem long after sunrise—but when the meal was finished, the reason became apparent.

"Maeve and I discussed your position last night," began Magnus. "We think that we should let the Abbot Marcus know that you are alive and with us. I'm going to set out for Clonmacnoise this morning. I estimate that the journey there and back will take me three days. We think it right to inform you of what we are doing. You may remain here until I return. I expect that the abbot will come back with me."

Fursey looked at him dully, but said nothing.

"Don't you agree that we are doing the right thing?" asked Maeve gently.

Fursey laboriously gathered in his thoughts.

"I suppose so. Is there any danger that the abbot may have me arrested and put on trial for sorcery? My life has been of little value to anyone; still there are pleasanter ways of terminating it than on a funeral pyre."

Maeve unaffectedly slid her hand across the table and laid it on his. A lightning thrill shot through Fursey so that he trembled all over. He looked up at her dumbly, and saw with emotion that her eyes were bright with tears.

"Dear, dear Fursey," she said, "we don't believe that you are in any danger. Ever since it was believed that your disembodied spirit manifested itself at Clonmacnoise eight months ago and saved the monks from destruction, your case has been examined and argued over, and the abbot and community are convinced that a grievous wrong was done you in the first place in expelling you from the monastery. They are good men; and the fact that you are still in the flesh, is no reason for them to reverse their judgment. I'm sure that they'll take you back. In any case Magnus promises that if treachery is contemplated, he will ride ahead and give you warning, so that you may escape to the hills."

Fursey felt that there was nothing that he could say. He went out of the house with Magnus and helped him to saddle his horse. The soldier was gay and whistled as he went about his final preparations.

"I'm looking forward to this journey," he confided. "It's good for a man to feel a horse between his legs and a sword by his side, and to be riding out into the free air once again."

He turned to wave his hand as he rode away. Fursey returned to the cottage marvelling that anyone should rejoice at being separated from Maeve for three long days. He sat in a corner of the hut surreptitiously watching her as she went about her work. Each time he looked at her he experienced a tiny shock of surprise. Her face as it had been when he first knew her, was indelibly engraved on his mind, the face of a girl with her hair blown back by the wind, a girl with lively eyes, and one who was always laughing. That had been only a year ago, yet there was considerable change already. Her hair was more neatly kept, her gaze, though still kind, was steadier; and there was a firm competence about her mouth which he had never noticed before. At last Maeve became embarrassed at so frequently encountering Fursey's dog-like gaze, and she indicated to him ever so gently that in the hut he was in her way. She suggested that he should go for a little walk outside, but to be sure to be back in time for the midday meal.

He rambled disconsolately in the neighbouring fields and cursed his ill-luck that he was without the love philtre. He reflected darkly on the base ingratitude of the cow who had so ill repaid his kindness to her. This would have been a glorious opportunity for the use of the love potion, a shot of it in the porridge when Maeve wasn't looking, and the woman was his. There was no doubt but that she had changed; yet steady eyes, well-kept hair and a competent mouth were attractive to him, and he still believed her to be without peer among womankind. When he reflected that she was married to an oaf like Magnus, entirely unappreciative of her excellences, he ground his teeth impotently. The fact that Magnus had left her unguarded for three days while Fursey was in the house, was an added injury. It meant that the hearty soldier did not consider him a serious rival.

He was sitting silently at the table after the midday meal when Maeve came from the door to tell him that the small boy Benignus was enquiring for him. Fursey immediately brightened.

"That youngster is not a relation of yours or of your husband's?" he enquired.

"No," she replied.

"Nor a friend?"

"No."

"I formed the impression that he is a particularly offensive little brat," said Fursey.

Maeve laughed. "I'm afraid that he is. He's a neighbour's child, and he's rather spoilt."

Fursey rose and left the hut, picking up a heavy stick which he had noticed behind the door. The boy was waiting outside.

"Eh, mister," he said belligerently, "you promised me something for delivering your letter."

"I have it for you here, my little man," replied Fursey smiling benignantly. "Let's walk up to the road, and I'll give it to you there,"

They walked up the track, Fursey's hand resting benevolently on the boy's shoulder. When they reached the road,

Fursey tightened his grip and gave the boy a couple of unmerciful skelps with the stick. The child fled down the road howling for its mother, while Fursey returned to the cottage in a state of great satisfaction. He remained in the best of good humour for the rest of the evening.

On the afternoon of the third day there was a clatter of hooves on the track outside: Fursey experienced a sudden fright, but he went to the door with Maeve. Magnus was outside helping the Abbot Marcus to alight from his horse. Fursey stood with a sad smile upon his face looking at the man whom he had once loved and respected so much.

"Ah, Fursey," was all that the abbot said, but he laid his hand kindly on Fursey's shoulder. They entered the cottage together. Some time passed in the usual commonplaces about the weather and the crops while the abbot sipped a bowl of milk which Maeve had placed before him. When courtesy had been satisfied, the abbot rose and suggested that he and Fursey should take a little stroll. As they climbed the track to the road Fursey noticed with sorrow that the abbot had become bowed and old. For an hour they paced the road together. The abbot spoke of the sense of guilt which had lain so long upon his spirit.

"As long as I have known you," he said, "I do not remember that you ever told me a lie. A year ago when you were being sorely tempted and harried by demons in your cell at Clonmacnoise, you told me of your experiences with no attempt at evasion or concealment. You did not pause to consider whether such admission on your part would perhaps prejudice me against you. When I consented to your expulsion from the monastery as a means of ridding the holy settlement of the demons which had attached themselves to your person, I did so with an uneasy conscience. We were clearly sacrificing you for the good of the community. You will appreciate how difficult it was to preserve order and good discipline while devils lurked in every dark corner saluting with cuffs and blows all who encountered them; and when even my oldest and trustiest monks were being subjected to temptations of the lewdest character imaginable by shameless female demons dancing in and out of their cells at all hours of the day and night."

"It was hard on me all the same," said Fursey quietly.

"It was hard," admitted the abbot, "but it was imperative to rid the settlement of its terrible visitants. And our judgment proved to be right: when you went, the demons went with you and troubled us no more. I said just now that I've never known you to tell me a lie. I'm therefore prepared to accept without further question your assurance that you have been completely cured of your sorcery. On my way hither I stopped at Cashel to inform the Bishop that you were still alive, and of your happy deliverance. He agreed, grudgingly I'll admit, that no further action should be taken against you. I observe that you are unwilling to give me a detailed account of how you have spent the last ten months, but I shall not press you on that score. I'm sufficiently convinced of the worth of your character to be certain that those months have not been spent in evil-doing. In short, I'm prepared to take you back into the monastery. Your old position paring edible roots in the kitchen awaits you. In a year's time if you continue to give satisfaction, I promise to consider seriously your possible promotion to the office of Laybrother in Charge of the Poultry."

"What a little world he lives in," thought Fursey, "yet it was once my universe."

"Well, what do you say?" queried the abbot. "Are you willing to return?"

"I appreciate your magnanimity," replied Fursey, "but I can't go."

The abbot did not speak for some minutes, but continued to pace the road. At last he halted and turned to look at his companion. Fursey was grieved at the unutterable sorrow in his eyes.

"Why?" he asked.

"Things have changed," muttered Fursey. "I've changed. I've seen the world, and bitter and cruel as it is, I belong there now. I cannot go back to the cloister."

The abbot said nothing more; but he looked very old and very bowed when they helped him on to his horse an hour later. He declined to permit anyone to accompany him, but walked his horse slowly up the track and disappeared around the bend without even once looking back.

Fursey sat in the darkest corner of the cottage, leaning forward with his elbows on his knees staring at the fire. He gazed at the playful flames, not because he was interested in them, but because he was afraid to encounter the eyes of the others. Magnus sat at the table with set brows oiling his leathern shield. When that operation was completed to his satisfaction, he began to polish his sword, grunting occasionally as he discovered a speck of rust. In the background Maeve clattered dishes very determinedly. She kept her back to Fursey. At last she approached the table with a platter in either hand.

"Move those things," she said sharply to Magnus. "Do you expect us to eat our supper off the floor?"

Magnus raised his head and looked at her loweringly. Then with a sudden gesture of vexation he swept his armament from the table and stalked through the open doorway. He sat down on the ground outside and continued his work. Maeve, with heightened colour, began to lay the table. Fursey sat, his heart throbbing painfully, until she curtly summoned him to his meal. He shuffled over to the table and seated himself. Magnus came in a few moments later, lifted a chair and planting it very firmly, flung his huge frame on to it so that it creaked. He pushed a couple of plates aside and set his elbows firmly on the table as if to assert that he was the master of the house. The meal proceeded in silence. Fursey, who was normally a considerable trencherman, found difficulty in swallowing each mouthful. Magnus ate doggedly staring at a spot in the centre of the table. Maeve seemed to have little appetite. Fursey was afraid to lift his eyes, but her long, white hands were within his radius of vision, and he noticed that she toyed with each morsel and raised very little to her mouth. When at last she spoke, Fursey dropped his knife with the fright of suddenly hearing her voice cutting through the silence.

"I must say," she commented in a tone of icy exasperation, "that after all the trouble Magnus went to, to bring the abbot here; and after the hardship the abbot himself endured in travelling such a distance at his age, it's most annoying that you should calmly refuse his offer to take you back to the monastery. What will the abbot think, I'd like to know?"

Fursey stared at his plate, too miserable to attempt a reply. There was a low grunt from Magnus.

"Leave me out," he growled. "I enjoyed the ride to Clonmacnoise and back."

"Why did you refuse to go?" persisted Maeve.

Fursey raised his eyes to her face. It seemed to him that never had she looked as beautiful as now, with the pale flame of anger flushing her cheeks. He felt as if he must burst into tears. Magnus lifted a bone from his plate and cracked it between his teeth.

"Leave the man alone," he said indistinctly. "What he does with his life is his own affair, and no one else's. Maybe he doesn't like psalm-singing. I know I wouldn't."

He flung the end of the bone into the corner, and heaving himself from his chair, lumbered across to the doorway. He picked up his sword as he went and, wandering across the yard, passed through the wicket in the thorn fence. Fursey saw him crossing the field, idly cutting the heads off the thistles and nettles.

Fursey crept out of the house too the moment Maeve had turned her back. He circled the hut almost on tiptoe and, gaining the road, wandered some hundreds of paces along it, until he found a convenient bank on which to seat himself. He remained there for a long time listening dully to a carefree bird tinkling in the hedge. He knew that as far as Maeve was concerned, he had worn out his welcome in the cottage and that it was expected of him that he would take his leave. He wondered how much longer he could stay before they put him out. It was obvious that he should without further delay proceed to the quenching of Magnus. But how was he to kill Magnus without Maeve knowing it and perhaps even denouncing him to the authorities as a murderer? The affair must be made to look like an accident. His thoughts raced ahead, and he saw himself gently comforting the widow, one manly arm about her waist as she sobbed on his shoulder, while Magnus lay in the corner looking very dignified in his martial furniture, and the neighbours thronged the cottage shaking their heads and saying what a nice fellow he had always been. But how was the affair to be made look like an accident? One scratch of the poisoned bodkin would be enough. If only it were later in the year, he could perhaps persuade Magnus to go picking blackberries with him, and when Magnus wasn't looking, scratch him deftly with the poisoned bodkin on the thumb. But as yet it was only the month of May, and it was in the highest degree unlikely that he would be permitted to remain in the cottage until the blackberries had ripened in the autumn. Maybe he could persuade Magnus to come for a swim, and could scratch his back as he was letting himself down some thorny bank into the water. Magnus would think it was a straying bramble that had injured him, and would think nothing of it until he found himself unexpectedly in his death throes. It didn't seem a very good idea, but Fursey was unable to think of a better. He sighed as another difficulty came into his mind. How would he set about winning Maeve's affections when Magnus was safely under the clover? Fursey had not the remotest idea as to how one set about making love. He rose to his feet and began to pace nervously back and forward. He realised that he must set in motion every bit of brain he had, for he was at a crossroads in his life, and his future happiness depended on his now using his share of wit to the best advantage. Yes, he must seek instruction in the matter of engaging Maeve's affections. But from whom? Why, obviously from the man who had gained them already—from Magnus. He had been successful with Maeve. Fursey must therefore defer quenching this valuable source of information until he had learnt how Maeve's maiden heart had been beguiled by her present husband. He turned and walked slowly back towards the cottage, secretly pleased that the inevitable assassination had been deferred for the time being, for at the back of Fursey's mind there lurked the uneasy thought that his onset on Magnus might fail and result in the outraged Magnus killing him.

When he re-entered the hut, Maeve had a splinter of burning wood in her hand and was lighting the taper on the table. Magnus was sprawled before the fire, heavy with food or thought. It was snug and comfortable within; and as Fursey's eyes accustomed themselves to the thick peat smoke, he looked appreciatively around the kitchen at one object after another, the hearth, the chairs and table, the plates and the food, and all the other furnishings of a home. He gazed longingly at the stout walls and the door. Outside was night and terror. Uncertain things were abroad, men and beasts, equally dangerous. But in here there was safety. He told himself that, come what might, he would obtain possession of this cottage and never wander the unfriendly roads again. He looked across at Maeve. How graceful she was as she moved lightly to and fro intent on the final tidying of the house before she laid herself down for the night. What a contrast, he thought, to her dull, thickset husband. It seemed to him that he had rarely seen an uglier piece of merchandise. He was like a bullock you'd see looking at you over a hedge, trying to assemble its thoughts and not succeeding.

"I've been thinking," said Fursey aloud; "I've been thinking of my position here. I feel that I should not trespass any longer on your hospitality. I feel that it's time for me to leave."

Maeve turned her head. Her face was bright. "It's late now. Wait till to-morrow morning anyway."

"Thank you," Fursey replied quietly.

As he rose to go over to his bed in the corner, he saw that Magnus' eyes were fixed on him. The soldier said nothing, but rose some moments later and yawned.

Fursey slept little. It was only when he was lying on his bed that he realised how hurt he was at Maeve's ready acquiescence in his departure. The realisation that he wasn't wanted was a bitter one. He knew now that he would have to leave on the morrow, and he considered desperately whether he would go back to Cuthbert on the mountain and beg him for a love philtre. But he realised that such a course would be the merest madness. He was convinced that Cuthbert's exasperation on seeing him return would be such that powerful magic might well be set in train with deplorable results. He wondered dolefully what it would feel like to be turned into a frog and spend an uncertain life beside a stream dodging the birds, or worse still to be imprisoned for a thousand years in a bottle. The thought of such a fate affected him powerfully and his forehead became damp with sweat. He dismissed from his mind all thought of the accursed mountain and, rolling over, pressed his hot face into the pillow. In an agony of self-pity, he asked himself where he would go and what would become of him. Before long the ebb and flow of Magnus' snoring began to shake the air of the cottage. Fursey listened indignantly, his plump fist clutching the hilt of the poisoned bodkin in his pocket. As the jarring note attained a high pitch and stumbled once or twice before receding, Fursey formed a desperate resolution. On the morrow he would somehow or other kill Magnus, having first questioned him as to how he had won Maeve.

He rose very solemnly on the following morning and shaved himself with Magnus' flint razor. The master of the house was friendly, making breezy remarks on the fineness of the day, a fact which any fool could see for himself. Maeve moved about the cottage demurely. Fursey spoke little, but kept his hand in his pocket and watched Magnus closely for an opportunity to give him a surreptitious nick with the bodkin. He felt that the situation was desperate, and was quite prepared to kill Magnus and forgo previous questioning as to how a woman's affections are best won. As the breakfast neared its end he had made up his mind to drop his knife on the floor, and when under the table recovering it, to draw the bodkin and prick Magnus in the hindquarters so gently that the lethal nick would be mistaken for the action of a splinter in the chair. But before he could put the plan into execution the soldier pushed his plate away from him and, rising, stretched himself with a mighty yawn. The unpleasant fellow was constantly stretching himself as if the house was too small for him and as if he wanted to push off the roof. Fursey rose, too, and went around the table so as to be near his host. His right hand was closed tightly over the handle of the weapon in his pocket.

"I've made up a package of food for you to take with you on your journey," said Maeve to Fursey.

Magnus turned and looked over his shoulder with affected surprise.

"What journey?" he asked.

"Fursey is leaving now."

"Nonsense," retorted Magnus. "You can't turn a man out on to the road when he hasn't made up his mind where he wants to go. Stay a week, Fursey. That will give you time to look around you. You want to stay, don't you?"

Fursey glanced from the broad, smiling face of the soldier to the set countenance of the wife. Her lips were drawn in a thin, hard line.

"Yes," he replied softly, "it would suit me to remain for a few days more."

Magnus clapped a huge hand on his shoulder. "Then stay. I like to see a man about the house."

Maeve turned her back and went quickly to the corner, where she began moving and gathering plates. One fell from her hand and smashed itself on the floor.

Magnus moved lazily through the doorway into the fresh morning sunlight outside. Fursey trailed out after him.

"Women!" said Magnus contemptuously, and he gave Fursey a broad wink.

CHAPTER X

During the ensuing days Magnus spoke little; he seemed preoccupied, full of heavy thoughts. He was considerate and kind in his dealings with Fursey, but Maeve remained formal and polite. Fursey tried to make himself useful, he fed the hens and chatted to the cows, knowing that cows yield the most milk when kept in good humour. From time to time he seized a broom and swept the floor with such thoroughness that Magnus began to complain of the gritty quality of the porridge, and Maeve had to take the broom from Fursey and tell him that she preferred to perform that office herself. Fursey, when he was alone, shook his head and told himself that she had become a very managing kind of woman, and thereafter confined his labours to the hens, amongst whom he became very popular. They soon realised that he always had his pockets stuffed with food, and they came tearing from all directions the moment he was sighted. He hoped vaguely that by making himself useful about the little farm he might prevail on its owners to retain him as farmboy, and that he would so gain time and could wait for a suitable opportunity to execute his fell purpose. It came into his mind from time to time that perhaps Maeve was in love with him and that her anxiety to get rid of him had its roots in feminine psychology, which, he was beginning to realise, was in the highest degree peculiar. When this possibility first struck him he made his way along the nearby stream until he found a deep pool surrounded by trees. He studied his countenance in that green mirror. It reflected a round, foolish face, thatched with prematurely white hair. He noted that his snub nose was without character, and had to admit that his general expression was far from intriguing. Whatever way he contorted his features they stared back at him with a look compounded half of astonishment and half of fright. He sighed and sadly admitted to himself that his looks were not such as to beguile a woman's heart. Still, the thought remained with him, and he often sat by himself pondering the possibility. He remembered how she had come to be affianced to Magnus. Her father had wished to re-marry, and she had felt that there was no room for two women in the one house. Magnus had been attentive and masterful, and so it had come about. Perhaps she had never really cared for Magnus at all. Much of his time Fursey spent in daydreaming. He saw himself in heroic attitudes. He imagined one of the cows going mad and coming rampaging into the cottage where Maeve, unconscious of her danger, was calmly making a pie. He heard her screams and burst in the door. In a moment he had the infuriated beast by the horns, and the two of them were in death grips on the floor. So powerfully was he taken up by his dream that he went around to the back of the house and looked over the stockade at the two cows to see whether he could detect any signs of incipient insanity, but he had to admit that they were the most harmless looking pair of browsers he had ever seen, seemingly incapable of even a bad thought.

One night as he lay on his bed with his mouth wide open watching the curious play of the firelight on the ceiling, he heard Magnus and Maeve deep in argument. She spoke rapidly and with determination, insisting that Fursey must leave the house. Magnus answered growlingly that it would be inhospitable and unchristian to turn out on to the road a man who had no means of subsistence. As Fursey held his breath and listened, the thought again struck him that perhaps Maeve was in love with him and was trying with womanish wile to keep the wool down over Magnus' eyes. Perhaps all this time she had been striving to keep her deplorable brute of a husband in ignorance of her real feelings while she waited for Fursey to do the manly thing. A wild impulse gripped him, urging him to spring out of bed and run across the floor at Magnus, brandishing the bodkin, but caution supervened. He detected a note of genuine bitterness in Maeve's voice as she persisted in her entreaty. At last he heard Magnus impatiently and wearily consenting.

"All right, all right," he said. "I'll tell him that he must go in a couple of days."

Fursey lay motionless and played with a new thought. Could it be that Maeve, cleverer than her husband, divined Fursey's tender regard and distrusted her own strength in resisting any advances which he might choose to make. This was a pleasant thought. It made him see himself as a formidable lover. He shook his head at himself for being such a sad rogue and, smiling happily, fell asleep. He slept the whole night through with a self-satisfied smirk on his chubby features. When morning came he sat up in bed, remembered the argument of the previous night and told himself coldly that he would kill Magnus that day.

He chatted affably during breakfast and announced his intention of leaving the territory on the morrow. He said that he once more felt the itch to wander abroad, and he understood that the scenery in the south was very remarkable. Landowners would no doubt be glad of his services now that the peat-saving season was at hand, and later in the year there would be the harvest. Perhaps some farmer with a shrewd eye for a good workman would entrust him with the care of a flock of sheep. He had always wanted to be a shepherd and learn to blow music through a rustic pipe. A man of spirit, he asserted, need never be in fear of hunger. If the worst came to the worst, he could always join some gang of gallant bandits or offer his services as a fighting man to some robber lord, such as The Wolf of Ballybunion. Magnus and Maeve listened in silence to his flow of talk until it petered out at last somewhat lamely. Magnus emitted a windy sigh.

"We'll miss you," he said heavily.

Maeve said nothing, and Fursey plunged hurriedly into a further account of the gay and careless life which might be enjoyed by a man of lively mind like himself, who had no responsibilities. He prattled on, the words stumbling over one another, for he was embarrassed by Magnus' apparent sincerity. When they rose from the table, he suggested gaily to Magnus a last walk together to a lonely tarn in the mountains a couple of miles distant from the hut. The soldier readily consented, and they set out, Fursey full of self-confidence and delighted with the success of his guile. It was a grey, cheerless day. The sky was overcast as they crossed the waste of bog and swamp and came at length to the tarnside. Fursey chose for their seat a spot at the lake's edge, from which the rock dropped sheer into the waters below. He had continued to chatter amiably during their walk, the moody Magnus scarcely answering his absurdities; but now as they sat with the deep, still water beneath their feet and the awful cliffs rearing themselves above, Fursey talked less and in a more subdued key, until at last he too became silent. It was a lonely spot, an area of gloom, where no birds ever sang and where winds rarely came to stir the long grasses by the lakeside. To Fursey the tarn was familiar. He had visited it several times during the preceding week and had chosen it as a fit spot for the terrible deed which he contemplated. Both men sat motionless. Fursey had sunk his right hand deep in his pocket and fastened it over the hilt of the fatal weapon. It seemed to him that the wild beating of his heart must surely be heard by his companion. It was a relief to him when Magnus spoke.

"So you're really determined to go away to-morrow?"

"Yes," he replied softly.

Magnus frowned down at the water.

"Well, I suppose I can't hold you against your will. But I'm sorry that you're going, and I'll certainly miss you. Apart from the fact that I like the company of men, I've come to have a great liking for you personally."

Fursey stirred uncomfortably and changed the subject.

"I'm not a man who will ever settle down for long in the one place," he declared. "Though you mightn't think it, I have a considerable dash of the adventure spirit in my system. Roads lure me, and the hope of finding adventure around the bend."

Magnus bent his heavy brows on his companion.

"You surprise me. I shouldn't have thought it."

"Oh, yes," squealed Fursey, "I love adventure. In the course of an interesting career I've bested many a dragon and noonday devil; but, strangely enough, success with women has always evaded me. You're a man of the world. Maybe you can explain the reason for that?"

"Women?" responded Magnus. He spoke with difficulty as if the subject filled him with almost unutterable gloom.

"Yes," chirruped Fursey, "females, those amiable and gracious creatures who crown our lives and efforts."

" 'Crown our lives' is right," said Magnus lugubriously; "more efficiently than a warrior might do with a two-handed sword."

Fursey was at a loss to understand this military jargon, so he tried again, hoping to get a plain answer.

"In brief, how should one set about engaging a woman's affections?"

For some moments Magnus did not answer, but gazed dully between his feet at the water wrinkling in between the stones.

"The matter is very recondite," he said with an effort. "I knew nothing about women when I fell in love with her ladyship beyond in the cottage, so, being a practical man, I consulted an aged female soothsayer who lived in a hole in a hill a long distance from here. She was very aged and had the reputation of knowing everything. I often doubt now whether she did. If she was so very knowledgeable, it doesn't seem to have done her much good in life. I had to climb halfway up a cliff face to get to the rockery in which she had set up residence. I found her huddled in rags and filth, gnawing a crust and trying to warm herself over a spark."

"She must have been an interesting old lady," said Fursey breathlessly. "What did she say about love?"

"She said that the whole matter resolved itself into a very simple formula, that every woman wants a man to be at the same time sweetheart, father, companion and child to her."

"I see," said Fursey.

"She said that if a man designs to engage a woman's affections, he must first be masterful, then he must chase her, metaphorically of course—"

"Of course," agreed Fursey.

"—then he must pay homage to her elusiveness. He mustn't press the chase too hard, but must seem to tire and be on the point of giving up in despair. Then he must show fresh determination and chase her again until she surrenders. After that he must never again assert his superiority in word or deed."

The light in the sky had changed, and Fursey frowned at the merry sleekness of the water.

"Did I understand you to say that the aged soothsayer held the operation to be a simple one?"

"She did."

"It doesn't seem simple to me."

"Nor to me," agreed Magnus.

"If only I could read," said Fursey, "I'd like to have it down in writing. Did you try this simple formula with Maeve?"

"No."

"Yet you won her."

"Yes"

"Would you recommend me to plan my future conquests on those lines?"

"No, unless you're some class of an acrobat. In my opinion life is too short. I'd rather fight a battle any day. At least you know who hits you."

Fursey threw a rueful glance at his companion and began to experience great depression of spirit.

"I don't know," declared Magnus, "why a man who longs for adventure should wish to weight himself down with the heart and hand of a lady."

"I've never seen a woman swoon for love of me," confided Fursey. "I freely admit it. I feel that their coldness in my regard is a challenge to me. I suppose that's why the subject interests me—the fascination of the unachieved."

"I expect that's what's at the bottom of it," agreed Magnus, "but it's crazy. Marriage corks the adventure spirit. Thereafter we merely wait in comfort for death."

The two men sat staring gloomily at the black ooze of water.

"I wish you wouldn't go away," said Magnus suddenly. There was a huskiness in his voice which affected Fursey powerfully. "If you go I'll have no one to talk to. You can stay with us as long as you wish. You don't eat much anyway, and you can make yourself useful about the house and farm. Will you not change your mind and remain?"

Fursey said nothing. A little smile came about the corners of his mouth, half sad, half bitter. He drew the poisoned bodkin from his pocket, looked at it for a moment, and then with a flick of his wrist sent it spinning into the dark waters below.

"What was that?" asked Magnus, startled by the sudden movement.

"I've told you a host of lies," said Fursey. "I don't want to go away to-morrow. I hate adventure. I'm afraid of the roads and what may lie in wait around the corner. I'm terrified of hunger and hardship. All I want from life is a small house with strong walls to keep adventure away from me. That and something else."

He could hear Magnus' heavy breathing, but he did not raise his eyes. He sat, a pathetic little figure, crouched on the slab of rock, staring ahead of him, his two hands clasped between his knees.

"What was that you flung away?" came Magnus' voice.

"A poisoned bodkin. One scratch would have meant death. I coaxed you here this morning so as to kill you. That has been my intention all the while I was in your cottage. When I had killed you, my design was to take Maeve, who to my mind excels all other women."

He was conscious of a choking sound proceeding from his companion, but still he did not look around. He expected to feel himself seized and flung into the tarn in the wake of the bodkin, but nothing happened. When he turned his eyes at last to look at Magnus, the big soldier was staring at him round-eyed.

"Well, aren't you the frisky fellow!" gasped Magnus. "And why didn't you do it instead of throwing away your weapon?"

"I've learnt," said Fursey mournfully, "that it's no use trying to be wicked unless it's already in a man's nature to be so."

"Philosophy now, by the powers above!"

"It's a great truth," said Fursey gravely. "It took me a long time to learn it."

"And all the time you were thinking of giving me a dig with that thing?"

"A nick would have been enough," explained Fursey. "It was smeared with a most potent poison."

"It's a good thing for you that you didn't try it," snorted Magnus. "I'd have mangled you."

"You don't seem to understand," said Fursey patiently. "You would scarcely have had time to retaliate. One scratch would have put you into paroxysms."

Magnus stared at him with unbelieving eyes; then he gave a sudden shout of laughter.

"By God, you've more manhood than I credited you with. Aren't you the hardy rogue? And were you really planning to murder me all the time you were eating my bread and salt?"

"Yes," admitted Fursey sheepishly, "that was my damnable intent. Did you never suspect me?"

"Not at all. I was convinced that you were a harmless, poor slob."

Fursey puffed out his chest, well satisfied that his manhood was vindicated.

"But," said Magnus suddenly, "if you're in love with Maeve, why didn't you carry her off when I gave you the chance? You can't say opportunity was lacking. I gave you three days."

"You don't mean to say," said Fursey incredulously, "that you wanted her carried off?"

"Well," admitted Magnus somewhat shamefacedly, "I had a sort of hope. After all, there was a broomstick handy behind the door."

"In other words," said Fursey stiffly, "you're telling me to my face that I'm a liar. You didn't believe me when I told you that I was cured of sorcery."

"I did indeed," replied Magnus hastily. "Please don't take it that way. Of course I believed you; but, situated as I was, I couldn't help hoping that a little of the old magic still clung to your person, just enough to raise a broomstick into the air.

I'm sorry if what I've said seems to imply a deviation from the truth on your part. I really didn't mean it that way."

Fursey stared haughtily at his companion until a sudden realisation of the turn the conversation had taken made him slide all at once from his attitude of injured pride.

"What's that?" he gasped. "Do I understand you to say that you want to get rid of Maeve?"

Magnus nodded dumbly.

"Why?"

"Have you not noticed about her a sharp, shrewish look?"

"I have not," retorted Fursey indignantly. "The most I'll admit to, is that there is in her air a certain self-sufficiency."

Magnus shook his head gloomily. "There's more than that."

"I'll thank you to keep a civil tongue in your head when you're talking about her," said Fursey hotly. "You seem to forget that I'm in love with her."

Magnus began to stutter an apology; then he stopped and hung his head. He glanced up at Fursey shyly. Some moments passed. Very slowly the soldier's face cleared as his mental machinery began to stir. The apologetic look made room for a look of surprise. His countenance slowly flushed and his brow darkened.

"Look here," he said angrily. "That woman is my wife, and I'm not going to listen to her being insulted."

"It's you who insulted her," snapped Fursey.

Magnus emitted a, sudden roar. "What are we talking about? You have me all confused. What right have you to be indignant about anything? You're nothing but a stygian villain, eating my bread and all the time resolved on the incivility of prodding me with a poisoned bodkin!"

"I see that you're determined to hurt my feelings," said Fursey. "That's all the thanks I get for saving your life."

"Saving my what?" howled Magnus.

"Oblige me by not raising your voice. I decline to continue the discussion unless it is carried on in the key usual to gentlemen when they meet to discuss their affairs. There is nothing so vulgar as raucous howling."

"Tell me how you saved my life?" repeated Magnus weakly.

"By not prodding you with the lethal blade, of course. Only for my laudable restraint in the matter you'd now be lying here, completely black in all probability, with a dozen vultures squatting around you in a ring. Am I to get no thanks for that?"

"I'm sorry," said Magnus humbly. "Will you take my hand and we'll be friends."

Fursey took the soldier's proferred palm and gave it a dignified shake.

"Where did we get to in the discussion?" asked Magnus uncertainly.

"I admitted that I loved your wife, and you on your part admitted that you wanted to get rid of her," replied Fursey primly. "We got that far and no further. You expressed surprise that I hadn't already abducted her during your misguided efforts to have me lodged in a monastery. We may as well dispose of that idea at once. I'm not prepared to attempt her abduction for two excellent reasons: Firstly, I don't think the use of force a good initial basis for a subsequent happy union of heart and mind; and secondly, I don't think I'd succeed. She's a muscular woman and might inflict an injury on me. Do you think there's any possibility of her going with me voluntarily if you turned your back for a moment?"

"No," replied Magnus dolefully. "Unfortunately she's sore assotted on me, and she thinks you're a horrible little hop-o'-my-thumb."

"Oh, does she?" replied Fursey huffily. "If she's not careful, I'll take my affections elsewhere."

"No, don't do that," put in Magnus hastily. "I'm sure we can come to an arrangement. I have been hoping that you would at least consent to remain in the house for a month or two, so that I'll be able to slip away to the war in the north. After all, a husband has certain obligations to his wife, and one of them is not to leave her alone and unprotected. Maeve, like all women, is subject to astounding fancies if left alone at night. She begins to be afraid that there are bandits in the cupboard and that every noise outside is a demon creeping up on the house. Women are very dependent on us."

"Are they?" muttered Fursey.

"Yes," said Magnus, surprised. "I thought everyone knew that. Well, the position is that I've grown weary of that woman's apron strings. I can't go out and pick a quarrel with a friend in a tavern but I feel those apron strings tightening. I feel all the time that I'm being played like a fish. When I pull hard she lets out the line a little, but she never lets go. I'm sick and tired of it, and I'm determined not to spend my life sitting at her feet. You can be her pet and warm yourself before the fire for the rest of your life for all I care. I have a solution which is in the highest degree watertight. I'll go across to Britain. When we were in Britain last summer the King of Mercia felt my muscles and offered me service in his army any time I wanted it. I undertake to have a message sent home within a month to the effect that on a well-fought field my body was dug out from beneath a heap of slain and subsequently buried with martial pomp and circumstance. Maeve will fall in a swoon, and both you and she will go into mourning. In a half-year's time she'll have got used to the look of you around the house, and eventually she'll consent to marry you. I assure you that it is merely a matter of habit with women. They get used to men just the same as they get used to the furniture. Never fear, she'll accept you in the long run in spite of your looks."

Fursey was conscious of the liveliest emotion. He clutched Magnus' fist again and shook it warmly.

"It's a most brilliant idea," he said excitedly, "and it has the advantage of being highly respectable. I was always against irregular unions. After all, one has a duty to society to preserve appearances."

"You'll stay then?" asked Magnus eagerly, "and look after Maeve until you receive intelligence of my demise?"

"Of course I will," responded Fursey; "and after it, too, if she'll have me."

Magnus' honest face glowed with satisfaction as he rose and began to lead the way back towards the cottage. The peaty soil under Fursey's feet was soft and springy, the lark which soared overhead seemed to pour down its congratulations. Fursey walked with his face raised to catch every playful breeze. His whole being was suffused with a strange, uneasy feeling of happiness. As they neared the cottage he spoke in a loud whisper to his companion.

"When do you plan to leave?"

"In a few days," muttered the second conspirator.

As they passed through the wicket in the thorn fence, Fursey began to wax nervous.

"Will you tell her now that I'm not leaving to-morrow after all?"

"Yes, of course," replied Magnus roughly. He turned on Fursey a piercing eye as he noticed that the latter had begun to lag behind. "Don't tell me that you're afraid of a woman."

"Oh, no," lisped Fursey. "Of course not."

They ducked their heads in the low doorway and entered the cottage. Magnus kicked a chair out of his way and took his stand near the fire. Maeve seemed to sense that something was afoot. She put down a bowl of buttermilk which she held in her hand and turned to look at them across the fire. Through the drifting smoke Fursey could see that she was quite calm and self-possessed.

"We men have been talking," said Magnus. "I'm riding north to the war in a few days' time."

Maeve glanced calmly from her burly husband to Fursey quaking in the background. She said nothing. Magnus went to the corner and picked up his spear. He tested the stout ash between his great fists. When he spoke again, he avoided looking at her.

"I won't be gone for long," he lied; "perhaps for a few weeks. In the meantime Fursey will stay here to guard the house."

Maeve turned and picked up the bowl of buttermilk as if nothing had happened.

"Fursey is our guest," she said quietly. "He is welcome to stay as long as he wishes."

Fursey stumbled out of the cottage in Magnus' wake, scarcely conscious of where he was going. He stood outside trembling in every limb.

"A very formidable woman," he said shakily.

Magnus' brow was set in hard, firm lines. He walked to the corner of the cottage, while Fursey trailed along in his rear. Then he weighed the spear carefully in his hand, raised and flung it so that it stuck quivering in the palisade. Two startled cows went scampering across the field.

"Mark my words," said Magnus darkly, "she's up to some devilment."

On the evening of the following day Fursey was sitting at the base of the tree, his mind blank, gazing at the sun's afterglow in the west, when Magnus emerged from the cottage and took his arm in a grip which made him squeal. The soldier led him some distance from the cottage before he spoke.

"There's a complication," he hissed.

"What?" asked Fursey blankly, not knowing what his companion was talking about.

"She says that she's going to present me with a pledge of our love."

Fursey gawked at Magnus with his mouth open.

"Don't you understand, you clodpoll? She's going to present me with a squawker."

"Oh," said Fursey.

"I wouldn't be surprised if it's all on purpose. This is a woeful complication."

"I don't mind," said Fursey brightly. "I'll adopt it."

Magnus scowled at him. "Do you think that I'd entrust my child to a ninnyhammer like you"

He stalked away. Fursey gaped after him, and then went over and sat down once more beneath the tree.

For two days Magnus moved about morosely. Fursey tiptoed in and out of the cottage, fearful of attracting attention. The soldier, when he spoke to his wife, addressed her with a rough kindliness. Maeve paid little attention to either of them. She seemed to live in a world of her own, remote from mundane things. Fursey watched her anxiously as she sat for hours on end by the fire, smiling slightly to herself.

"She despises us both," Magnus confided to Fursey a couple of days later as he sat on the grass outside the door savagely polishing his sword. It was already dusk, but the soldier had sat there since sunset. "She hasn't told me so, but I know it. She finds herself on the level of creation, and for all she cares the two of us may go and drown ourselves. She has another allegiance now. She is complete."

Fursey could not think of anything to say.

"She knows what we have been planning," continued Magnus fiercely. "She hasn't said so, but I feel it. And the curse of the thirteen orphans on her, instead of telling the two of us what she thinks of us and blistering the hides off us as we deserve, she chooses to be soft-spoken and gentle! Why doesn't she let fly at us? Why?"

"I suppose," said Fursey miserably, "it's not in her nature."

Magnus flung down his sword on the grass.

"I'm remaining here," he declared. "You'll have to go. Now and forever my legs are entangled in this house. I should have known that marriage is the end of adventure. Here, help me to gather up my weapons."

He rose and picked up sword and spear. Fursey clumsily gathered up the shield and corslet. "What are you going to do with them?" he asked dully.

"Put them in the corner beyond the fire where the dust can gather on them."

They entered the cottage, and Magnus piled his weapons. Maeve was sitting by the fire, but she did not raise her head. Fursey looked about him, but then remembered that he had no possessions to take with him.

"Fursey is going," said Magnus.

Maeve, brooding smilingly over the fire, did not seem to hear.

"Fursey is leaving us," repeated Magnus, touching her gently on the shoulder.

"Goodbye, Fursey," she said, but even then she did not raise her head.

Fursey walked across the kitchen and out of the house. Magnus stood beside him at the door. For one moment the two defeated men looked at one another, then Fursey turned and made his way up the track. It was dusk. He did not pause, but began to plod slowly along the road which led over the hills into the unknown lands in the south. In the dim light, against the mighty backcloth of creation, the tumbled mountains and valleys over which the shadows of approaching night were gathering, he seemed a negligible figure. He was indeed a negligible figure, a small, bowed man holding his torn coat tightly about him, not only for warmth, but as if to keep from the vulgar gaze his terrors and the remnants of his dreams. And so, as he goes down the road, he is lost to view in the gathering shadows, glimpsed only for a moment at the turn of the track or against the vast night sky, just as we have managed to catch a glimpse of him through the twilight of the succeeding centuries.

Last spring I walked the road from Clonmacnoise to Cashel, and from Cashel to The Gap. Fursey and the others are still there, trampled into the earth of road and field these thousand years.

ACKNOWLEDGEMENTS

The publisher would like to thank those who helped see this book into publication: Mary Rose Callaghan, Jesse Campbell-Brown, Máiréad Casey, Michael Dirda, Nick Galante, Meggan Kehrli, Ken Mackenzie, Jim Rockhill, Jonathan Williams, and the family of the late Mervyn Wall, who offered their invaluable assistance and kind support.

The Return of Fursey was first published by The Pilot Press Limited, London (1948).